Murder Stalks A Mansion

A Newport Mystery

By

Anne-Marie Sutton

ISBN: 1-4107-9217-X (e-book)
ISBN: 1-4107-9216-1 (Paperback)

Library of Congress Control Number: 2003096911

This book is printed on acid free paper.

Printed in the United States of America
Bloomington, IN

1st Books - rev. 02/23/04

For Marie, my grandmother

Author's Notes:

This book could not have been written had I not spent so much time in the wonderful city of Newport, Rhode Island. The idea for the story grew in my head during my frequent walks on the Cliff Walk where for months I worked out the details of the characters and plot.

While many of the places mentioned actually do exist, I have created the house called Kenwood Court from my own imagination. There are references to many of the famous families of Newport, but the Kents and the other characters in the mystery are all fictitious.

I hope the reader will enjoy reading, as much as I have had writing, this novel, inspired not only by those marvelous Newport houses and their history, but also by the charm and enchantment of the entire city.

CHAPTER ONE

The dream had shut down in her mind in the same sudden way that the computer screen faded into nothingness when she turned off its power. The sound of the alarm clock had wakened her. Six a.m.. Caroline Kent didn't need to open her eyes to know the time.

"Another day, another dollar," her father used to enjoy saying as he went off to the office each morning.

Caroline sat up. She looked at the photograph of Reed in its silver frame on her bedside table.

"I miss you," she said softly.

For several seconds she stared wistfully at the picture. Kenwood Court was quiet. Finally, she leaned back against the pillows, inhaling the ocean air from the room's open windows. The day's weather looked promising. She was glad. The Hargreaves were arriving in Newport today, and Caroline wanted everything to be perfect for their stay.

At last she rose and went to one of the tall windows. The view of the water's catching the first rays of light was splendid. Caroline watched the slow lumbering waves washing up onto the cliffs below the house. The early autumn sky was clearing as the fog lifted from the water. She had a vague memory of hearing the fog horns during the night.

"If only Reed were here, we could be out there together," she said to herself. Reed had been a good sailor, often sailing these waters off Newport.

But the thought, like her dream, quickly left her. It could not be.

Caroline glanced up at the old kitchen clock. It was ten minutes past eight. She heard Mattie's footsteps on the back stairs.

"I've put the tea cakes in," Caroline said to the old cook as she entered the room.

Mattie Simpson nodded curtly and reached her angular arm for a blackened pan hanging over the massive stove.

"What are you making, Mattie?"

"French toast," Mattie answered without looking up from her work. She had cut three thick slices from the loaf and now was beating the eggs. "Missus says she has a taste for some."

"Is Mrs. Kent coming down for breakfast this morning? We've a lot to do before the new guests come today, and Jan is late as usual. The Hargreave family is coming right after lunch."

"Excuse me, Mrs. Caroline, but I told the Missus it's much too chilly this morning for her to be up until she's got a good hot breakfast into her. You're young, and I know you can—"

"I'm sure you're right," Caroline said, speaking evenly over Mattie's fretful voice. "My mother-in-law needs to conserve her energy. I believe she plans to work in the garden today."

A gruff sound emanated from the old woman's thin lips. Caroline concentrated on taking a breakfast tray from the shelf.

"We don't have to give that family lunch then?" Mattie asked.

Caroline turned to see that Mattie was removing a bowl of strawberries from the big steel refrigerator.

"No, we'll start them with tea in the afternoon." Caroline frowned as the cook spooned the fruit around the pale yellow French toast. "The strawberries are for the guests' tea, Mattie."

"I'm just taking a few."

"All right, but they are expensive. You know we have to watch—"

Mattie slammed the cover on the plate and picked up the tray. Caroline watched the erect back of the slim figure leaving the room and sighed.

By the time Jan Lowry entered the kitchen through the service porch, Caroline had rehearsed several times what she was going to say to her young employee about the importance of being punctual.

They had agreed on the previous day that Jan would be at work at eight, half an hour earlier than her usual arrival.

"Jan, you must realize that today is going to be exceptionally busy, and I—oh, God, the cakes!" Caroline's hands flew to the oven door.

"Those smell good," Jan said as she hung up her jacket on a peg by the door. She had an amiable face, round and rosy, framed with long blond hair. "Would you believe the crowd of tourists is already forming at The Breakers?" Jan shook her head. "I never understand what people see in that ugly pile of stone. Your house is so much nicer. It's got to be one of the prettiest mansions in Newport."

The young maid walked to work each morning by way of the Cliff Walk, the three mile stretch of pathways and steps along the high rocky sea wall of the Atlantic Ocean. Each day she passed The Breakers and several of the old Gilded Age houses fronting on the ocean before coming to the path that led up to the Inn at Kenwood Court.

"You know we don't call them mansions, Jan. Especially in front of the guests. This is a cottage. That is what they have always been referred to by the wealthy in Newport, and that is the word the guests expect to hear us use."

"Yes, I understand. I was just saying that Kenwood Court is a nicer... cottage... than The Breakers."

"I suppose so," Caroline said as she put the cake pans on racks to cool.

"Of course Kenwood Court is much smaller, but a house can be *too* big, don't you think?"

When Caroline didn't answer, Jan continued. "It's too bad you don't have the money to fix this place up." Her own house was on the more humble Easton's Beach side of the Cliff Walk, and it had taken some time for Jan to understand that Caroline's owning a house like Kenwood did not mean she had no money worries. "I was looking at the gazebo this morning. That must have been beautiful."

"I don't know," Caroline said. "I first saw the house after it was put up for rent."

Only the once, Caroline thought. When Reed and I came so that he could talk to the tenants. She had waited in the morning room. The Kents had called the house Kenwood then. When she had opened the inn, she had fancied up the name by adding *Court*.

"I guess you'll have the money now with all the people who want to stay here since you opened up your house as a hotel."

"The Hargreave family is coming right after lunch," Caroline said. "You'll have to make up the beds. I've put the linen in each of the rooms." Why was it so hard for her to get Jan started on her work each morning?

"How many bedrooms does this family need? All of them?" Caroline shook her head. "Didn't you say they were taking the whole house for this weekend?"

5

"They are, but they don't need all the bedrooms."

"But they want the whole house. Isn't that strange?"

"They are coming to celebrate a special wedding anniversary in the family. They want the privacy. And it is the off-season. Reservations are slow. They'll be here until Sunday."

"I bet it's a fiftieth."

"There are three married couples coming, and I've put them in the three big rooms along the west wing. There are three other guests, all needing single rooms. Two of them will be in the smaller rooms at the front of the house. However, Nelson Hargreave specifically asked that the third be given an extra large room, so I've earmarked the corner suite in the east wing for that guest."

"Oh," Jan said, raising her eyebrows. "That sounds intriguing. Who's so special?"

"Mr. Maurice Hargreave, Nelson Hargreave's uncle."

"Oh, I see. He must be the one celebrating the wedding anniversary. No, that can't be right. You said he was a single."

"I'm having trouble keeping them all straight myself. I know Nelson's mother and father are the ones who are having the anniversary. Maurice, I believe, is the father's brother."

"The only one you've met is Nelson?" Jan asked. "Not this Maurice?"

"Yes, Nelson came down from Boston to make the arrangements. Why Maurice Hargreave is a special character I'm sure we'll soon find out. Now, I think you'd better get started on the beds."

6

Jan shrugged and reluctantly left the room. She was the second chamber maid Caroline had employed in the last six months since she had begun running her late husband's family home as an inn where, as the advertising promised, "guests could experience life in Newport in the grand old manner at stately Kenwood Court."

The first maid, Henrietta, had been a middle-aged sour woman whom Caroline suspected of drinking while working. Guests noticed her sullen manner and put-upon demeanor, and Caroline was glad when "Henny," as she liked to be called, left after two months, complaining that the work was too hard and the guests too demanding. Henny and Mattie had been a formidable domestic team for an inexperienced innkeeper to manage.

Caroline brushed a strand of her fair brown hair away from her forehead.

"Everybody told you not to do this, but you wouldn't listen," Caroline reminded herself. "This was your idea, and now you have to make it work."

"She's eaten every bit," Mattie announced proudly as she strode into the room. With a flourish she lifted the cover of the empty dish for Caroline's approval. "I don't know why she has to use up all her strength on it, but the Missus says she has to clean up that rose garden before the frost comes. I thought that kind of work was George's job."

"George only comes in two days a week, and he can't keep up the grounds on that schedule. Mrs. Kent helps him by doing some of the pruning and weeding."

"It's not a proper job for the *mistress* of the house," Mattie said, her voice underlining the rank she assigned to her Missus in the household.

Caroline wanted to say who was in charge these days at Kenwood, but instead gritted her teeth, determined not to show the other woman that she was bothered by her disapproval.

"I don't know what Mr. Reed would say if he were still here."

"A lot of things have changed in this family, Mattie. I'm sorry you can't accept that."

"Why, the people who you call the 'guests' wouldn't have been welcome here at Kenwood in the old days. Not proper ladies and gentlemen. I remember when I cooked dinner at this very stove for the British ambassador and his wife. Twenty six we had that night. Mr. Reed was a boy. He watched from the gallery on the second floor as the guests arrived. I was young then, like you are now, Mrs. Caroline, but it comes back to my mind as if it were yesterday. I can tell you the menu by heart."

"Mattie," Caroline began slowly, "try to realize that the old days are gone. We can't afford to live like the Kents once did. You knew when you came back to live here with us that we planned to open the house as an inn. The guests must come first."

"Yes," Mattie said acidly, "they get Missus's strawberries."

8

"Newport is changing. Many of the old houses have been bought and turned into inns and bed and breakfasts."

"But this is Kenwood! We used to have three gardeners."

"It's not my fault, Mattie," Caroline said, holding back the words which said she hadn't been responsible for the family fortune's being lost. "I'm doing the best I can."

"You are a hard worker, Mrs. Caroline. But the Missus shouldn't be doing the things she's been doing. Mr. Reed—"

"Mrs. Kent wants to do her share."

"Missus is much too kind to complain."

"I appreciate your sharing all this with me, Mattie," Caroline said, moving toward the doorway to the pantry. "Sometimes it's good to clear the air. But now I have work to do."

As Caroline left the kitchen, she wished she hadn't been able to hear Mattie's petulant voice declare, "Well, that's what I think. And you won't get me to change my mind."

CHAPTER TWO

The big black BMW hesitated before turning left at the intersection of Memorial Boulevard and Bellevue Avenue. The light was green, but traffic on Bellevue Avenue in front of the Tennis Hall of Fame was at a standstill as pedestrians crowded into the striped crosswalk in the middle of the block.

"You ought to keep going, Nelson. Otherwise you'll miss this light." His wife's filtered, elegant voice had been silent for most of the trip from Boston, and hearing it now startled him. He turned to see her face, but it was turned to the window, watching the traffic as if it were her special responsibility to do so.

"I don't want to get stuck in the middle of the intersection, Kae." He heard the sound of a honking horn. Nelson cautiously moved the BMW a few feet forward, a gesture that failed to placate the driver behind him who leaned on his horn in one, long accusing blast.

"You'd better go." This advice came from the back seat.

11

Harold Hargreave turned his body around to look through the rear window. It was a laborious motion.

"That guy behind you is upset."

On the seat next to Harold, his wife Donna also turned around to see. She, too, had some difficulty rotating her short, thick figure.

"Well, there is nothing I can do now," Nelson remarked to his brother. The green light had turned to yellow, and his decision to stop had proved to be the right one.

Nelson looked around the intersection now and studied the people on the street. From their dress he thought they were mostly tourists, drawn to the fabled Avenue for a look at where the nation's richest families had once made their summer homes in Newport. Everyone seemed to be wearing sensible walking sneakers. Nelson doubted if any of them were staying at lodging of the caliber of The Inn at Kenwood Court. There was a bus parked further along on Memorial Boulevard, and Nelson guessed some of these sightseers were even day-trippers, here for a few hours to tour the mansions and pick up a Newport souvenir T-shirt.

The blaring sound of the horn told him that the light had turned green again and Nelson turned, the intersection clear for him to go forward.

"Oh, look, Harold, there's a restaurant that looks nice."

Harold obediently looked in the direction of his wife Donna's pointing finger. She waved her small hand at the timbered block of stores surrounding the Newport Casino. "And all those stores. Oh, Kae, let's go shopping together tomorrow."

Kae Hargreave leaned back against her seat. She was beautiful, thin and haughty as a model.

"That's an idea, Kae," her husband said lightly. "I ought to get work done while we're here, and you two can certainly have the car tomorrow."

"Oh, Nelson, stuff it," Harold said. "This is supposed to be a vacation."

"It's Mother and Father's anniversary party," Nelson corrected.

"Well, you and I..." Harold hesitated before continuing. "And Brian are paying for it. And I'm going to enjoy myself. I hope the food's good at this place."

"It's highly rated," Nelson said brusquely, "and probably one of the best places to stay in Newport."

"What is this place anyhow? How did you find it?"

"Yes," Donna said, "I couldn't find it in the guidebook."

"It's new," Nelson explained patiently. "I saw an ad in the *Boston Globe* magazine and drove down to see it. Mrs. Kent opened it in the spring. Kenwood Court is her family's—actually her late husband's family's—the Kents' old summer home."

"And she takes in paying guests?" Harold asked, the suspicion creeping into his voice. "One of those old Newport families... I bet we'll get chicken à la king every day for lunch."

13

"Mrs. Kent is a young woman, and it's a sad story, really. As I understand it, her husband died last year in an automobile accident. They had only been married a short time."

"She told you that?" Donna asked. She was leaning forward to hear every word.

"I'm afraid I asked. Or rather made what turned out to be an unfortunate comment that elicited that information. My guess is there isn't much money, and she needs the income."

"How old is she?" Donna asked. "You said she was young."

"Not much more than thirty, I'd guess."

"How is she in the looks department?" Harold asked.

Nelson sighed and began to wonder if this idea of bringing everyone together for a long weekend in Newport was such a good idea after all.

"Harold," he began, speaking slowly. "Not only is this our parents' fortieth anniversary, but I'm sure you do remember that Father will turn seventy next year. I thought this getting together would be a good time for us all to start thinking about what is going to happen at Hargreave Industries now that Father is at retirement age."

"There is no retirement age at Hargreave Industries. It's our company, for Crisakes! Besides, father hasn't said anything about retiring."

"Has your father said anything to you, Nelson, about retiring?" his wife asked.

14

"No," Nelson admitted, "but it's got to be on his mind."

"Father will never leave the office. What else would he do all day?"

"What does he do all day in the office now?" Nelson spoke his question before thinking and immediately regretted it. "I only meant that I think he's ready for retirement. And I'm sure Mother would like to travel."

"You don't know what you're talking about," Harold said.

"Yes," Donna said, "Lionel comes to the office every day and Maurice never puts any pressure on him. Your father gets paid very well. Why would he give that up?"

"He'll still own his half of the company. He'll have a good income."

"Father doesn't care about money," Harold said with conviction.

"Or Hargreave Industries," Donna said.

"The point is…" Nelson was determined to have his say. "We should talk about who is going to take Father's position in the business. It seems to me that the time has come for the family to sit down and discuss how the company will be managed in the future. Uncle Maurice isn't going to be running things forever."

"Even if it seems that way," Kae murmured.

"And you want this someone to be you, dear brother?"

"Oh, sure," Donna said. "And you think Miss Tina Tart is going to stand by and let you take over the whole place? Nelson, I've always thought you were pretty smart, but now I have to wonder."

To imagine Tina running his family's company made Nelson's blood rage. He looked at his wife in the hope that she might be readying a response to support him. But, Kae was looking out of the window. Large, princely houses lined both sides of the Avenue. They had just passed The Elms.

Maury, their Uncle Maurice's only son, had been dead for three years now. The time had come to go beyond Maurice's original plan to name his son the successor. Surely Nelson's father Lionel could be made to see the importance of advancing his eldest son's interests. And this weekend together in Newport seemed to be the time to settle things once and for all in Nelson's favor.

"Cha—teau—Sur—Mer."

Emily Hargreave read the sign out loud in her best school-girl French accent, enunciating each syllable and accentuating the middle word, sounding like a Frenchman trying to say the English word *sewer*. When she was finished she looked at her husband quizzically. "Do you like it, Lionel?"

"Like what, Emily?" He had been looking straight ahead, focusing on the road, concentrating on his driving and his own thoughts.

"That house. The one we just passed. Didn't you see it? I didn't much care for the design. I guess because it's French. I've always been partial to English country houses. Oh look, Lionel, there's another mansion. What do you call that architectural style?"

"I don't believe Newport is famous for strict adherence to architectural style, Emily." He still didn't take his eyes from the road. "You must remember that these are the houses of the robber barons of the nineteenth century. These people took lots of license with their houses, mixing styles all around."

"Well, that was a nice history lesson." Her voice, as well as her face and body, was tiny, bird-like. Her hair had gone gray, but she kept it neatly coiffured.

"I meant no offense. You asked about the architecture."

"I wonder where The Breakers is. I suppose you know that is the house that belonged to the Vanderbilts."

Lionel nodded. "Old Cornelius was probably the biggest robber baron."

"There is another Vanderbilt house. There were two brothers, Cornelius's grandsons actually, who built mansions in Newport. Marble House, that's what the other one is called. It should be along here on Bellevue Avenue."

"We have to turn off soon, I think." Keeping his eyes still looking ahead, Lionel took a neatly folded paper from the breast pocket of his tweed jacket. "I have Nelson's directions."

17

"Here, you'd better give them to me," Emily said, taking the paper from her husband's grasp. "You can't read and drive."

"Yes, dear," Lionel said. He knew his wife meant to be kind, but he wished she didn't give the impression that he was incapable of the simplest of life's tasks.

"It looks like a left turn to get to the Inn at Kenwood Court." Emily Hargreave frowned, studying the directions. "Nelson says that we should pass a small green road sign for the turn-off to The Breakers. It's on the left, too. I didn't see that, did you, Lionel?"

"I see one of those green signs up ahead," her husband said. "Maybe that's what he means."

"Then we should be turning soon after that. Oh, isn't that house lovely? Lionel, look." She was staring to her right at a large cream-colored house with tall columns and a sweeping brace of entrance steps. "I would love to live in a house like that."

"Do you know what the bills for a place that size would run?"

"I don't care. I wish it were mine."

"We couldn't afford it."

"I bet Maurice could." Her tone had a bitter edge to it.

"Don't be foolish, Emily. Even my brother doesn't have that kind of money. Why, those old houses have morning rooms and billiard rooms. Now what would you do with a billiard room?"

"I said I don't care. I wish I could live in a house like that."

"Look at this place where we're staying. Kenwood Court. The owners have to rent out rooms, turn their house into a hotel to keep from selling it."

"I wish you wouldn't act as if I'm silly for suggesting we have a nice house."

"We already have a nice house."

"That's not the point."

"Where do I turn?" Lionel asked impatiently.

"We could have a mansion to live in if Maurice paid you your fair share from the company."

"You don't know what you're talking about. Maurice has always treated me fairly. I wish you would believe that."

Emily was silent, hurt. Lionel sighed and turned his attention to estates on Bellevue Avenue which they were now passing one after another.

"I know we've gone too far. We should have turned off further back there. Let me see those directions." He took the paper from her hand which was resting limply in her lap. "Let me see."

Lionel drove the Lincoln into an open driveway. He realized that he had entered the parking lot of one of the mansions open to the public. The house was called Rosecliff.

"Look, Emily, this is a pretty house."

On the seat next to him, his wife continued to look down at her lap. Lionel studied the directions. After a minute or two, he put the car in gear and backed out again. He wished his wife would speak. She hadn't once looked up to see the house.

Why did she always have to bring Maurice into everything? Wasn't it enough that Lionel had to work for him, take orders from him? Couldn't Emily see that throwing his subservient position up to her husband only made him feel the pain all the more?

This weekend in Newport had been planned to celebrate their wedding anniversary, but it was not the kind of thing Lionel would have chosen if he had been consulted. A quiet week away on one of the Caribbean islands was always his favorite getaway. After all, being married forty years was not the same as being married fifty years. You expected a fiftieth anniversary would be a family occasion. No, spending this time with his family, if it had been left up to him, would not have been his choice. Emily had liked the idea, however, and he had been forced to go along with it. The children had suggested it, she said, and she wanted to please them. Children. Three grown men. Why did he have to please them? One day he'd only have to worry about pleasing himself.

Lionel turned the dark blue car left through the open gates of Kenwood. A modest marker etched in the beige stone revealed the house's name. The setting was bucolic. A grove of beech wood trees, their autumn leaves already turning color, stood along the front of the property, bordering the winding drive. The old gate house, a rock square now empty but still imposing, continued to guard the entrance. Beyond it an old yew hedge screened the west side of the property.

Slowly Lionel maneuvered the car around the curve past the gate house, and now the main house came fully into their view. Emily was looking out of the windows on both sides of the car, switching her focus left and right. She was happy now.

"Why, it's a beautiful house," she said. "Like something in a picture book."

Lionel looked at the house and had to admire it. The Palladian windows with their graceful topping curves were trimmed in white against a gray facade. There were two compact wings on either side of the main wing. This house, unlike some of its discordant neighbors, had never been given over to inventive architects. Lionel found himself pleased.

He stopped the Lincoln behind the BMW, which was already parked near the front door. Nelson came out of the house immediately. He helped his mother from the car. She seemed almost to float as she rose noiselessly out of the car. Blinking against the bright afternoon sun she looked around at the house and lawn.

"Didn't I tell you it was wonderful, Mother?" Nelson crowed. "Didn't I say it was just the place for you and Father to have your anniversary party?"

"It's wonderful."

"It was built in the late 1800s by Stanford White for the Kent family, who still live here."

Nelson turned as Caroline came out through the heavy oak front door.

21

"And here is Mrs. Kent herself. Mrs. Kent, my mother and father."

Caroline smiled a practiced hostess's look of welcome as she came toward her guests' car.

"Good afternoon," she said pleasantly. Lionel liked her immediately, noticing the clear green crystals of her eyes. Her soft, full mane of hair was the color of pecan shells. He wanted to shake her hand, but felt that was not done in the circumstances. "Welcome to the Inn at Kenwood Court," Caroline said. "Please come inside. I have tea ready in the salon."

"I was just telling my parents that the house was designed by Stanford White."

"Yes, it's one of his earliest efforts. Very elegant, I've always thought. None of the gingerbread of some of his later summer cottages. Although he did have to please some very difficult clients."

"It's very good," Lionel said. He had remained by the car and was looking up at the house.

"Where is Brian?" Nelson asked his father. They were the same height and their eyes were level with each other. "I thought he was driving up with you? I talked to him last night, and he promised me he was coming."

Lionel gestured with one shoulder in the direction of the back seat. Nelson peered down through the Lincoln's back window.

"He's been asleep the entire trip," his father said.

Both men looked at the slender figure curled in a crab-like position on the back seat. Nelson opened the door.

"We're here," he said. "Wake up."

Brian turned lazily out of his ball and looked up. In stature and appearance he most resembled his mother, although his coloring was darker than both of his parents.

"Come out and meet Mrs. Kent," Nelson said.

"This is my brother, Brian Hargreave, Mrs. Kent."

"Well, hello," Brian said to Caroline as he emerged from the car. He had recovered from his sleeping state and was taking in Caroline with his piercing black eyes. Brian extended his hand and shook Caroline's.

"Mr. Hargreave," Caroline nodded, as Brian still held to the tips of the fingers of her right hand.

"I think your mother would like to go inside," Lionel said.

"Of course, Father." Brian let his grip on Caroline's hand slip.

"Come on, Mother," Nelson said, "Harold and Donna are inside with Kae. Maurice had some things to finish up at the office. He and Tina should be here in an hour or so."

Lionel took his wife by the arm. "Let's get you some tea, Emily. I'm sure you could use a restorative."

Brian looked at his watch. "I might like a drink. Is that possible, Mrs. Kent?"

"Yes," she answered agreeably. "Whichever you prefer."

Lionel guided Emily up the marble steps. As he held the door, he watched the others. Caroline walked ahead of his two sons. Behind her Nelson seemed fixed on his own thoughts. He carried his tall frame stiffly. In contrast, Brian walked easily, his lean frame lithe and energetic. His eyes were bright, like a cat's on his prey, and they were trained on Caroline. Four days of family togetherness, Lionel mused. What will we be like at its end?

CHAPTER THREE

The sun's rays were fading as Louise Kent sat down heavily onto an old garden seat in the shadows of a majestic beech wood tree. She was a small woman, but today she felt weighted down by her arms and legs. She was tired and ready to admit it.

Caroline's parting words as her mother-in-law had headed out to the garden were fresh in her mind. "Don't exhaust yourself, Louise. You know you don't have to finish everything today. We don't usually get frost until late in October."

Louise realized that it was Mattie's disapproval of her working about the house and grounds that was responsible for the caution. Why couldn't the stubborn old woman understand that it was important to Louise that she help with the household chores? She loved Kenwood; it was the first home to which she had come as a young bride. It was where she and Frederick had had their wedding reception. Here was where she came every summer when Reed was a boy. More than their big duplex apartment in New York City, it was *home*. That Caroline had made it possible for her to return to it meant everything to her, and she intended to do her share of the work now that so many things had changed. The Inn at Kenwood Court might be a hotel to the rest of the world, but the gardens and a small part of the house were still her very own home.

The fortunes of the Kent family were now at the lowest point in their history, with the exception of the period just before the Civil War when Henry Kent lost two ships plying the China Trade routes in rapid succession. The Lloyds' policies, unfortunately, had been written to cover only half the value of the ships and cargo, and the family wealth was drained while two succeeding generations worked hard to revive it.

Bad business judgments did not plague the Kents for more than another hundred years until Louise's husband Frederick, reflecting still the family's belief that their fates would be enriched in the Far East, against all advice, resolved to back a British syndicate drilling for oil in the China Sea. The venture failed, and Frederick died soon after the loss of the money.

Louise and Reed, who was twenty-seven at the time of his father's death, were left to handle the situation. They had been shocked to find that Frederick had committed everything to the failed scheme except the deed to Kenwood, which he had mortgaged. By the terms of his father's will, the property—and his debts—were left to Reed. The young man, newly graduated from law school with a future which once seemed assured, now found himself under the burden of clearing up his father's estate and providing for his mother.

Louise had some family money, but nowhere near enough to maintain her former lifestyle. She and Mattie moved to a smaller apartment in New York City where Mattie functioned as cook, maid and housekeeper. Kenwood was put up for rent, attracting a family of Texans who gave lots of black-tie parties where all the waiters wore white gloves. They were not popular with the members of local society, who were quick to report all their comings and goings to Louise in New York.

But, it was not the loss of the family's money which Louise had minded, as much as she missed being at Kenwood. As Reed worked hard and began to prosper as a lawyer with an eminent Wall Street firm, his mother had begun to hope that one day there might be enough money for the family to be able to live at Kenwood again. Reed had met and married Caroline, and Louise hoped that once grandchildren came, he would want to bring them for summers in Newport.

And then Reed's death had changed everything. He had been driving home from a conference in Albany late one night during a rain storm, missed a curve in the road, swerved and was killed instantly by an oncoming car. Her only son was dead at the age of thirty-three.

For both of Reed's survivors, Caroline and Louise, the anguish was almost too much to bear. Caroline, an actress on the off-Broadway stage, lost all interest in her career. For three months, she stayed in her apartment and grieved. Louise feared she might be on the verge of a breakdown. Then the impossible happened. Caroline seemed to find some determination deep within herself to go on.

Louise remembered the day Caroline had invited her to live at Kenwood, which she had inherited from Reed, along with the still unpaid mortgage.

"How can we do that, Caroline?" Louise had asked. "How can you afford it? Do you realize how much it will cost to live there?"

"Yes," Caroline said. She was smiling. Louise thought it was the first time she had seen her smile since Reed's death.

"Where will you get the money, Caroline?"

"I have a plan," Caroline said simply. And she did.

Kenwood was to become a hotel, the Inn at Kenwood Court. Caroline had worked out all the details. Louise marveled at it all, although it seemed risky and she had said so.

"I know," Caroline agreed. "Everybody is telling me that. Mr. Clarke is especially angry with me. I'm using what capital Reed left me." Archibald Clarke had been the Kent family lawyer since Frederick's time, and a more conservative attorney did not exist. "But I've made up my mind, and nothing is going to change it."

And transform Kenwood into a hotel they did. Louise was often astonished by her daughter-in-law's energy and determination. Grief over Reed's death drove Caroline. It was her way of coping.

Louise Kent looked across the lawn at the rose garden where she had spent her day's labors. It pleased her to look at her work and to know that she had helped to save expenses by doing it herself.

What was it Jan had said yesterday about the path from the Cliff Walk? Louise had asked her about a fresh scratch on her cheek.

"Oh, it's those brambles on the path coming up from the Cliff Walk," Jan had said, touching two rough red streaks of dried blood on her face. "I wasn't paying attention, I guess. I pushed the branches aside, but one of them snapped back and hit me in the face. You know how wild things grow along the Cliff Walk. Caroline said George will cut them back before winter."

"I can see to that, too," Louise told herself, rising determinedly from the wooden seat. No need to wait for the gardener to be paid to do it.

Arriving at the path she saw that it was in a real state of disrepair. With a gloved hand, Louise reached for one particularly menacing clump of shrubbery and cut at it with her pruners. As she worked, bottom branches became entangled in her trousers. Furiously she pulled her leg away from the branch. Sticky seed pods from a low-growing plant covered the cuffs of her pants and her shoes. As she tried to brush them off, she found they clung to her gardening gloves. Her tired body began to feel frustration and fatigue.

Louise surveyed the path. This was going to be a bigger job than she thought, one that should be started on another morning when she was fresh and full of energy. Gathering up her tools in her basket, she decided it was time to end her day's work.

As Louise walked toward the gazebo, her memories of all the happy times spent there flooded back to her. She began to remember the pleasant summer afternoons with Reed in the shelter of the gazebo's cool walls, nights with Frederick looking at the stars and shimmering lights of the Middletown coastline beyond Easton's Beach.

As she approached the gazebo she could see through the open window that there were two people inside. These must be some of the new guests Caroline was expecting. The Hargreaves. Louise was still getting used to the idea of sharing her old home with a succession of strangers, who paid for the privilege.

"I'll take a quick peek at them," she said to herself.

Looking through one of the windows, she saw a man near her own age seated comfortably on one of the wicker chairs. He had a thick chest, and his wide face was florid with a border of receding jet black hair exposing a large forehead. On the table in front of him were spread out papers and files, one of which he was reading with deep concentration. The other occupant of the room was a slender young woman, heavily made up with short hair that was artificially yellow. She tapped her high-heeled shoe impatiently on the stone floor.

"Stop that, Tina. I can't concentrate, girl," the man barked.

The young woman flinched. Her face darkened, but her body became still. At last her companion put down the file. Louise could see his eyes. They were deep in his head, black and bright like two burning coals.

"Well, Maurice," Tina said, "what is your decision?"

Maurice looked around the gazebo and nodded approvingly.

"I'll have my lunch out here tomorrow. Make arrangements for the kitchen to send down a tray."

"I thought you would want me to telephone Mark Fitzgerald." Her gaze trailed to the file.

"I like working here. I appreciate your suggesting it. It's quiet except for the sound of the ocean waves. Yes, I'm glad I took your advice and walked down here this afternoon. It's given me a chance to clear my head and settle some things."

"Such as?"

"Oh, several things," Maurice answered. "You know this country is changing, Tina. There are a lot of business opportunities out there that didn't exist a few years ago."

"You always have so much on your mind, Maurice. Mark Fitzgerald can't do everything for you. He has enough to do as the company's lawyer. You know I could take more of the responsibility of running the business off your shoulders. Why don't you leave me to deal with some—"

Tina reached for the top file. Before she could touch it, Maurice's large hand covered it. His companion quickly recovered herself and stepped back with a tiny two-step and finished her sentence.

"—of the less pressing details of the business. You know you can trust me."

"Do I?" Maurice purred. "I wonder."

"Maurice," she said, looking straight at him. "I don't like what is going on. You owe it to me to be frank about the Townsend Crest merger. Is it going through or not?"

"I'm happy with the way things are progressing. That's all you need to know. Mark is working out the details. Why do you think you should be brought in on the negotiations?"

"You know perfectly well," she said with flashing eyes, "that I want more responsibility in the company. The merger would give me that opportunity. You owe me, Maurice."

"Tina, you keep talking of what I owe you. After Maury died I made sure you were well provided for. You have no financial worries." He paused and then added, "Do you?"

"Of course not. Money has nothing to do with it. When Maury died, you told me I was still part of this family. You said I could have this job with the company. Don't tell me you don't know what I expect. I'm the only one in the family capable of taking over from you."

"My dear daughter-in-law," Maurice said, his voice light and cheerful, "I expect to be running my business for a long time to come."

Maurice stared directly into Tina's eyes. She met his gaze with a return one of the same gale force. For a second both antagonists pondered the next move. Tina spoke first.

"Sometimes, Maurice," she said, "I could kill you."

Outside the gazebo, Louise could not help but suck in her breath in astonishment at the tone of the threat. Despite her natural patrician aversion to eavesdropping, she had stayed at the window after she caught sight of Tina's expression. Louise found herself unable to take her eyes from the hatred on the woman's face. Did the object of so much loathing have any idea of its existence?

Louise moved back from the window. "Really," she said to herself, "it would be most awkward to be found here."

Suddenly she was conscious of movement from around the other side of the gazebo. There was the imperceptible crunch of feet walking on dead leaves. Someone else was in the vicinity. As if on a tour of the garden, Louise began strolling leisurely and made the full circle of the summerhouse. There was no one in sight. She frowned and, as she did, she saw the shrubbery of the Cliff Walk pathway part.

"Well, hello," a bulky figure in a nylon track suit called to her in a hearty voice. "I was just having my daily constitutional."

Louise stared at the newcomer as he strode toward her. He appeared to be perspiring heavily. Was he another of the guests? It was often confusing. Sometimes tourists wandered on to the grounds from the Cliff Walk.

"Harold Hargreave," he said, extending his hand. "My family is staying here this weekend."

"Louise Kent," Louise said as her hand was grasped by a sweating palm. Should she say she was happy to meet him?

"Nothing like the sea air to work up an appetite."

"No," she said as she scrutinized him. Harold Hargreave bore some resemblance to the man in the gazebo, but seemed soft where the older man looked hard. "And I believe we have a lovely dinner planned for your family this evening." She sounded like the brochure Caroline had made up for the Inn.

"Well, that suits me fine," Harold boomed jovially. "I could tuck into a horse. Exercise does that to me, you know."

"No, I didn't," Louise said.

"Well, I'll see you later at dinner."

He smiled at her and trotted up the pathway toward the house. As Louise followed his retreating figure she saw a dim silhouette near the rose garden. As her eyes focused into the orange sun, she saw it was Mattie. Louise called to her.

"Do you need me in the house? Does Caroline want me?"

Louise reached the cook's side and repeated her questions.

"Them Hargreaves is here," Mattie said, her voice making no attempt to hide her disapproval of them. "Mrs. Caroline is fussing all about the place."

"I'd better get cleaned up so I can help with dinner," Louise said.

"What were you doing down there by the Cliff Walk?"

"Inspecting the path, if you must know." Louise's voice had more than a hint of querulousness, and only her fatigue stopped her from adding "Miss Busybody" to the end of the sentence.

"Well, you look a proper mess, with your hair full of leaves and things."

Louise involuntarily stepped back. She thought Mattie was going to put her hands on her head and pick out the leaf mold and bits of twigs.

"I *said* I'm going up to take a shower."

"I'll run your tub," Mattie said. "You need a good soak." She turned and began walking toward the house.

"I'm having a shower," Louise said to her back. "It will be quicker. I can wash my hair."

There was no response from Mattie, and as Louise pushed her tired legs up the hill she wondered if indeed she would be allowed to wash herself in the way which she preferred. Somehow, the closer the two women got to the service porch, the more she doubted it.

CHAPTER FOUR

The decanter of vodka in the library drinks' cabinet had been full earlier in the afternoon. Now after Brian Hargreave poured another drink from the elegant cut glass, he calculated how many days' worth of alcohol it now contained. One more. Perhaps two, if he were careful. He had been sitting, drinking in the library of Kenwood Court ever since he had arrived, not even bothering to go up to see his room or to change his clothes.

But, why should he be careful? Especially with such smooth tasting vodka to consume. He wondered if all the bottles contained premium brands and lifted the stopper of the scotch to investigate its quality.

"Mixing your drinks, Brian? I wouldn't advise it."

Brian raised his eyes up from the bottle's open mouth and looked at the round figure of his brother with indifference.

"The scotch is good, Harold. Can I pour you one?"

"I'd rather have a beer, thanks for asking. Is there some? What do we do?" He looked around the spacious room. "Do we ring for it?"

"Oh, no. It's all right here, part of the guest service," Brian said as he opened a low door in the cabinet to reveal a small refrigerator. "Bass ale, Guinness, Heineken. What would you like?"

"I could get used to this," Harold said. He grabbed for one of the brown ale bottles. "This is living. What do you think, little brother?"

"I think this bar is going to make putting up with all of you palatable."

"You're a nice fellow, Brian, when you want to be." Harold took a long, noisy pull on the Bass. When he was finished, a contented belch, smelling of malt, came from his mouth. "Why don't you try to get along with us this weekend instead of always looking down your smart-ass nose at us all the time? We're really not so bad."

"All of you?" Brian asked. "Are you including Maurice and Tina in your group of the not-so-bads?"

"Well…not so bad, not so good." Harold laughed and finished off his ale. "I'll take another of these."

Brian opened the refrigerator.

"How's your doctoral thesis coming?"

"All right," Brian shrugged.

"What does that mean? I thought you were the brains in the family. Maurice can count himself lucky you never went into Hargreave Industries. You would have given him some competition."

38

"I prefer studying history to manufacturing junk."

"What's your trouble?"

"My work is on the Sack of Rome, you might remember. I'd like to go to Italy next semester and do some research on the burning of the libraries by the barbarians in the fifth century."

"Why don't you?"

"Where would I get the money on a graduate assistant's salary? Italy's damned expensive these days, especially Rome."

"Ah, money, the elusive commodity. We all could use more."

"Some Hargreaves seem to have enough."

"Ask Mother," Harold said. "She always indulges you."

"She gives me the money now to live. I can't ask for any more."

"There's always Maurice." Harold smiled mischievously.

"Believe me. I'm so desperate that I've actually thought of doing that."

"The problem," Harold said with a smile, "is that I've never known our Uncle Maurice to admire scholarly pursuits. Somewhat of a barbarian himself, don't you think?"

"Yes, our very own king of the Visigoths."

"The who?"

"The vandals who burned Rome. Maurice would applaud their efforts."

"What are you talking about, dear?" Emily's diminutive form entered the room. She had changed into an ankle-length, aquamarine

39

silk dress for dinner. Clusters of diamonds glowed in her earrings and around her neck.

"Maurice, Mother," Harold said. He raised his bottle. "We're drinking to all the barbarians. Will you join us? Brian, do the honors. A drink for our mother."

"Hush, Harold. Please don't joke about Maurice. He and Tina were right behind me coming down from upstairs. They've stopped to talk to Mrs. Kent, but they'll be here any minute."

"You know, Mother," Harold began, "you've got to get over that irritating habit of yours of avoiding family friction. Otherwise what's the fun of being a Hargreave?"

"What would you like to drink, Mother?" Brian sat his empty glass down carefully. He didn't want her to see he was drunk.

"Some sherry, please, Brian. And after you pour it, I think you ought to change your clothes for dinner."

He nodded. A perfect excuse to escape the room.

Caroline was coming across the grand hall on her way to the library with a tray of hors d'oeuvres when she had met Emily coming down the main stairway.

"Oh, Mrs. Kent," Emily said, pausing on the bottom step. "Where should be we be?" There was a touch of tentative excitement in her question which Caroline found appealing.

"We're serving drinks in the library," Caroline said. "It's right through that hallway. I believe some of the family are already there."

"Thank you."

"How are you enjoying your stay, Mrs. Hargreave?"

"Oh, everything is wonderful. Your house is lovely, like a palace."

"I'm glad you like it," Caroline said.

"Lionel and I went to visit The Breakers after tea. It was breathtaking. Can you imagine living there? So many rooms."

"It was built for a different era, Mrs. Hargreave. The Vanderbilts had a large staff." Caroline looked around the hall and smiled. "It's so difficult these days keeping one of these houses running."

"Oh, I would love to live there, even for a week. I want to see more of the mansions, but I don't know how much more Lionel will do. I know he found it boring."

Emily paused in her narrative as she saw Maurice and Tina walking down the stairs.

"Oh, I should be going into the library. You must see to your other guests." She hurried away.

"Mrs. Kent," Tina said. "May I speak to you?"

Caroline waited as the couple approached. An unexpected question about the nature of their relationship flashed across her mind, and she admonished herself for thinking of it. Guests could have any relationship they liked.

"Mr. Hargreave wants his lunch in the gazebo tomorrow," Tina said. "He'll be working there all day."

"Fine. There's no need to come to the dining room. Anyone is welcome to have a tray in their room, or on the veranda if the weather cooperates."

"This is a fine house, Mrs. Kent," Maurice said. "My suite is extremely comfortable." It took a second or two for Caroline to realize he was dismissing Tina, who must be used to his ways, because she was moving on toward the library. A second or two after she was gone from sight, Brian came out of the same corridor. He stopped when he saw Caroline with his uncle.

"Thank you," Caroline said to Maurice, conscious of Brian's staring at them.

"I like the set-up here. Relaxing, yet gracious and elegant all at the same time." He glanced at his nephew, taking in his appearance. "I like the formality of things here."

Brian, nodding to Caroline, moved past her and started up the stairs. Neither man acknowledged the other.

"When I get back to Boston, I intend to recommend your establishment to some of my friends. It's a good place to come for some quiet thinking."

"That's very kind of you, Mr. Hargreave. I would appreciate that. We are ideally suited for business retreats. The grand salon can be set up for meetings."

"By the way," Maurice continued smoothly, "you'll have another guest coming tomorrow. I hope you can accommodate him."

"Of course."

"Mr. Fitzgerald should arrive after lunch."

"That's no problem."

"Good. I thought it wouldn't be."

As Caroline circulated through the library with the tray of appetizers, she found herself studying each of the Hargreaves in turn. She had been a drama major at Yale, and it was second nature to her to look for physical mannerisms and voice inflections in everyone. How a glass was held, a comment replied to, a look given when its owner thought no one was watching. Observing such details was basic for an aspiring actor, and noticing these characteristics was an old habit Caroline had not broken.

Now as she answered questions about tourist attractions in Newport and gave suggestions on the best shops and restaurants, she began to form impressions of the Hargreave family. They reminded her of the solar system, many planets revolving around one sun.

Caroline was almost certain that Lionel was the older of the two brothers. He was tall, graying, distinguished-looking, yet he held himself in the background, preferring the perimeter of the family gathering to the center stage his sibling occupied.

"Excuse me, Mrs. Kent." Caroline heard a female voice behind her and turned around to see Donna's hand reaching for one of the cheese straws on her tray. Next to her, Kae Hargreave's look of disgust followed Donna's fingers as the food was plucked up.

43

"My, these are good," Donna said, her mouth closing over the flaky pastry. A few buttery crumbs stayed on her pink lipstick.

"Would you care for anything, Mrs. Hargreave?" Caroline asked Kae, who pulled back and shook her head as if the mere closeness of the tray was as offending as its calorie-laden contents.

"Have one of these cheese things," Donna counseled her. "I could eat them all."

"I'm sure," Kae said.

"We should ask Mrs. Kent for the name of a nice place to have lunch tomorrow, Kae," Donna said. "Let's get an early start, do lots of shopping, have lunch, and then—"

"I don't think I'll go shopping tomorrow."

"But, you said before that you would. You promised," Donna pleaded.

"I said I don't want to go."

Caroline watched as Kae walked away. She joined Maurice, who was momentarily alone in front of the fireplace. They began a conversation, which appeared to disquiet Nelson's wife. Caroline decided to clear some of the drinks' glasses which had begun to accumulate around the room. Eventually she drew near enough to the fireplace to hear some of what the two Hargreaves were saying.

"I can't wait for an answer." Kae's tone was rigid.

"You won't have to," Caroline heard Maurice say lightly. "I can give it to you in one word. No."

"You don't want trouble at a time like this, Maurice."

44

Caroline pretended to inspect an imaginary water ring left by one of the glasses on a table.

"A time like what? I don't know what you think you know, Kae, but—"

"Stop it," Kae hissed. "Don't play games with me. I'm not one of your feeble blood relations. I want out. You have to let me out."

"You know what you signed when you and Nelson married. You know what you get in the event of a divorce."

"That's not good enough, Maurice. I know what you're doing. I can ruin you."

Caroline could not help looking at Kae Hargreave. An unflattering line had hardened around her mouth.

"I wouldn't if I were you," Maurice said. "No good comes of being greedy, Kae. Take my advice and avoid the temptation."

"You're not in a position to give advice, Maurice."

Kae turned and looked around the room. When she found her husband's tall figure she strode in his direction. Maurice Hargreave watched her with an impassive stare and drained the last of his drink.

CHAPTER FIVE

Early the following morning Lionel slipped out of the bedroom in the west wing that he shared with his wife. He passed his son Brian's room and then the one which Tina occupied. Her door was right before the entrance to Maurice's suite, and Lionel wondered if there was also a connecting door between the two.

"Do you think Maurice and Tina are having an affair?" Emily had asked him several months ago. The question had not dawned on him previously, and he had answered quickly in the negative. That her question might have deserved a positive response, however, was an unpleasant idea that had continued to absorb him.

Lionel tapped gently on his brother's door. He knew him to be an early riser, up with the sun to get on with his day's work.

"Come in." Maurice's voice was full of energy. Lionel opened the door and entered the room. He found himself in an expansive sitting room with soft, upholstered chairs grouped in front of a marble fireplace. A wood fire was burning in the grate.

47

Maurice was sitting in one of the chairs, wearing a dark robe over his paisley silk pajamas. His full attention was on a sheaf of papers in his hand. Lionel thought how many times he had seen his brother in exactly this same position, head down, eyebrows drawn together, the thin line of the pensive mouth moving slightly as he concentrated.

"Lionel," Maurice smiled as he looked up. "I'm glad you've come. I've just been going over this one more time. Everything's in order. I've gone ahead and signed everything myself." He handed his brother his pen.

Without a word, Lionel took the pen and the document. His eyes skimmed the pages.

"So, this is it," he said solemnly after he had signed the papers. Why did it feel so hollow to know it was done?

"And you are satisfied?"

"I told you I would have liked the other matter to be included."

"You said you understood why it could not be in writing. Legally—" Here Maurice shrugged his shoulders in that way that Lionel had seen so often. "Well, no counsel would advise including it. Not in this age."

"But I have your word?" Lionel pressed.

"You have."

Lionel was watching his brother's face carefully for signs that there was truthfulness behind his words. He had seen him often say

48

one thing, affecting complete candor, while meaning something entirely different.

"This is important to me, Maurice. I've got to trust your word."

"Mark is driving down later today. He'll have the final documents. Meanwhile everything is taken care of."

"Good."

"What will you do?" Maurice asked.

"I shall have to talk to Emily, of course. It is her decision now as much as mine."

"You haven't told her yet?"

"I thought we agreed it best to wait." Wait, he thought, until there was no turning back. "Emily has been so happy coming here for our anniversary. I'm not a sentimental person myself, but a woman often is."

"I'm happy we're all here with you. Getting the family together these days is not an easy thing to do." Maurice's voice was easy, friendly.

"I suppose I haven't thanked you properly for giving up your time to do this. I know how you dislike being away from your business."

"I'm glad to do it," Maurice said expansively. "I'm sure I owe you a few debts from over the years. This is my way of making them good."

Lionel digested his brother's comment for a second or two before speaking. His tone was diffident. "As I said, it's for Emily. I owe *her*, you see."

"I'm sure I can understand. I wasn't as lucky as you in the choice of a wife." His first wife Phyllis had left him shortly after the birth of their son. Then, like her offspring, she had died young from the ravages of cancer.

The second of Maurice's wives, a photographer whom he had met while she was working on a profile of him for a business publication, sued for divorce after five years of acrimony. Lionel heard she had afterwards married a rancher and moved to Montana. Maurice had been alone now for almost ten years. Or was he? Lionel looked around the room for a door to Tina's room.

"What are you and Emily planning for today?"

"Mrs. Kent suggested a restaurant on the water for lunch. It's at the other end of the Cliff Walk near the Easton's Beach. I thought a quiet time together would be in order... to celebrate our anniversary alone before the big dinner tomorrow night. We're going to walk there later this morning."

"Isn't that a long walk?"

Lionel frowned. "Mrs. Kent said it's about half an hour's walk. I think we can make it there."

"Don't take offense, Lionel. I didn't mean to suggest—"

"I'm not offended," his brother cut him off. "I just wish you didn't always think I was a complete fool."

50

Maurice got to his feet. He put his hand on the taller man's arm. It was a gesture of conciliation, but Lionel remained stiff. All he wanted to do now was leave the room.

"After all these years," Maurice said, looking up at his brother, "I'd like to think we've become friends."

"So much has happened." Lionel's voice was starched.

"Let's forget the past, Lionel, and only think about the future."

"I don't know if I can," Lionel answered. His eyes drifted toward the yellow flames in the fireplace. Their dancing shapes had a calming effect on him, and he understood why his brother liked having the fire lit. "Perhaps after this weekend is over, things will be different between us."

As Nelson Hargreave sat at the breakfast table later that morning, his body was anxious. His early morning run had failed to quiet his uneasiness, and now Nelson ignored the chatter of his family which filled the dining room.

"Nelson, Nelson? Are you listening?" His wife's voice jolted him out his thoughts. "What are you doing today? I've asked you twice."

"I'm sorry, Kae, what did you say?"

"What are your plans for today?"

"Oh," he said. "Mrs. Kent gave me a brochure for a tour that tells the history of Newport through its architecture. It stops at two of the Preservation Society houses, and I thought we might take it today." He looked at his watch. "The bus leaves at ten, and we can catch it if we leave here at 9:30. It's just before nine now."

"You're going on a bus tour?" Tina asked from across the table. She had been pouring Maurice another cup of coffee. "That sounds tacky."

Nelson scowled at Tina. "It will be very educational. I'm sure that wouldn't interest you."

"Spend the whole day riding the bus, Nelson," Maurice said amiably. His black eyes twinkled. "You have the time."

"Yes, Nelson," Tina said. She gave her father-in-law a conspirator's smile.

"See that my briefcase is brought down from my room," Maurice said to her. "I need some papers. I've had Mark Fitzgerald get the figures on Townsend Crest's sales compared to ours. I want to review them."

"What papers do you have, Maurice?" Nelson asked crossly. "Sales are my responsibility and Mark Fitzgerald is our lawyer, in case you've forgotten how the organizational chart reads at the company. If you want information on sales, you should ask me."

"You know I'm interested in what Townsend Crest does these days."

"How would I?" Nelson fingered his coffee cup restively. "You keep everything in your own head and don't seek advice from the rest of us."

Brian gave his uncle an angry look and stood up. "I'm going back to bed," he said to no one in particular.

"The tour sounds lovely, Nelson," his mother said, pretending she hadn't noticed Brian's exit. "Your father and I went to The Breakers yesterday."

"I'd like to go with you, Nelson," Kae said, "but I've already promised Donna I'd go shopping with her." From across the table, Donna registered her surprise.

"But, I thought you said last night that—"

"I've changed my mind. Mrs. Kent told me there were good antique shops in Newport, and their prices were reasonable."

"Planning to re-decorate, Kae?" Maurice asked. His keen look in her direction caught her husband's attention.

"I thought I would take the car," Kae said to Nelson.

"Well," Nelson hesitated.

"Take the Lincoln, Nelson," Lionel said. "Your mother and I are going to walk to our lunch. That way Kae and Donna can use the BMW."

"Thank you, Father," Nelson said. "Shall I come upstairs with you while you get your keys?"

Lionel had produced a set of car keys for Nelson from his pocket, and that had been another missed chance to talk. Now as Nelson stood on Bellevue Avenue, holding a purple ticket in his hand, waiting to join the other passengers on the tour bus ready to take him

53

through the architectural ages of Newport, his father's actions continued to puzzle him. How much did he know about Maurice's sudden interest in promoting a merger with one of their competitors? Lionel appeared very disinterested in the topic.

Once aboard the bus Nelson studied his fellow passengers before choosing a seat in the vehicle's middle next to a lean young woman with close-cropped blond hair. His eye picked her out as a foreigner. German, he thought. Or perhaps Scandinavian.

"May I?" he asked, pointing to the empty seat beside her. "Is this seat taken?"

She shook her head and Nelson settled himself into the seat, finding room for his long legs. He placed the shopping bag he was carrying between his feet.

"Thank you," he said. She inclined her head slightly, and Nelson wondered if she understood English. "It's a pretty city," he said, nodding toward the window.

"I like it very much. There are many beautiful houses," she replied in measured, accented tones. German. He was pretty sure.

"Are you interested in architecture?"

Before she could respond, the voice of the driver came over his microphone.

"Please take your seats, ladies and gentlemen. We'll be starting off on our tour of historic homes and buildings of Newport in just a few minutes. But first let me acquaint you with some of the

54

history of the beautiful city of Newport, Rhode Island, the 'city by the sea'."

The German woman leaned forward in her seat to catch every word of the commentary. Beside her, Nelson relaxed against the cushion and let his mind range to Maurice's announcement at breakfast that Mark Fitzgerald would arrive later that day. His thoughts were interrupted when he caught sight of a black BMW turning across the intersection near where the bus was parked. He strained forward to see it, and his wife's profile in the driver's seat was unmistakable. The passenger seat was empty.

What had she done with Donna? He thought their plans had been to leave the Inn at Kenwood Court together around ten. Nelson knew his way around Newport, and Kae was off track for both the harbor shops and the antique district. What was his wife up to? He repeated the question to himself, and he found he had no answer.

As Caroline left the kitchen after the breakfast dishes had been put away, she came into the foyer to see Harold coming down the main staircase. He was wearing a windbreaker and carrying a book.

"Hello, Mr. Hargreave," she said pleasantly. "Are you going outdoors?"

"I'm going to finish my book," he said, holding up a worn Tom Clancy paperback.

"The veranda at the back of the house gets the sun. There are some comfortable chairs out there."

"Perfect," he said. "I don't suppose you read this kind of thing," and he held up the book once again for her inspection, "but once I start, I can't put it down."

"I know what you mean. Why don't I bring your lunch out to you there?"

"Oh, don't trouble."

"It would be more convenient for me. That way I can get the dining room ready for tonight's dinner."

"That's fine then. You don't have too many in today, I see. Everyone taking the opportunity to shop and see the sights." He laughed as if he shared some camaraderie with her. "Maurice and Tina working as usual, though. Maurice is in the gazebo again today?" His voice lifted as if in question.

"Yes. He's lunching out there at noon."

"Outdoor lunch sounds good for me, as well," he said as he made his way, book in hand, for the veranda.

It was a few minutes past one o'clock when Caroline put the silver buffing cloth down on the worn wooden counter of the pantry and looked at the time. Soup was on the menu tonight and the tureen, which had come into Reed's family at the end of the nineteenth century as a wedding present for his great-grandparents, had needed polishing.

"I don't have the hang of this yet," she said, sighing to herself over the passing time.

Her own upbringing in an upper middle-class Connecticut suburb had not provided her with the charmed youth which the Kent family had given Reed. But there had always been help to clean the house and take care of the messier side of running a busy household. Caroline and her sister had been called upon to do little. Their parents had been more interested in enriching their daughters' lives with lessons and travel than in teaching them how to do the chores.

Getting the inn up and running had been a challenge for Caroline as she mastered domestic skills she had never planned to acquire. While she couldn't say she found all her new work challenging, the fact was that the manual work distracted her from thoughts of Reed and what might have been.

Now as she put the soup tureen aside, Caroline remembered that she had yet to collect the luncheon trays.

Jan had helped her to deliver them, taking Brian's to his room while Caroline had taken the tray down to Maurice in the gazebo.

"I knocked and went in the room like you said we should do," Jan reported back to Caroline a few minutes later in the kitchen, "but I didn't see him in there. I heard his water running so I left it. I didn't want him to come out undressed or anything."

"That's fine, Jan. Now you can take this one to Harold Hargreave on the veranda. If I go, he'll talk me to death. And this last one is for Tina. She's working at her computer in the morning room."

In the kitchen, Caroline checked her watch again. Almost quarter past one. Jan was busy upstairs, getting the bedroom ready for Mark's arrival. Caroline would have to clean up the lunch service.

As she slipped out the back of the house, Caroline could see Harold on his chair on the veranda, book in hand. He waved to her.

Caroline walked across the lawn toward the gazebo and felt the gentle warmth of the sun's rays on her back. The sky was blue and cloudless, and over the tall shrubbery at the back of the property she could see the glistening silver band of the Atlantic Ocean. It was at times like these that she felt positive about her decision to leave Manhattan and come to Newport. How many people could boast one of the world's oceans at their doorstep? The smell of the chrysanthemums in the perennial garden next to the gazebo was pungent, and she paused to enjoy their strong scent. Their colors were warm and bright, and she decided to come back later to cut some for the house.

Entering the gazebo, her eyes went immediately to the tray, with its crumpled napkin and clutter of empty dishes, which was sitting on the table near the door. Without meaning to she looked at her watch again. It was 1:25. It was only then that she looked for Maurice and saw him slumped over in his wicker chair, his neck hanging at a jagged angle. For several seconds she was confused. Soup tureens, flowers to cut, luncheon trays and dirty dishes to be washed had all been joined in the jumble of her thoughts. She stared hard at Maurice Hargreave and realized that her heart's hope that he might move because he had heard her come into the room was irrational. She took a few hesitant steps toward him, and her foot kicked an object on the stone floor.

A gun. It seemed so unfamiliar a sight to Caroline that she bent down to examine it. Then something told her not to touch it, and she only stared closely at the weapon. It was a small handgun. Not a revolver, but the other kind, the kind that had the bullets in the clip in the handle. Her father had kept a similar German pistol his father had brought back as a war souvenir.

She turned her attention again to Maurice, staring bewilderedly at him, then looking back at the weapon on the floor. The room had an eerie stillness.

Cautiously she stepped nearer to the chair. Maurice had been sitting back in the chair, his left side turned to the door, she surmised, when he was hit, causing him to slump forward. She didn't know much about such things, but she thought one would bleed freely from a gunshot wound. She looked at his broad chest to see if there was blood. There didn't appear to be a wound. Had he actually been shot? When she moved around the right side of the body, her question was answered.

Maurice had been shot on the side of his head, an inch or so to the left of his right ear. She stared at the hole, ugly and red. There wasn't as much as blood as she thought there would be. It was not liquid now, and she looked with both horror and fascination at the wound's circular entrance. He must surely be dead, but supposing he wasn't?

She listened close to his chest for the sound of his breathing, but there was none. One of the body's hands was hanging at his side, and she touched his wrist for a pulse but felt nothing. She had to will herself not to give in to the feeling of sickness rushing over her.

"He's dead, isn't he," declared a familiar voice.

Caroline jumped with fright and leapt to her feet. Standing in the doorway, his gray eyes harsh and cold, was Lionel Hargreave. He stared at his brother as he walked toward him. Lionel had noted the gun and carefully walked a route which led around it.

"I suggest you call the police, Mrs. Kent," he said. His voice was even, composed. "This is a responsibility for them."

"I believe that under the circumstances you should be the one to return to the house and have the police notified. I will stay here with the body until someone in authority comes." Then she added what up to then had been unconscious in her thoughts.

"You, after all, will be considered one of the suspects. Therefore I should remain here to see that nothing is touched or—" And she glanced at the gun on the floor. "Removed from the murder scene."

Lionel started to speak, but didn't. Instead he nodded and left the room.

CHAPTER SIX

The first uniformed patrol officers to appear asked Caroline to wait outside the gazebo for the arrival of the detectives. She was surprised to find the police more interested in securing the house and grounds than investigating the summerhouse. While one of the officers waited with her, the others went to ascertain who was present in the main house. The officer who stayed behind, a young woman with a nameplate that said *Williams* did not engage Caroline in conversation, but periodically gave her a solicitous smile while Caroline stood awkwardly on the path.

The afternoon sun had left this side of the gazebo, and the cool breezes off the water began to chill Caroline. She was wearing the light-colored slacks and a long-sleeve black turtleneck, which only an hour earlier had begun to feel warm as she had worked. To keep from thinking about the cold, she started to collect her thoughts about what she had seen in the gazebo.

As soon as Lionel had left to call the police, she had made a quick examination for clues like earrings, cufflinks, buttons and the like which the murderer could have left behind. She supposed that expecting to find some evidence was melodramatic on her part, but she wanted to make sure. There had been nothing, and she had even gone as far as to look at Maurice's hands to see if something had been clenched within.

Nothing in the room had seemed out of the ordinary. There were no signs of the well-known struggle. What did it mean? That Maurice knew his murderer and did not fear him... or her? Had Maurice Hargreave sat calmly in his chair while the assailant walked behind him and put a bullet in his head?

Suddenly she remembered Mark Fitzgerald, whom Maurice had been expecting to arrive sometime after lunch. *Had* he arrived? Where was he now?

Mentally she added Mark to her list of suspects, which she now realized could include other employees of Hargreave Industries or business associates who might have had a grudge against Maurice. Her impression was that Maurice Hargreave had been a man who did not care if he made enemies. It was probably well-known that the family had traveled to Newport for the weekend. Anyone could have tracked Maurice to Kenwood.

Had someone been watching the house? Caroline shivered at the danger this new possibility implied.

Further speculation on who Maurice's murderer might be was ended as Caroline saw two men in street clothes walk down the path toward the gazebo. As they neared, Officer Williams greeted them with a deferential manner.

"No one has entered this building since we arrived, Lieutenant," she said, gesturing to the gazebo. "Everything is just how we found it."

"Thank you, Officer Williams," the lieutenant said. He was a tall, good-looking man with black, curly hair and the wide shoulders of an athlete. As he spoke, his companion took a notebook and pen from his breast pocket. The second man was middle-aged, with graying sandy hair and the beginnings of a paunch.

"Mrs. Kent?" The lieutenant turned to her. She nodded and automatically extended her hand. His deep blue-black eyes were giving her a professional once over. She judged him to be about thirty-five.

"I'm Lt. Nightingale, detective squad." His handshake was firm and quick. "And this is Sgt. Davies." Caroline held out her hand to Davies, who juggled his book and pen into one hand to shake hers. He was an average-looking, sturdy cop, and his presence helped to put her at ease. "You are the owner of the house? Kenwood I believe it is called."

"Yes. My mother-in-law and I live here. She is Mrs. Kent also." Sgt. Davies made a note of this, and Caroline realized she had to be careful how she expressed herself. Her words would be evidence in the case.

"Is your mother-in-law at home now?" Nightingale asked. Caroline said that she was, as well as Mattie and Jan, who made up the household staff. She added that Mattie lived in and provided Jan's home address. Sgt. Davies was writing at a rapid clip. "The dead man, Mr. Maurice Hargreave, does not live here?" Caroline swallowed and explained the details of Kenwood's being an inn, and the fact that Maurice was one of her guests.

"How many guests do you have staying with you presently, Mrs. Kent?" Davies asked.

Caroline spoke the names as if from a list. She explained who each member of the family was and the relationships among them. She went back to the day when Nelson Hargreave called to inquire about reserving the house for the anniversary party, his inspection visit, and ended with the family's arrival yesterday.

"So all the male Hargreaves are blood relations, and none of the women are," Nightingale said thoughtfully.

"Do you find that to be significant?" Caroline asked.

"The significance, or lack of it, will be part of my investigation," the lieutenant said. She thought that his manner was condescending. She also realized that he did not intend to answer her questions.

"Let's start with your finding the body, Mrs. Kent. I don't suppose you noted the time."

"Well, I didn't look straight at my watch as soon as I saw the body, if that's what you mean, Lieutenant." She hadn't meant to sound curt, and she could see that the tone of her voice had surprised him. "I looked at my watch as I came into the room. It was 1:25."

"Exactly? Exactly twenty-five minutes past the hour, not twenty-four or twenty-six?"

"I believe it was 1:25." Caroline held out her wrist. He looked at her watch, then at his own.

"It keeps good time. All right, 1:25. How long do you think you had been in the area of the gazebo prior to that time?"

"It's hard to say. A minute, two minutes, that's all. Who can tell the difference between a minute and half a minute? Let me see," she said slowly, seeing the lieutenant's look becoming impatient. "I was in the pantry and looked at my watch, and it was a little past ten after. Twelve minutes after," she added quickly before he could interrupt. "I had to wash my hands, put the silver polish away. I walked through the kitchen, Mattie asked me a question, I answered it." She took a breath. "I went out the back door and waved to Harold Hargreave. He was on the veranda—"

"We'll get to where everybody else was in a minute," Nightingale interjected. "Keep going with your movements."

"Well, as I said, I paused just a few seconds. And then I walked down the path to the gazebo. No, no, I'm wrong. I stopped by the perennial garden. That's around the other side of the gazebo. I was there a minute or so, a few minutes probably." Davies had been writing hastily as she spoke, and now she looked at him for some accounting of the time at that point.

"I've got it all, Lieutenant. I'll sort it out later and make a time line."

"Tell me now exactly what you saw when you entered this structure here," the lieutenant said, pointing to the gazebo. "Did you see anyone around the grounds? Besides Harold Hargreave."

"No, no I didn't. If anything it seemed quieter than usual. Sometimes you can hear people on the Cliff Walk. The pathway through the shrubbery there leads to it." The detectives looked at the path with some interest. "My mind was on all the work I had to do. I didn't even see the body when I first came in. All I was thinking was to take the tray, get back up to the house, and do everything I needed to do before this evening."

"Let's go inside the gazebo now, Mrs. Kent," Nightingale said.

He led Caroline and Davies into the summerhouse and stopped a few feet into the room. Caroline's eyes went immediately to Maurice's body still sprawled over in the chair in its frozen pose. The detective appeared to take no particular interest in the dead man as he turned his head slowly in a 180 degree arc to take in the entire room. Caroline marveled at his dispassion.

"Is this what you saw when you entered?" Nightingale asked her. She nodded. "How far did you come into the room? Did you touch anything?"

"I was looking at the tray." She pointed to the object, now beginning to look conspicuously untidy with its plate of hardened food stains, the dirty cutlery and the soiled napkin which surrounded it. There was also a glass with the dregs of iced tea and a withering slice of lemon. "I didn't look at Mr. Hargreave at first. I guess I was preoccupied, as I said. Eventually I went to see what was the matter with him. He looked so odd like that."

"What time had the tray been brought to him? Did you do that yourself?"

"Yes. Mr. Hargreave asked for his lunch at noon, but I think I brought it down a little before that."

"How early?"

"I was in the kitchen at quarter to twelve, I remember that. But it was just after that I came out with the tray."

"Was Harold Hargreave on the veranda at that time?"

Caroline nodded.

"So," Nightingale said thoughtfully, "you would have brought the tray sometime around ten to, would you say?"

Again Caroline nodded in agreement and detailed her impressions of her first trip to the gazebo, then returned to her second. She added her kicking of the gun to this version, which Davies noted with more than casual attention on his pad. The familiar frown returned to Nightingale's face, and he again made a lengthy visual examination of the space.

"And you didn't recognize the gun?"

"No, definitely not."

"Did you see Lionel Hargreave actually enter the room?"

"I was looking at Mr. Hargreave's face. I didn't even hear his brother come in. Mr. Hargreave startled me. Lionel Hargreave, that is."

"Too many Mr. and Mrs. Hargreaves in this case," the detective said disagreeably. "And did Lionel Hargreave touch anything?"

"Oh, no," Caroline said vehemently, "I made sure that he did not. In fact, I insisted that he be the one to go to the house to telephone to the police."

"And why was that, Mrs. Kent? I would have thought you might have preferred to leave such a morbid sight."

"Oh, honestly, Lt. Nightingale, you can't think me to be that dense." He raised his eyebrows. "I knew immediately that everyone in the family would be a suspect in Maurice Hargreave's murder."

"And why was that?"

"I just expected they would be," she said uneasily, twisting the slim gold band she wore on the ring finger of her left hand.

"That's an important statement, Mrs. Kent. What are you basing it on?"

"Perhaps I shouldn't answer that." Saying one of the Hargreaves might be a murderer was a serious charge for her to make.

"And perhaps you should." His deep eyes reflected determination. So this is what it was like to be questioned by the police.

"It's only my impression, of course. With guests, you can't help but observe things." She was still wavering, but Nightingale expected more. "The Hargreaves didn't give the impression of being a harmonious family, Lieutenant. Maurice is... was the head of the family company. I had the sense that he enjoyed being in control a little too much." She was thinking of the way Maurice had watched Kae walk across the library on the previous evening.

"You got the impression he controlled the family?" Caroline nodded reluctantly. "And they disliked him for doing this?"

"I don't think that they were happy about it."

"Did you like Maurice Hargreave?" The question came unexpectedly at her.

"Me? Why would that matter?" When he didn't answer her question, she knew she had to respond to his. She thought about it for several seconds, and then said, "I had no reason not to."

She was surprised to see him smiling.

The arrival of the crime scene team caused the detectives to suspend their questioning of Caroline. Lt. Nightingale's full attention was given to the newcomers as he gave them their instructions. As the photography and the careful measuring started, Caroline left. The gazebo had become a buzz of activity, and she was strangely reluctant to leave it.

Walking up the path back to the house, she realized that the feeling of nausea was gone. Seeing Maurice for the second time in the company of the two plainclothes men had somehow made the whole thing seem unreal. That Maurice was allowed to lie dead, untouched bordered on her being in one of those dreams where inexplicable things happen in what are otherwise ordinary and familiar settings.

A man carrying a medical bag pushed past her without comment, hurrying down the lawn. Two uniformed officers, who were looking in the shrubbery and flowers for any signs of evidence, ignored his passing. "How single-minded they are," she said to herself. "Each has their own job."

Would the entire house be searched? Caroline supposed it would be necessary. The realization of what effect Maurice's death would have on her business crowded on Caroline's mind. The house had to be kept full of guests for her to survive financially. Being at the scene of a murder investigation would not be the ambience visitors to the Inn at Kenwood Court would expect. There were some new guests coming on Tuesday. Should she call them to cancel their reservations? How could she, in good conscience, welcome them without explaining the presence of police in every nook and cranny of Kenwood? What had she called the estate in her brochure for the house? "A gentle oasis taking you back in time."

Now the house was more fit for the setting of one of those murder mystery parties she had often seen advertised, but never expected to host herself.

Feeling guilty that her thoughts were on her own financial situation, Caroline tried to find sympathy for the Hargreaves who had lost one of their family. But again she had the distinct feeling that it was one of them who had killed Maurice. It was a horrible thought. Until today they had seemed like any other visitors to the house.

Caroline let herself into the house through the service porch. The kitchen and pantry were empty, and she walked out into the grand hall where a police officer was on duty. He directed her to the morning room where she found another officer standing guard. Although the room was full of people, no one was speaking.

Louise, Mattie and Jan were sitting on one side of the room across from those of the Hargreaves who had been found in the house. Lionel and Emily, with her husband's protective arm around her, sat side by side on a sofa. Brian was seated on the other side of his mother, a somber look on his face. He looked up as Caroline came into the room, and his intelligent eyes met hers with a questioning look.

Harold was sitting in one of the chairs, his paperback gripped in his hand. Tina sat across from him in another. Only she, of all the occupants in the room, seemed to be showing any signs of grief, as she nervously played with the hem of her short skirt. Her eyes looked red, and her face was drawn.

71

Louise rose and came toward Caroline. They embraced. Caroline found herself fighting back the urge to cry. Now she was beginning to feel that the death was true and not a dream. As the two women separated, Louise continued to hold her daughter-in-law's hands in hers. She rubbed them soothingly and turned to the officer.

"Do you suppose we could have some tea brought in?" Mattie rose, relieved for the chance to leave the room. "You can send someone with Mattie if you like, but I think we could all do with some. Your officers, too, if you wish," Louise added. "Mattie can prepare some coffee as well."

The officer spoke on a walkie-talkie device and soon a uniformed policeman appeared to escort the cook to the kitchen. Caroline looked at the faces left in the room. It seemed as if they were all waiting for someone else to break the silence. Finally, it was Harold who spoke. His voice sounded almost cheerful.

"I suppose there's no doubt that he's dead, Mrs. Kent?"

Caroline stared across the room. Again Brian's eyes locked on to hers, but she held his stare for only a moment.

"No, Mr. Hargreave," she said to Harold. "Your uncle is dead."

Tina muffled a sob, and Harold shot her a disgusted glance.

"Really, Tina, this theatrical display of sorrow over Maurice is a bit much."

Tina looked up, her face now angry. Before she could speak, Lionel turned to his middle son.

"Harold, may I remind you that there is a policeman present? I suggest that you refrain from saying anything."

Harold only shrugged, making no rejoinder. He fingered his book as if he wanted to open it. Caroline saw that there was a bookmark placed near the end.

Lionel directed his next comment to the police officer.

"I wonder, Officer, if you could tell us how long we will remain here. My wife should lie down. You can see this has been a shock to her."

Everyone looked at Emily, who was staring vacantly ahead.

"Lt. Nightingale instructed me that everyone is to remain here until he can speak to them. If the lady is ill, I can ask him about allowing her—"

Emily interrupted his comments. "No. No. I don't want to lie down. I want to stay here." Lionel tightened his fingers about her shoulder.

"It's going to be all right, my dear," he said tenderly. "I'm here to take care of you."

"Maurice," Emily said weakly, and Lionel whispered something into her ear. Caroline was not close enough to hear clearly, but she thought she caught the words "can't" and "anymore." Was Lionel telling Emily that Maurice could not hurt either of them anymore? If Lionel Hargreave meant his words as a comfort to his wife, they seemed to be having no effect.

CHAPTER SEVEN

As Caroline sat waiting with the Hargreave family in the morning room, she once more began to have feelings of being in a dream world. She was staring at the others in the room through a hazy, half-asleep lens over her eyes. She longed to open a window.

"Officer. Officer, excuse me." Caroline looked up. Tina was trying to get the attention of the young policeman. "I wonder," Tina began with an artful shift of her eyes. "Could I be excused for a few minutes?" She paused, letting the officer get the meaning of her request.

"There's a powder room right off the foyer," Caroline said.

Tina seemed to have recovered her composure as she left the room under the watchful eye of the officer. She was no longer displaying any sorrow over her late father-in-law's demise, and Caroline considered the possibility of Tina as a suspect.

"Alibis," she said to herself. "We will all need alibis for the time of Maurice's death."

Caroline knew that she had taken Maurice his lunch at ten to twelve when he was definitely alive. When she had come back at 1:25, he was dead. Roughly an hour and a half. But, he had eaten his lunch. The tray proved that. She had brought him a sandwich of lobster salad with a plate of mesclun and some fruit. She supposed he could finish that in half an hour. That would mean he was done eating about 12:20.

Also, the blood was dried around the wound, and she knew that was important to the time. Would it take twenty-five minutes for that to occur? If that was reasonable, she would assume that the murder happened no later than one o'clock, and no earlier than quarter past twelve. Caroline shifted in her seat as her mind became energized. Where had everyone been between 12:15 and 1 p.m.? She would begin by putting together what she knew.

Across the room Brian was sitting, staring out the window. Caroline hadn't seen him since breakfast, and she remembered that Jan had said she had not seen him when she had left his luncheon tray. The water had been running in his bathroom, and Jan took that as a sign he was inside. But, suppose he hadn't been? Suppose he was lurking outside the gazebo, waiting for his chance.

Caroline frowned. Her eyes fell on Harold as he sat, absorbed in his own world. His alibi would be that he was reading all the time, but who had witnessed it?

Lionel had been on the murder scene at 1:25. He and Emily had said they were going to lunch at the end of the Cliff Walk. Had they? Could either of them have returned before one? Caroline had no way of knowing.

Tina was back now, and the sound of her heels walking across the parquet floor snapped the silent atmosphere. Caroline turned to Tina and her alibi. Tina was someone she had seen in the house, and Caroline concentrated on reconstructing that part of the day.

After delivering Maurice's tray, Caroline had gone back to the kitchen. Mattie was there, rolling out the dough for some fruit tarts, and Louise was slicing the apples. Jan had just come back from taking Harold his lunch. Tina's tray was the last on the counter.

"You can take Mrs. Hargreave's lunch to the morning room, Jan."

"O.K.," Jan said.

"And we need to get the bedroom ready for Mr. Fitzgerald. We'll put him in the old study in the west wing." The room was part of a suite once used by the master of Kenwood for his private contemplation. The space had no bathroom, and Caroline kept these rooms as the last to be assigned to guests. A hall bathroom serviced both guest rooms, and she hoped Mark, as a man, would not mind the lack of privacy.

And then Tina had appeared in the kitchen doorway. Caroline reached back into her memory to view the scene clearly. Mattie and Louise were working at the table. Tina seemed fascinated by the rapid movements of Mattie's hands as she handled the pastry.

"What is that you're making?" Tina asked Mattie. A frigid look from the cook was the response she received.

Louise, who was presiding over a large blue bowl of peeled apple slices and a mountainous pile of red skins, answered in a calm, deliberate voice. "Apple tarts." She looked at Tina sweetly. Caroline suppressed a smile.

"Can I use the fax machine?" Tina turned to Caroline. There was a file folder in her hand.

"Right now?" Caroline remembered asking.

"Maurice wants some documents sent immediately."

"All right," Caroline said. She wondered if she should direct Tina to her office, but decided instead she ought to take her there.

And then she had been unable to extricate herself from conversation with Tina Hargreave. Caroline used the old smoking room at Kenwood as an office. Family photographs from the last hundred years lined the room's walls, and Tina looked at them with interest, asking innumerable questions. Caroline found herself giving a history of the Kent family, with all the Newport connections. It had been time-consuming, and Caroline noted now how much time she had spent in her office with the suddenly inquisitive woman. Caroline was trying to figure out exactly how long they had stayed in the room, when she realized that a police officer was standing directly in front of her.

"Mrs. Kent," he said gently.

"Yes?" His manner was so polite.

"Lt. Nightingale wants to see you."

"Certainly," she said, jumping to her feet. She followed him out into the foyer. The lieutenant was standing looking up at the chandelier hanging from the high ceiling in the grand hall. It was very ornate, as most original fittings in the house were, and Caroline wondered what he was making of the house.

"Mrs. Kent," he said, transferring his gaze to her, "I wonder if I could have a room to use for my interviews. I am ready to start taking statements from everyone."

"Of course. Let's go back to my office. I think you will find that comfortable."

The detective followed her through the house. Instead of leading him across the grand hall, she went instead through the back hallway which led past the kitchen and the back stairs. Before he entered the old smoking room, he took a look inside the billiard room, which was across from it. Caroline stood and watched while he took in every detail of the house and stored it away.

Inside the office his approval of the space was clear. "This is fine," he said unnecessarily.

"Is there anything else I can do for you?" Caroline asked. She was hoping she might be freed of the obligation to remain in the morning room with the others.

"Yes," he answered. "Actually I had a few more questions for you." She nodded. "I want you to try to tell me everything you did today up until the time you found the body."

79

She gave the information quickly in an organized way for she had already had the time to order her thoughts.

"Thank you. That was very helpful."

"Do you think anything I've said is important?" She asked the question before she realized what she was saying, and his face darkened. "I mean," she stammered, "does it help you to figure out when the murder was committed?"

"We'll be looking for hard evidence to determine that. Now, I'd like to talk to your mother-in-law."

"It's just that the more I think of it, the more Tina Hargreave's actions this afternoon were suspicious. I thought—"

"Thank you, Mrs. Kent," he cut her off. "I'll see the other Mrs. Kent now."

"Of course," she said. He had turned his attention toward the desk, which had her paperwork spread out on it. "Let me move that so you can sit down." Deftly, she scooped up the papers and cleared the desk. As he put his hand on the chair's back she slipped quietly out of the room.

When Hank Nightingale talked with Louise Kent, he found he could learn little more than he already knew about the Hargreaves. He was impressed by Caroline's mother-in-law. She had a wellborn manner, yet she was easy to talk to and anxious to help. When Louise Kent told him that she had spent the times relevant to the murder in the kitchen, he was surprised to discover that she was there to help her cook prepare the inn guests' evening meal.

Hank had grown up in Newport in a decidedly middle class family. Their lives had been largely untouched by the proximity of the wealthy residents of Newport and their lavish homes. His father had worked in an insurance agency, and his mother taught in the local public schools. Theirs was a private parallel existence to the glamorous public side of the city. The elder Nightingales endured Newport's tourists as a constant, but unwelcome nuisance, especially in summer when the traffic was unbearable and the noisy rental party houses sprang up in every neighborhood.

Hank's parents' opinions had been his own when he was younger. But ten years in the Newport Police Department had brought him regular contacts with all the elements his parents steadfastly ignored. He had been called to several of the mansions over his career. Crime struck in them as well in the lesser dwellings around town. He'd seen the rich up close and hadn't found them to be much different from his own bourgeoisie parents and their friends. His impression of both Mrs. Kents was that they were gracious and casually unpretentious about their drop in status from society matrons to hard-working innkeepers.

The house was comfortable and attractive. Nightingale liked its simple design, but he could see that there were signs of wear throughout the residence. The grounds were overgrown and lacking much of the formal planting usual for a Newport mansion. The

81

gazebo, where the murdered man had been found, needed restoration. He wondered how much of the decision by the Kents to turn their home into an inn was driven by financial hardship.

Ben joined Hank in Caroline's office. The veteran sergeant was used to his role as assistant on an inquiry, and he settled comfortably in a chair waiting to get started on the formal interviews.

Hank had established himself behind the big carved wooden desk. Before sitting down he had studied the photographs on the wall, pausing to ponder the studio shot of Caroline and Reed on their wedding day. He would have to ask the lady of the manor about the whereabouts of the gentleman in the picture at some point. Would she believe that it was his professional duty to do so or would she take it as an invasion of her privacy? He had no clear feelings on either position. He planned to ask.

Lionel Hargreave was escorted into the room and given a seat across from the two detectives. His demeanor was calm, detached. Hank would have bet that the man was capable of murder, but it was early going. No sense to start with prejudices. Instead he smiled his professionally disarming smile and began a process he had done many times in the past and always found stimulating.

"I understand from Mrs. Kent that your family is here to celebrate your wedding anniversary." Lionel nodded. "Fortieth, isn't it?" The man across the desk nodded for a second time. "I would offer my congratulations, but under the circumstances of your brother's

82

death…" Here Hank watched Lionel carefully. "You may not appreciate such sentiments."

"My wife was much looking forward to the family dinner party tomorrow," Lionel said, shaking his head. "It's ironic in a way that my brother would upstage our celebration."

"Was that something he often did?"

"Maurice was not a grandstanding type of person. Rather, he always seemed to be the center of attention. Even when others might be thought to deserve more notice." Lionel leaned forward in the chair.

"I know one of the things you want to learn about is my brother's character, who he was, isn't that right?" Now it was Hank's turn to nod. "Well, I'm sure you will hear from everyone that Maurice was a difficult person to get on with. He was domineering and expected all of us to jump when he barked." He pondered his last statement and added, "And I suppose we all did."

"Did you like your brother, Mr. Hargreave?"

Lionel looked as if the question was being asked of him for the first time. He took his time to answer it.

"No, I can't say that I especially did. Not that I hated him. Please know that. We were two different people. Even as children. My father Joseph was a difficult man, you see. Maurice took after him. Always a go-getter, always planning."

"Your father or Maurice?"

"I was referring to Maurice, but my father had those traits as well. He was a successful self-made man. There's no end to the ego that develops in a person in that circumstance. My father made his millions, and Maurice took the business even further."

"But you, yourself, are employed in the family firm?"

"Yes, as president."

"And just what is the firm's business?"

"The company started in 1938 as a manufacturer of table china. Now we have an entire line of china and giftware. We employ almost 300 people." He said it without pride. "Maurice runs the business. He's the chairman."

"Is the company prosperous?"

"There are no money problems, if you are thinking of that as a motive for Maurice's murder. We're all generously paid."

"Who actually owns the business?"

"Maurice and I inherited equal shares from our father."

"So you receive profits as well?"

"You must know in a small business we keep our profits down through clever book work," smiled Lionel.

"No, I didn't."

"Everybody in the family is on the payroll. We all get nice paychecks and company cars and lots of expenses covered. It's all legitimate, but a bit unethical, I've always thought."

Hank took in this information and digested it.

"What happens to the ownership of the business now that your brother has died?"

Lionel hesitated before replying.

"That's a good question. My father had expected Maurice and I would pass the business on to our four sons. Maury, that was Maurice's son, died three years ago. He would most certainly have taken over from Maurice."

"Why Maurice's son, and not yours?"

"He was like his father, and Maurice would have wanted it that way. My two sons, Harold and Nelson, would have continued to hold major responsibilities in the company. As they do now."

"Your son Brian is not employed in the family company?"

"No," Lionel said. "It's not his particular interest."

"But what will happen to your brother's half share?"

"I'm sorry to say I do not know the terms of Maurice's will. I had always expected to retire from the business before him, and I do not know what he intended would happen to his share. He has lately been talking with another manufacturer about the possibility of merging the two companies. The Townsend Crest Corporation has a product line which is similar to ours. But it's just in the talking stage."

"And would you continue to pursue that, Mr. Hargreave?"

Lionel shrugged. "I doubt it. It never seemed a good idea to me."

"Thank you. Now, let's go through your day, Mr. Hargreave. What happened after you finished breakfast?"

"My wife and I lunched out. We thought it would be appropriate to share a quiet meal together during the weekend." His face showed distress, and Hank wondered if he was thinking of his brother's death or his wife's disappointment.

"Where did you go?"

"We walked along the Cliff Walk to the restaurant just at the end by the ocean beach."

"Easton's Beach?"

Lionel nodded.

"What time did you arrive at the restaurant?"

"I think it was about quarter to twelve. No earlier than that. We had reached the beach about 11:30. I remember Emily wondering what time they began serving. We took our time looking at the view. Then we saw people being seated on the terrace so we went up and got a table."

"Did you pay the bill by credit card?"

"Cash, I'm afraid. No record."

"And can you tell me what time you left the restaurant?"

Again Lionel hesitated and then began shaking his head.

"At my age, Lieutenant, my eyes are not constantly on my watch. I felt I had the leisure of not caring what time it was."

"Try, Mr. Hargreave," Hank said patiently.

"I suppose we may have been there forty-five minutes or so. We didn't hurry, at any rate. Afterwards we walked on the beach again."

"And how long did you walk?"

"Fifteen, twenty minutes. I'm not sure. And then we started back along the Cliff Walk. I know the walk back to the inn takes about a half an hour because that's what Mrs. Kent told us before we got started."

"And you went straight to the gazebo when you returned?"

"Yes, I did." His tone was definite this time.

"Mrs. Kent thinks that you arrived shortly after 1:25."

"She's probably right. I can't dispute her statement."

"And your wife?"

"Emily?" he asked sharply. "What about Emily?"

"Why didn't she go with you to the gazebo?"

"She was beginning to feel tired from all the walking. I wanted her to rest. She went straight to our room."

"Why did you want to speak to your brother at that particular time?"

"Do I need a reason to speak to my own brother?" He bristled, then recovered his composure. "I knew he planned to work there during the day and thought I would take a minute to tell him how much I appreciated his coming to Newport with us. It meant a lot to Emily to have the whole family here, and I thought that was as good a time as any to thank Maurice for coming down here for the weekend."

CHAPTER EIGHT

After Lionel was gone, Hank and Ben went over his statement. "He's the cagey type," Ben said.

"Yes," Hank agreed. "I had the definite feeling that we were getting the sanitized version of things."

"Too bad about not using a credit card. We could have had a time check there."

"Get on the restaurant anyway. Someone will remember seeing them, and we'll try to get some times."

Hank stood up and stretched his back while walking to the door to ask for the next Hargreave. The officer waiting outside in the passageway handed him a business card.

"This gentleman has been waiting to see you, sir. He's most insistent that he be interviewed next."

Hank looked down at Mark Fitzgerald's card in his hand.

"Senior vice president and chief counsel," he read. "No Hargreave here," he said looking up. "When did he arrive?"

"About fifteen minutes ago." Hank looked at his watch. It was ten after four. "He demanded to know what was going on, and Sgt. Weber had a time calming him down. He even wanted to see the body. But it had just been taken away. He's most upset, sir."

"Is he?"

"Mr. Nelson Hargreave has also come in, Lieutenant. A few minutes before this Mr. Fitzgerald."

"All right. Thank you, Dickson. Let's have Mr. Fitzgerald next."

Word was sent to the morning room, and Mark Fitzgerald responded rapidly to the summons. He strode importantly into the room and went straight to the desk, putting both of his palms face down on it. He was fair, probably just under forty years of age, of medium build, well but conservatively dressed, and angry.

Leaning forward, Mark spoke in harsh tones. "What is the meaning of this?"

It was such an absurd thing to say that Hank could not suppress a smile. He loved witnesses like this one. The opportunity to question pompous asses like Mark Fitzgerald was one of the things he got up for in the morning.

"The meaning of which *what*?" Hank asked. "*What* happened? *What* I'm doing? Or *what* you're doing, Mr. Fitzgerald, coming in here on your high legal horse to harass a duly sworn-in officer of the law?"

"Don't give me that policeman's right rigmarole, Lieutenant. My client was murdered several hours ago. I want some answers."

"First of all, we don't know yet when Mr. Hargreave met his death. The report on that will not be ready for quite a while. Secondly, now that you're here, why don't you give me an accounting of your movements for the last several hours, and we'll see what you know about *what*—" And he said the word with an exaggerated swag of his head. "Happened here."

If Mark Fitzgerald was used to his manner being effective with legal adversaries, he was not successful on this occasion with besting Lt. Hank Nightingale of the Newport Police Department.

Hank waited calmly while Mark sputtered some further attempts at intimidation and then waved him to a chair.

The questions put to Mark Fitzgerald began very simply. Peevishly he told the two detectives that he was the close, right-hand man to the late chairman of Hargreave Industries. Maurice had requested him by telephone late on the previous afternoon to make an appearance today. He had come when called, leaving the offices outside Boston shortly before two o'clock. He had stopped for a sandwich on the way.

"Who can corroborate this alibi?" Hank asked.

"Alibi!" Mark Fitzgerald fairly shrieked the word. "Are you telling me I am a suspect?"

"Right now this case is wide open on suspects. Any or all of you may have been in on it. I have it on good authority that Maurice

Hargreave was not a popular man. Disliked." He decided to test a theory. "Hated, you might even say."

"I did not dislike or hate Maurice," Mark said, "and that is strong language, Lt. Nightingale. Maurice was a tough, exacting businessman. All I can say is that he treated me well, and I like to think he trusted me. Believe me when I say I had no reason to kill him. Quite the opposite."

"Why did he want to see you so suddenly?"

"He said he had some documents he wanted me to look at."

"They couldn't be faxed?" He glanced at Caroline's machine on a side table. "I understand this machine here was at his disposal."

Mark paused before answering. He seemed to be debating with himself. Hank rubbed the back of his neck which was beginning to ache with fatigue.

"Well, Mr. Fitzgerald?"

"I do have some obligation to my client, Lieutenant, even though he is dead. You see, I'm not sure what Maurice wanted me to see. I think I can guess, but I don't want to. This is, after all, a murder investigation. I want to tell you only facts, not conjectures."

Hank had to agree that this was a reasonable statement on the part of the attorney so he tried another tack.

"Are you by any chance an executor of Maurice Hargreave's will?" Mark nodded. "Did you draw it up?" Again, Mark moved his head in the affirmative. "Will you tell me the provisions? Specifically what happens to his share of ownership in Hargreave Industries?"

"It passes to his brother Lionel."

Hank was startled by the information, and he did not try to conceal his surprise.

"Maurice changed his will soon after his only child died of cancer three years ago," Mark said with a superior tone in his voice. It appeared to please him to go one up on the policemen. "While his son Maury was alive, he had been the heir."

"I see," Hank said, still trying to put this piece into his puzzle.

"A powerful motive, don't you think, for a man to murder?"

Hank had no reply. Even though Mark's words mirrored his own thoughts, he would never give the impudent man the pleasure of conceding as much.

After Mark had left the room, Hank and Ben took a break for the coffee which Jan brought in for them.

"It can't be this simple," Hank said.

"We have to hear from a few more people, Lieutenant. Who knows? They may all accuse each other."

"Yes. We'll have to examine the papers Maurice had in the gazebo."

"How will we know if this special document is among them?"

"I don't know. Let's see that list again. How many Hargreaves are left?"

Ben passed over the paper. Hank looked at it and frowned. Too many Hargreaves, he thought again.

93

"Ask outside if the rest are back yet. Kae," he said, "and, let's see here. Donna. The two shoppers."

"This is going to take a lot of legwork to check these movements about town. This would have to be the day everyone decided to sightsee, shop or stroll."

"Perhaps the murderer planned it that way," Hank suggested.

"You mean somebody wanted a pretty clear coast?"

"Yes. Mrs. Kent mentioned that the youngest son, Brian, had asked how to get to the Redwood Library. He's a historian and wanted to do some research or something. It was unexpected that he felt ill this morning and didn't go out as he had planned."

"That's suspicious in itself," Ben said.

"We'll see if anyone saw him moving about the house during the middle of the day. As I see it, the murder took place during the time between when Caroline Kent brought the lunch tray to the gazebo at 11:50 and when she returned at 1:25. She said the blood was already drying on the wound. That backs back the time of the shooting. Possibly to no later than around one o'clock."

"So we're looking at where people were between 11:50 a.m. and 1 p.m. That's still a good stretch of time."

"We'll wait for the medical report. The doctor might fix us up with a better earlier time, something well past noon. The lunch tray was empty, don't forget," Hank said. "He had to have some time to eat. Why don't we find out if Mr. Hargreave was a slow eater or a fast one? Surely his family would know that."

94

"The murderer could have dumped the lunch to confuse the times. He, or she, might not know that the autopsy would examine the stomach contents."

"What would be the purpose?"

"The time," Ben said. "The crime would seem later than it was."

"Hmmn. Where would the food be dumped? We've come across nothing on the grounds."

"Maybe the murderer ate it." Hank scowled. "All right. It's farfetched, I agree. But possible. Don't forget that Harold Hargreave... he was supposed to be out on the veranda at lunchtime."

Hank argued no more. He knew Ben liked to come up with some interesting possibilities in every case by suggesting a point or two that would add an uncommon dimension, pleased that he was the first to come up with the new reasoning. Hank indulged Ben's habit. Once in a while he had an intuition that had proved helpful.

When Emily Hargreave came in to be questioned, her story matched the one which her husband had previously told. Moreover, she could be no more sure than he of specific times. Hank was uncomfortable pressing her beyond her forthcoming admissions. The woman was clearly in a state of unrest. She answered the questions mechanically, her voice rarely changing pitch but remaining at a low whisper, which was often hard to hear. Several times Ben Davies was forced to ask her to repeat important details.

Emily finished her account by explaining that when she and Lionel had returned from lunch she went straight up the pathway to the house, leaving her husband to make his way to the gazebo on his own. No, she didn't walk close enough to see inside the summerhouse. She had gone to her room and was lying down because she had felt tired after their walk. With a slight shyness she admitted to having had some wine with her lunch and conceded that she might have felt sleepy due to that, inasmuch as she generally did not drink alcohol with her midday meal. She had no idea her brother-in-law was dead until after Lionel had notified the police of the crime. Her husband had roused her from her sleep with the news.

Hank could not find a wedge into any of her statements, which paralleled so closely those of her husband. That Lionel had gone over with her what they would say during the time they had been together in their bedroom seemed obvious. Was it to his benefit? Or hers? He shook his head and looked across the desk at Emily Hargreave. She looked in need of further sleep.

"Why do you think your brother-in-law Maurice agreed to come down to Newport for several days to celebrate your wedding anniversary, Mrs. Hargreave?"

Emily started slightly in her chair. Her hand went to her lips. She furrowed her brow pensively, but did not speak.

"By all accounts," Hank said helpfully, "he was a dedicated businessman. He lived for his company." Hank thought he detected a flutter in her eyelids on the word 'his.' It would seem to me that

96

spending much time away from the office would be unusual for such a person."

Emily nodded tentatively. Hank pressed carefully forward.

"Were you and your husband close to his brother? Is that why he came?"

Emily seemed to be searching her mind for the precise answer. Some time passed before she replied to his query.

"I don't know why Maurice decided to come with us. My older son made the preparations and my other two sons, Harold and Brian, were happy to come into the arrangement with him. I was very pleased that my sons and their wives wanted to be with us for our wedding anniversary."

"But not Maurice and Tina Hargreave? Would you have preferred if they had stayed away?"

"They are part of our family." She spoke softly. "Tina is Maury's widow, and we must all include her in family things. She feels slighted, you know, if we don't."

"How would you describe the relationship between Tina Hargreave and her late father-in-law?"

Again Hank had the feeling that Emily was thinking carefully of the right thing to say.

"Maurice loved his son. It was a great blow to him when Maury died. He suffered so at the end." Emily faltered. "It was not something my brother-in-law could accept. The money, you see.

Maurice was used to its buying everything. It couldn't buy Maury's life."

"I see," Hank said, picturing the grieving father as a real human being for the first time since he had seen Maurice Hargreave's corpse. "And that is why Mr. Hargreave continued to remain close to his son's wife? To feel close to Maury?"

"It may be the answer to it all, Lieutenant," Emily said with sudden conviction. "Tina's not a particularly endearing person, and I think we all have wondered what Maurice was planning for her future."

It struck Hank immediately upon this comment that he wanted to see Tina Hargreave next. He thanked Emily and had Dickson escort her out and take the order to bring in Tina.

"Now what are they hiding, do you think?" Ben asked. "The two of them got that story straight enough."

"That's for sure. Neither of them seems very grieved over the dead man."

"That was a good point to ask why Maurice came with them. That makes it seem the murder *was* planned in advance."

"The gun will give us the clue to that. If we can prove that it was brought here by someone who planned to use it on Maurice, we will be closer to the truth of this case."

"Mrs. Kent didn't recognize the gun?"

"No, she was definite on that. She said there are no guns kept in the house."

"You think the Hargreave family are the suspects then?"

"It's logical to assume, isn't it? I don't see any sign that there was a robbery. And unless it turns out that there is a serial killer at work on the Cliff Walk, my money's on that family."

Hank looked restlessly around Caroline's office, his thoughts unexpectedly moving toward her. "That's why I am concentrating on the family first. They all came here together on a holiday. Maurice was probably more relaxed, his guard down. It was a perfect opportunity for somebody."

Hank picked up a letter opener from Caroline's desk and idly struck the palm of his left hand with the blade. "Somebody brought that gun along on the trip. I'd bet on it. It's an old handgun, a Colt .32. I don't think they've been made since the end of World War II. It's the kind of gun somebody kept in a bedroom drawer, or in the study, for protection. Probably had it for a long time. Before they take the gun to the lab we should let these Hargreaves take a look at it."

"What about fingerprinting everyone here?"

Hank looked now at the letter opener in his hand. Seeing there was an inscription on it, he brought it closer to his eyes to read the words: *The Newport Reading Room * Henry Pierce Kent * Founding Member 1853.*

"Yes, that'll have to be done," Hank answered, putting the letter opener carefully down on the desk. "Have Jarvis start setting up for that. And let's check gun permits with Massachusetts. Oh, and make another note. Let's try to find out how it was first suggested that

Maurice work down in that gazebo. Was it his own idea, or did somebody put the idea in his mind?"

CHAPTER NINE

"I suppose I did that, Lieutenant," Tina Hargreave said complacently. She was giving Hank her full attention, contributing the impression of someone earnestly trying to help. Her eyes locked on Hank's each time he spoke.

"Why did you do that, Mrs. Hargreave?"

"Suggest that Maurice work in the gazebo?" Hank nodded. He was becoming uncomfortable under her stare.

"I thought Maurice could work undisturbed. Nelson, especially, was always hanging around him, trying to be involved in whatever Maurice was doing. Putting him down there made it a little harder for Nelson to bother him."

"Did Nelson often bother him, as you put it?"

"Oh, yes," Tina said.

"Why?"

"He was always trying to push himself forward in the company. You know," she said to Hank, smiling in an overly friendly way, "trying to find out things about the business that were not part of his responsibilities. Maurice kept a lot of the decisions for himself, and Nelson resented it."

"What exactly are Mr. Nelson Hargreave's responsibilities?" Hank asked.

"He is vice president of sales. We have a good size sales force and a network of brokers who handle our products. Nelson's job is to supervise them."

"Is he good at his job?"

Tina thought for a minute. "Yes, I'd have to say that he is. Nelson works very hard. I'm sorry if I might have given you a bad impression of him." Are you, Hank, wondered. A few moments ago, she had wanted him to agree with her assessment of Nelson's intrusive and boorish behavior. "Maurice was happy with Nelson's performance in sales. Our figures are up on a regular basis. No, Lieutenant, Nelson is valuable to Hargreave Industries. It was only that annoying attitude of his that can get on one's nerves. Like guests at a party who won't take the hint and leave when it's time. I'm sure you know the kind of person I mean."

Again she gave him the knowing look. Hank was careful not to make a sign that he agreed with her. Rather he decided on another line of inquiry.

"Tell me," he said. "What is your job within the company? Do you have a title?"

"Yes," she said, "I do. I serve as Assistant to the Chairman of Hargreave Industries."

"Assistant. I see. And what does that mean exactly?"

"Oh, that's hard to say in a few words."

"I can listen to many words. Give me some examples of what you do."

"Maurice is … was…" Here she paused dramatically and expelled a deep breath of anguish, which Hank let pass without comment. "A marvelous strategist. His mind was always on some new plan for improving the company. He knew everything about what was happening in the plant in manufacturing, in R & D, in the administrative and financial functions we had to carry out. His mind was a steel trap. Nothing got by him. I was always at his side. Whatever he wanted carried out he told to me. I took care of seeing that his orders were executed."

"Is that all?" Tina's expression indicated that she considered that work to be a great deal for one person to undertake. While Tina Hargreave wasn't his type, Hank speculated on whether a vigorous, forceful man in his sixties like Maurice Hargreave might find her the antidote to his own aging.

"I meant," Hank continued, "did Maurice discuss the business with you? Ask your advice, that sort of thing?"

"Yes. I can't say he always took my advice." Again there was the tone of some shared understanding between them, which Hank tried not to show he disliked. "Maurice was usually right on target

103

with things, but that didn't stop him from allowing that there might sometimes be a better alternative. Yes, he did seek my suggestions about things. It helped him, I'm sure also, to have a sounding board. Someone he could count on not to pass things on within the company. Rumors flow in a company the size of Hargreave Industries. Maurice knew anything he told me would be kept strictly confidential."

"I gather you don't believe he felt that way about the rest of his family?"

"I don't think so, no. Part of it was, well, you do want the truth, don't you?"

"I thought that was obvious, Mrs. Hargreave."

"Maurice did not have confidence in the abilities of his brother and two nephews to see the big picture at Hargreave Industries. I think he was happy to give them jobs he thought they could handle. I just don't think he thought much of their ability to help him manage the company. For that, he thought I was best suited."

"Yet he seemed to have placed a lot of trust in Mr. Mark Fitzgerald."

If Hank had said the devil, he could have gotten no stronger reaction than the one which came from Tina Hargreave. Her whole body stiffened, and her face seized up in an ugly sneer. Even Ben, who could only see her in profile from where he sat, looked shocked to see the unexpected, angry transformation in her.

"Mark," she fairly spit out the syllables, "Fitz—ger—ald."

104

"My impression from him," Hank continued steadily, "was that *he* is an integral part of Hargreave Industries."

"That's his impression of himself. It's too bad Maurice is no longer able to give you his opinion, Lt. Nightingale. Maurice and I did not share Mark's sense of self-importance."

"I see," Hank said thoughtfully. "Just one other thing, Mrs. Hargreave. We're checking everyone's movements today, as you might have guessed." Tina nodded solemnly. "Were you here at the house the entire day?"

"Yes. Even though this is a vacation for the rest of the family, Maurice and I kept up with things at the office."

"And that included sending some faxes earlier today, I believe." He paused to let her nod that this was true—entirely true, she seemed to be gesturing with an extravagant bending of her chin into her chest. "Do you remember the time you sent them?"

Now she paused. "I'm not sure," she finally said.

"It might be important."

"No," she said firmly. "It was lunchtime. I do remember that. After twelve o'clock, most certainly."

"Well, perhaps we can verify the time later on in our investigation."

"If you think it's important."

"And you visited the kitchen two times during that period?"

Tina looked confused. "The kitchen? Oh, yes, I had to talk to Mrs. Kent about sending the faxes."

105

"The second time?"

"The second time. To the kitchen? I don't recall a second visit." Hank watched her. "Oh, yes, I did go back for my lunch tray. I'd forgotten."

She smiled at Hank. It was a generous smile, and he glanced over at Ben. With a slight movement in his eyes, the sergeant signaled back. Ben Davies did not approve of Tina Hargreave.

After Louise had helped Mattie to make a tray of sandwiches for the police officers still on duty in the house, she sought out Caroline to share her experience of being questioned. It took her some time before she found her daughter-in-law sitting pensively in the advancing twilight on the loggia, the open-air room on the second floor which faced the ocean side of the house.

The loggia's ceiling was formed by the third floor above, and the space was enclosed on three sides by exterior walls extending out from the house. The fourth, the room's outside wall was fashioned with a waist-high balustrade and several supporting columns. The space had an air of languid timelessness about it, primarily due to its primitive view of sky and water and the rugged sound made by the waves pounding against the massive rocks supporting the Cliff Walk below.

Louise watched Caroline for several seconds before disturbing her. "Poor dear," she thought. "This has disrupted her plans for the house, just when things seemed to be on the right track."

106

Caroline turned as Louise made a movement toward her. She smiled weakly. "The air is pleasant, seasonable for this time of year."

"Yes," Louise replied. "We might have been able to serve the cocktails in the conservatory before seating everyone at dinner." Caroline only shrugged, and Louise added, "I'm sorry, dear. This has been a blow to you, I'm sure. It's rotten luck."

"It seems wrong to be looking at it that way, Louise. That man is dead."

"But we didn't know him, now did we? We can't pretend grief we don't feel."

"No, I don't feel grief as much as I feel... oh, it's hard to explain."

"Of course, Caroline, you found him. You must be still upset by that. You ought to have a drink of something. Would you like me to get it?"

"Are you prescribing brandy?" Caroline smiled again. "I'm not going to faint."

"Brandy is good for a great many things. I would recommend some. There is a decanter in our sitting room." Louise started to go, but Caroline put a hand on her arm.

"Don't bother. I would like your company just now."

Caroline lapsed into silence, and Louise sat in quiet companionship, watching her daughter-in-law's face closely. The lapping waves made heavy, melancholy sounds as they dragged themselves toward the rocky shoreline. In the distance, among the shadows on the lawn, was the dark outline of the gazebo.

"Who do you suppose did it?" Caroline asked.

"One of the Hargreaves, no doubt."

"There's that Mark Fitzgerald. He didn't turn up until well after 3:30, you know. He was supposed to have come right after lunch. Maurice had said that last night. I expected him to arrive earlier than almost four o'clock."

"Do you think he came early, killed Maurice, and then returned later?"

"I think it is possible."

"What else have you been thinking?"

"I was trying to remember everything that happened during the time when Maurice died. I must have seen something that is a clue."

"I was in the kitchen for the entire time. I told the detectives that. I ate my lunch there and helped Mattie. She's in a state, you know. The police at Kenwood!" Louise couldn't help but smile.

"She'll forgive *you*," Caroline said with a frown.

"Let's get back to the alibis." Louise was more interested in the murder. Mattie could wait. "What about Brian Hargreave? He was in the house all day."

"I didn't see him. Jan left the lunch tray for Brian in his room while I took the one down to Maurice."

"Did she talk to him? Did she see him?"

Caroline hesitated. "He wasn't in the bedroom, but she said she could hear the water running in his bathroom."

"Now that's significant. You could disguise that you are not there with the trick of pretending to be taking a bath."

"He seems an unlikely suspect."

"Why would you say that?"

"What would be his motive? He has nothing to do with Maurice or the business."

"Maybe." Louise had noticed the looks with which Brian favored Caroline, and she disliked them. Asking Caroline directly about it would be a mistake. Better to pretend she hadn't taken any heed of it. "The quiet ones can deceive you," was her only comment.

"I think there are other Hargreaves with a better motive, Louise. I've been wondering about Tina."

"Did you notice the way she was watching Mattie make the dough for the fruit tarts when she came in the kitchen for her tray? She seemed unusually interested in the ins and outs of a good pastry. Now that seems out of character, don't you think?"

"Yes, although we have to be careful to look for a meaning in everything. The woman may just be interested in cooking. We don't know that she's not a gourmet cook at home."

"I think that's extremely unlikely," Louise said, rolling her eyes. "That woman couldn't boil an egg."

"Tina and I went into my office at 12:20. I know because I looked at my watch again. I was so busy worrying about getting everything done, I looked at my watch every five minutes."

"How long would you say you were in the room together?"

"Quite a long time. Tina looked at all the photographs on the wall and asked me about the family."

"She did? That sounds tactless."

"I thought at the time her curiosity was natural. Now, I'm not so sure."

"We are getting into the time frame when the murder was committed."

"Yes," Caroline said. "She was also eager to talk about her own husband. It was an inconvenient time for me to listen, but I felt I could hardly be rude."

"What did she say about him?"

"That he had been a great help to Maurice in the business, that he was just like Maurice and his father expected him to succeed him as head of the company. I think she was very proud of him. I left her there to send faxes, about 12:40 I think it was. I had to make the excuse of needing to go back to my work. It was hard to cut her off."

"She was working on her alibi," Louise said with sudden sureness.

"What time did she come back to the kitchen for her tray?"

"I wasn't looking at the clock especially. I remember your coming back from your office and going into the pantry. I'd say she came back about ten minutes later, maybe less."

"Well do you think she could have slipped out of the study, ran to the gazebo, shot Maurice, and came back to the kitchen, all in that ten minutes?" Caroline asked.

"I believe she could run fast. Without those awful high heels, of course. She's got very muscular legs, I've noticed. Probably uses one of those personal trainers so she won't lose her figure."

"Somebody ought to have noticed her running through the house. I'm sure the police will check if she actually sent any faxes after I left, and who received them. They all come through with the date and time. How long did Tina remain in the room when she came for her lunch?"

"Again, now that you mention it, she lingered. She talked about the dinner, asking what the menu was, who decides what we serve."

"We must be close to one o'clock by now," Caroline said. "When Tina took her tray, would she have time enough to put it in the morning room, slip out of the house and shoot Maurice, all in the later time frame we have? She would have had to get out of the house by a door other than the kitchen, which is the most convenient for going down to the gazebo. That would add time to her trip. Plus, wouldn't Harold have seen her? I hardly think he would fail to mention that."

"It doesn't seem very likely," Louise agreed disappointedly.

"And what about Harold? He was right out on the veranda during the time when the murder must have been committed."

"He would have seen if Tina or Brian went down to the gazebo from the house. The veranda faces directly onto the back lawn."

"And, of course, he could have gone down to the gazebo himself and done the shooting."

"When did you see him, Caroline?"

"Both times when I was coming and going to the gazebo with Maurice's tray, but not any of the rest of the time. Harold didn't come inside the house?"

"Not that I saw." Louise paused and spoke thoughtfully. "I have noticed him to be a sneaky person, Caroline."

"In what way?"

Louise related her experience outside the gazebo yesterday when she had thought she had heard someone lurking about. "It was Harold coming from his supposed stroll on the Cliff Walk who was the first person I encountered. I didn't believe him at the time. I think he was on the other side of the gazebo listening to Maurice and Tina's conversation."

"Harold?" Caroline asked with curiosity.

"Yes." She frowned. "Heavens, Caroline! I'd almost forgotten with everything else that's been going on. It's got to be important."

"What's important, Louise?"

"It was what Tina said to Maurice in the gazebo yesterday when she was so angry with him. I've noticed, too, that she was all sugar and spice when the others are around, but when she and Maurice were alone, it was a different story."

"Louise, are you going to tell me what she said?"

"Oh, why, of course, dear. Tina said she would like to kill Maurice."

"That's what she said? Exactly?"

"No, not exactly. What she said was," and Louise frowned again, "was that sometimes she could kill him. That's it."

"Sometimes she could kill him? Louise, we've all said something like that at one time or another in anger."

"I have never said that," Louise replied with some vigor. "To say I would kill someone. No, I would not use an expression like that, even lightly."

"I think someone like Tina would."

"You didn't see her face. She hated that man, I'm sure of it. And Harold overheard her. He may have thought he could use it to his advantage by killing Maurice and blaming her."

"But how? What would be the evidence?"

"The gun. It may have been Tina's."

"But why did she bring it on this trip? No, Louise, that doesn't hold up. Whoever brought the gun, assuming it was one of the family, did so because they expected to use it. This murder was not done on the spur of the moment. It was carefully planned. This weekend has been carefully controlled by someone. Someone who used the family's trip to Newport as an opportunity to murder Maurice. I have been sitting here racking my brain, trying to remember everything I have seen and observed about this family since they arrived. There have been clues. We've got to see them. Somebody set this all up, and I'm going to find out who it is."

"I don't know," Louise said with some anxiety. "I know you think it's silly of me to read those detective stories, but I've learned one important thing from them. If the murderer finds out that you know his or her identify, you're not safe. If someone has killed once, they will kill again."

"I won't take any chances. I'm just going to add everything up. And keep my eyes and ears open from now on. If I have any evidence, I will go right to the police with it."

"Promise me that," Louise commanded.

"I promise," Caroline said firmly.

The police officers, who were still working in the gazebo, had turned the summerhouse lights on. Louise looked across the lawn at their hazy brightness. What had seemed not to touch their lives now did. Things must be put right at Kenwood Court.

CHAPTER TEN

Hank decided to begin his interviews with the three Hargreave brothers by seeing Brian first. The youngest son of Lionel and Emily arrived looking tired and wan. He eased his thin frame slowly into a chair without waiting for an invitation to sit. Hank was open to believing the man was suffering from some illness, probably the flu. He was therefore very surprised, after asking about his health, to see Brian grimace.

"You look ill, Mr. Hargreave," the detective explained. He watched the man closely.

"I have a hangover."

"I see," Hank said. "Is this something usual for you?"

"Are you asking me if I am often drunk? Am I suspected of killing my uncle in a drunken stupor?"

"You're right," Hank said easily. "That was an imprudent question." He hoped this apology would relax the man in front of him.

Brian's face showed intelligence, and Hank would tread carefully. "Did you leave the house at any time today?"

Brian shook his head.

"What did you do after breakfast?"

"I went up to my room and stayed there. I took aspirin and tried to sleep, but it was difficult. I've always heard of people sleeping one off, you know. I've never been able to," he said, shaking his head.

"When Jan Lowry brought up your lunch, she told Mrs. Kent she heard the water running in your bathroom."

"I'm sure she did."

"And you were in the bathroom?"

"Yes. It was one of many trips." There was no embarrassment. "And you didn't leave your room?" Again Brian shook his head. "Hear any activity upstairs?"

"The maid was cleaning in the morning. She vacuumed the hall outside my room. I shooed her away when she wanted to make up my bed."

Hank studied Brian's face. His first impression that it was unattractive was replaced by an awareness that there was something engaging about it. The eyes, he decided. Dark black rounds beneath a prominent forehead and heavy brows, which never seemed to blink. "I didn't kill Maurice."

"Somebody did."

"I don't know who in this family has the brains to do anything like that."

"Except you?"

"I've been trying to think who did."

"But not you?" Hank pressed.

"I said I didn't." His tone was didactic.

"What have you come up with?"

"A few things seem curious to me," Brian answered. "I haven't worked it all out yet."

"Well, if you think you have evidence, you'd better give it to me."

"No," he dragged out the syllable into two. "I can't be sure."

"Can you tell me something of your relationship with your uncle?"

"Maurice?" Brian looked surprised. "I don't think we have any at all. A 'relationship,' as you say."

"Have you ever been employed in your family's company?"

"No. I passed up the golden opportunity to bring more junk into the world."

"What is your employment?"

"I am a graduate student and teaching assistant at Boston University. This semester I am working on my thesis for my doctorate."

"In what field?"

"Italian history."

"Did your uncle approve of your career?"

"I never asked him."

"What about your father? Did he want you to come into the business?"

"I didn't kill my father."

Hank hesitated, unhappy at the direction of the interview.

"Look, Lieutenant." Brian was drawing on some energy now, and the color was coming into his face. "I'm sure you've found out by now that Maurice was the whole show at Hargreave Industries. My father was a cipher. That I would sit in some office like he did... or Harold and Nelson did... or become a clown in the circus... it didn't matter to my father one way or the other."

"What about your mother?" Hank was beginning to feel the germination of an idea.

"I'm sure my mother would say she wanted me to be happy."

"And are you?"

Brian looked at his watch. "I wonder if Mrs. Kent will be setting out cocktails in the library tonight. She usually does at this time of the day." He stared languidly at Hank. "After today's events, I should say we all need a few drinks."

"It will be some time before I can think about a drink," Hank said.

"Pity," said the man across from him.

*****

Mattie's stone-faced concentration as she worked on the Hargreaves' dinner greeted Caroline as she came into the kitchen. The cook was busy grating Gruyere onto a large yellow baking dish filled with coquille St. Jacques.

"What a pretty picture that coquille makes, Mattie," Caroline said. The smell was intoxicating.

"Hmmn," Mattie growled.

"Do you want me to trim the asparagus?"

When there was no response, Caroline began to work on the large bunch of asparagus which was sitting on the work table top. She gave Mattie a wide berth as she carried the baking dish to the oven.

"I can fill the salad plates as well."

Mattie shut the oven door with another grunt. The door hinges were old and it took a careful tug to move them closed.

"I thought them Hargreaves would be leaving tonight," Mattie said, "not having dinner."

"The police won't let them leave Newport."

"They can stay somewhere else, can't they? There's plenty of hotels in town."

"They have paid until Sunday," Caroline explained. "I expect the police will tell us if they think we shouldn't have them remain here." She hoped she sounded calm and reassuring to Mattie. As usual she was relying upon her acting training, making her voice sound more confident than its owner felt.

119

"One of them's a murderer!" Mattie cried. "They could kill us in our beds."

Caroline reached out her arm to Mattie, but the cook drew away. Suddenly she turned and gave her full attention to the contents of a pot on the top of the stove.

"I'll talk to the detectives, Mattie. I'm sure they'll advise us what to do." She felt helpless in the face of the woman's distress.

In how much danger were they? What could Lt. Nightingale do to protect them if there *was* a killer staying at Kenwood?

Hank was struck by Harold Hargreave's friendly and convivial manner as he came into Caroline's office. He looked around the room with frank curiosity, pausing to scrutinize several of the family photographs.

"Mrs. Kent's family has a long history in Newport," Hank suggested in a casual tone.

"Old money," Harold agreed while studying a picture of three women, dressed for a garden party, taken somewhere around the late 1920s.

"It's a nice kind to have," Hank said.

Harold turned away from the photograph and smiled. "Any kind of money, Lieutenant, is a nice kind to have."

Hank motioned for Harold to take the chair, and Ben began writing as Hank asked for the details of Harold's activities during the day.

"You want to know my alibi?" he asked brightly.

"That's one way of looking at it. But I'm also looking for verification of other people's alibis."

"Ah, yes. Now who can I alibi? Let me see." He scratched his jowl in an exaggerated manner. Hank was feeling the burning sensation across his shoulders again. Harold's attempt at being playful was wearing thin, but Hank resisted the urge to hurry him along.

"Certainly not the lovely Mrs. Kent," Harold declared at last.

"Caroline Kent?"

"I certainly wasn't referring to her sixtyish mother-in-law, although she is quite the grande dame, don't you think?"

"Why do you mention Mrs. Caroline Kent?"

"It's obvious, isn't it? She visited Maurice twice while he was in that gazebo. She could have done the filthy deed either time."

"What would be her motive, Mr. Hargreave?"

"Perhaps Maurice was refusing to pay the bill. Lodging in this place costs a pretty penny."

"I understood that you and your brothers were paying for your family's stay here."

"Are we now? Yes, that's correct. Nelson would not ask Maurice to contribute his fair share. My big brother never wants to get on the bad side of Uncle Maurice, you know. Although, he doesn't have to worry about that now, does he, Lieutenant?"

"What is your evaluation of your brother Nelson's work at Hargreave Industries? Is he a valuable employee?"

"Nelson? Of course. Place couldn't run without him. He sells the goods, don't you know. What would be the point of making the products we make if we couldn't turn around and sell it?"

"He's good at his job?"

"Excellent. Works like a dog. Typical first child. An overachiever. Older brother wants to be the man my father never could be."

"And you?"

"I'm the child lost in the middle. Baby brother is my mother's pet, of course. I'm just wedged in the center." He laughed self-consciously as he placed his open hands on his rounded stomach which stretched the limits of the shirt and pants he was wearing.

"But you do work in the family business?"

"Paper pusher, head of human resources. We don't have much turnover. Same faithful hands in the factory. Same tired faces in the office, sending out the bills and adding up the profits. I just make sure all the employees get paid, their taxes get sent to Uncle Sam and the Governor of Massachusetts, and everyone fills out a request for vacation time."

Hank nodded. It sounded like a good advertisement for the adventure of police work.

"Let's get back to your movements today. What time did you go out to the veranda?"

"Early. Way before lunch. I saw my wife off in the car, and I went back upstairs to get my book, and then I went outside. I suppose it was well before eleven."

"That's fine. Now how long did you remain on the veranda?"

"Until the big news broke. I had a Tom Clancy book, and you know those things really catch you up in the plot. I couldn't put it down. I just kept on turning the pages."

"You had your lunch out there, I understand."

"Yes, Mrs. Kent sent me out a tasty lobster salad sandwich and some of those greens that look like exotic plants. That cook of hers is a sour lemon, but she can dish out the food."

"I see. And you never left that chair? Let's see… from before 11 a.m. until Mrs. Kent sent your father up to the house to call the police at sometime after 1:30. Two and a half hours. Didn't you have to use the bathroom during that time?"

"I have a strong bladder, Lieutenant. I didn't feel the urge."

"And you read for these two and a half hours?" Harold nodded, smiling too confidently for Hank to be comfortable with this answer. "And who else did you see during this period?"

Harold looked surprised and shook his head. Hank felt a quickness in his stomach.

"You saw no one?" Harold again assumed the air of certainty and Hank added, "Not even your mother?"

"Mother?" Harold seemed bewildered, but he quickly recovered and said with a firm voice, "Oh, Mother. Of course."

Hank waited, but Harold made no other comment. It would be a stalemate unless Hank pushed. He chose to nod at Ben, who flipped through the pages of his notebook.

"Mrs. Emily Hargreave stated that she came up the path past the gazebo from the Cliff Walk to the house shortly before1:30 when she returned from lunch." Ben looked up from the page and squarely at Harold.

"Oh, yes. Funny I forgot that. You're right, Sergeant."

"You would swear that you saw her?" Hank asked.

"Swear it on the family Bible."

CHAPTER ELEVEN

"It keeps coming back to Lionel and Emily's story, doesn't it, Lieutenant?"

"We've got to do some real digging there. Their alibi better be watertight." He got up and went to the window. The view was of the path which led from the kitchen wing down to the gazebo.

"They're about the age that gun would match up with," Ben said.

"Yes. The gun. We need to see if anybody recognizes it."

Ben went to the door and as he was in conversation with Officer Jarvis, Nelson Hargreave made his entrance into the office. Hank turned from the window and indicated the chair. Nelson sat his tall frame down with an easy motion. As he resumed his seat at the desk Hank examined the gray eyes which the son had inherited from his father. The detective saw an energy in them that his father's had lost. Or perhaps never had.

"We're checking everyone's movements during the time when it appears Mr. Maurice Hargreave was killed. Obviously we'll need to check yours, Mr. Hargreave."

"Of course, of course. This is a bad business."

"Yes. Well, why don't you start with what you did at breakfast when the whole family was together?"

"Right. We were all at the table. I had plans to do some sightseeing." Nelson paused, and then added, "I suppose, Lieutenant, that Maurice's death means the family can't leave Newport now."

"No," Hank said. "We'll need you all here for a couple of days until we can check everything out."

"I had better make some further arrangements with Mrs. Kent about that. We're only booked until Sunday."

"Fine," Hank said. "Now let's get your story on paper."

Nelson took some slight from this abrupt change in topic, and Hank was forced to add, "You have to attend to family matters, and I want to make this as quick as possible. If you could tell me about your day…"

Nelson was mollified by the gesture and proceeded to document his morning's activities. He had thought his tour started at ten, and he had left around 9:30 to give himself time to park the car and buy a ticket. It began instead at eleven. He must have misread the schedule. It was a long tour, stopping at two of the Newport mansions, plus bus travel through the city. At the end of the second house tour there had been a rather lengthy commentary given by the tour guide while their bus sat parked in the parking lot of The Breakers. He remembered that the entire tour was over about quarter to two in the afternoon.

"And then where did you spend your time between 1:45 and the time you arrived back here?"

For the first time Nelson's composure looked less than sure.

"Do you carry a cell phone, Mr. Hargreave?"

"Yes." Nelson looked confused.

"I'm surprised your father didn't call you as soon as he knew your uncle was dead."

"I had turned it off. They had asked us to turn our phones off during the tour. I must have forgotten to turn it back on." He shook his head. "Of all times."

"I believe you arrived back here at 3:25," Hank continued. "Where did you go after the tour was over?"

"I stopped for lunch." Nelson hesitated and dropped his eyes for several seconds. Finally, he looked up, his face sheepish. Hank wondered what revelation the man was struggling with making. "I took a young woman I met on the bus to lunch with me." Nelson expelled his breath. "We had been sitting together and struck up a conversation and well, it seemed polite to ask her to have something to eat with me. There was a restaurant next to the depot where the bus let us off, and we both had said we were hungry. I thought there would be no harm in it."

"No," Hank said. He thought to himself, "I'm sure you didn't."

"She was a young German woman, you see. An architecture student. I'm sure she hadn't much money, and I thought she could use a good restaurant meal. And I was happy for the company."

"You have her name, of course?"

"Sylvie Becker. She said she was staying at one of the bed and breakfast places in the town. I'm sorry I didn't think to ask which one."

"We can check that out," Ben said, making a note.

Nelson seemed to feel better after his admission, and he sat back in his chair. Suddenly he changed his expression and asked with consternation, "Will my wife have to know this? I don't think she would understand."

"I doubt it," Hank said.

Nelson looked relaxed again and even allowed a small, satisfied smile to break out on his face. Hank studied him. Was he the kind of man who preyed on unsuspecting women he met casually on bus tours and in darkened movie theaters? He'd have to remind Ben that after he found out the name of Sylvie Becker's B & B, that it would be worth asking if she had brought a man back to her room on the afternoon of Maurice Hargreave's murder.

The old mansion seemed unusually silent to Caroline as she entered the library and turned on a lamp. The dark paneling and heavy leather chairs were warm and familiar. The Hargreaves had seemed to appreciate their cocktail hour the previous evening, and she thought she ought to be ready with drinks again tonight. Especially tonight.

"May I join you?"

The sound of a man's voice interrupted her thoughts. Caroline turned to see the moody face of Brian Hargreave waiting for her answer.

"Yes, of course, Mr. Hargreave. Would you like a drink?"

"Yes I would like a drink, and would you stop calling me Mr. Hargreave? My name is Brian."

"Yes, of course, Mr. …Brian."

"And would you stop saying of course?" he asked as he went over to the liquor cabinet. He knew his way around the fittings, finding the glass and ice and reaching for the vodka decanter quickly and efficiently. After he had poured his drink and was about to lift the glass to his lips, he turned to her. "Can I mix you something?"

"No," Caroline answered. He shrugged and drank from the glass. "Are you hungry?" she asked. "Can I put out some food?"

"The funeral feast?"

"The what?" She was taken aback.

"The celebration. The true celebration of why we Hargreaves have journeyed here."

Caroline stared at him, trying not to look shocked. Her first instinct that she should leave him alone with his drink was overruled by her curiosity over the meaning of his remark.

"Are you celebrating your uncle's death?" She looked pointedly at the glass in his hand.

"This?" Brian's eyes went from the glass to Caroline and back to the glass. The pupils darted like fireflies in the twilight. "I would drink whether Maurice was dead or alive. I merely meant to suggest that you are witnessing a celebration tonight."

"You said Maurice's death is why you came here." He absorbed the statement without any visible reaction. "Is that true?"

The man in front of her shrugged. His glass was empty now, and he started to refill it. "Are you sure you won't join me? May I call you Caroline? Have a drink with me, Caroline."

"I'm sorry, but I can't."

"Hotel policy? Can't drink with the guests?"

"It's not that." She could see that he was offended. "I still have lots of work to do tonight. I have nothing against drinking with my guests."

"Good, I'll take a rain check. Some evening, after you have finished your work." He accented the last word.

"You make me sound like Cinderella."

"Aren't you? You're like the girl in the story. Washing, cooking, cleaning. I never see you relax."

"This has not been one of my more usual days," Caroline said with some emotion.

"No, I suppose not. And now you have a murderer in your house."

"Who is it?" She decided to go for the direct approach.

"That's an excellent question."

"Do you know the answer?"

"Not me. I can assure you of that."

Did he mean he was not the murderer? Or was he saying he didn't know the identity of the killer? She was watching his eyes. She realized who his eyes reminded her of. Maurice.

"You didn't like your uncle, though."

"No, I didn't. But I also don't like a lot of people. And I'm not about to jeopardize my future by bumping them all off."

"Someone hated him," Caroline said, feeling sure for the first time. "Someone truly hated Maurice."

"Oh, I know several people."

Caroline's heart skipped a beat.

"And do you suspect one of them? Do you think you know?"

Suddenly the flame went out in his pupils, and he looked sad.

The last interviews had to be gotten through. Hank had seen all the male Hargreaves, and now it was time to complete his introduction to the family by seeing Nelson and Harold's wives. His curiosity concerning Nelson's wife was especially strong, but he decided to see Donna first.

"I can't believe he's really dead," Donna bubbled as she faced Hank across the desk. "Imagine. Maurice not at the center of all of our lives." She tried to suppress a smile, and a noise escaped from her

131

throat that was much like the sound of giggling. Ben looked up from his pad. Suddenly Hank was tired of the Hargreaves. There were too damned many of them in the case.

Altogether too mechanically, he began his questioning to determine his subject's movements throughout the day. He heard the story of breakfast repeated once more and the details of the planned anniversary celebration. For Donna Hargreave, the chance to dress up for a gala dinner in the baronial Kenwood Court was clearly a treat. For the first time he heard that the male members of the Hargreave family would be in black tie. He felt himself becoming more interested in the questioning now. She was almost childlike in her enthusiasm for the party, almost as if she hadn't quite understood yet that it was not going to take place.

Gently he nudged her past the subject of the Hargreave family party and back to recounting her day. He heard of the plans for the much-discussed shopping excursion with Kae and how Donna had worried whether they would actually be going. Patiently he heard of the BMW being driven by her brother-in-law's wife through the "cutest streets" of downtown Newport.

"And did you and Mrs. Kae Hargreave spend the entire afternoon in each other's company?" Donna looked surprised at the question. "You separated then?" he continued. "You didn't go to the same stores?"

"Kae is an antiques' person. A nut, if you ask me. She wanted to go in every one on that street right above the road around the harbor."

"And you weren't interested?" Hank asked.

"Oh, no. I wanted to look at clothes. You have so many cute stores here." Hank shuddered as Donna used the word *cute* again. It was not a favorite adjective in his vocabulary.

"What time did you part company?"

"Oh, right away. She dropped me off at one of the wharves and said she was going to park the car. There were no spaces anywhere around. It was about... let me see." She was thinking hard. "We left about quarter after ten, maybe a little later. I guess it may have been about quarter of eleven, maybe a little sooner."

"Shall we say approximately 10:45 then?"

"Is it important?" Donna asked nervously.

"Not at this point. What happened next?"

Donna recounted her swing through what seemed to be every store in downtown Newport, ending up with a list of her purchases.

"Did you stop for your lunch?"

"Oh, oh, of course. I almost forgot. Lunch! Can you believe it? I forgot to tell you about lunch."

The next rambling account told of her agreement with Kae while they were still together in the car that they would meet for lunch at 12:30 at the café that had been on the corner where Donna had been left.

"It seemed as good a place as any. We both knew where it was and the name. Kae said she'd be there at half past twelve."

"But she wasn't?"

"No, I waited for her to come, but finally she didn't seem to be coming. I went ahead and ate and got on with my shopping."

"So how did you find her again? You did come back together, didn't you?"

"Oh, yes. That was funny. I was walking along the other big street, the one that goes away from the harbor. Thames Street it's called, I think."

"Yes, that's correct." She pronounced the name of the street the same way the locals did by saying the word exactly as it was spelled, not the way most tourists in Newport made the *h* silent, as was done by Londoners who called their Thames River the *Temms*.

"I was walking along the street, and I was sure getting tired of walking. I was actually thinking of stopping for some coffee when I heard a horn blowing. It was Kae. She waved at me, and I went over and got in the car."

"What time was that?"

"Well, we came right here. And when we got to the inn it was a little after four. So I guess however long it takes for her to have driven us here."

"I see. And did Mrs. Hargreave give you a reason why she didn't keep her luncheon date with you?"

"She said she had gotten the name of some antique store up on Broadway. You have a Broadway in Newport, don't you?" Hank nodded. "She said she had started walking up there before she understood how far it was. By the time she got there, she realized she wouldn't have time to walk back to meet me in time."

"She couldn't have taken a cab?"

Donna's expression showed that she accepted she was not worthy of her relative's spending cab fare.

"So she had been driving around, hoping she'd see you?"

"That's it. She said downtown Newport wasn't a big place. She knew if she kept going around the harbor she'd spot me."

Hank leaned back in his chair and mulled over things. He was interested in what Kae had been doing for the whole afternoon and knew that it would be easy to check with every antique dealer in town. Most not only owned their own business but were their only employee. They were always in the shop, and they would remember their customers. He'd have someone start making the rounds the first thing the next morning.

As Donna's place in the chair was taken by Kae Hargreave, Hank was conscious of a prickling in his senses he wished he wasn't feeling. The woman was damned attractive. He watched as she sat on the chair, every body movement precise yet spare. He concentrated on finding just the right adjective for her. At last, *sultry* came to mind. The temperature in the room had become hotter with her presence.

"Thank you for being so patient, Mrs. Hargreave."

"Why don't you call me Kae?" she suggested easily. There was a gap in the conversation which was hard not to notice. He had been staring at her, and he was sure she noticed it.

Quickly he nodded his assent, and Kae spoke, as if besides everything else the witch was able to read his own mind. "There are too many Hargreaves in the case for us all to be called Mr. or Mrs.. Make it easy on yourself."

"Thank you, Kae," Hank found himself murmuring. Then in a stronger voice, he continued. "I suppose this has been an upsetting day for you."

"If you mean the death of Maurice, not at all," Kae answered. "It was bound to happen."

"What do you mean by that? That Maurice Hargreave was old enough to die?"

"Oh, no. The man was healthy as a horse. I meant that it was only a matter of time before he went too far, and someone had to take matters into their own hands."

"Let me get this straight," Hank said. His nostrils began to get the scent of Kae's perfume. It was not the thick, sensual fragrance he expected, but rather a clean, almost the smell of green grass in the sun, aroma. This was a new one for him, and he wondered if this was some new trend in perfumes he hadn't caught on to yet. "You expected someone to kill Maurice?"

"Of course."

"Oh? I must ask you why."

"You're a policeman, aren't you?" Kae smiled.

"That's what it says on my paycheck."

The comment amused her.

"He deserved it. Maurice was always pushing the bounds of what most people would consider the conventional way of doing things. His family suffered the most, but I think that was more because so many of them chose to be around him all the time, rather than because he singled them out."

"Do you count yourself among those who suffered?"

Kae raised her chin thoughtfully, and as Hank admired the firmness of her jaw line, she spoke. "Sometimes."

"In what way?"

"He knew everyone's weak spot, and that was where he attacked." Hank was about to ask what she considered her weak spot, but she gave him no opening. "Take my husband, for example. He is obsessive about his work. A perfectionist. He would like more responsibility in the family firm and, frankly, has earned the right. Yet, Maurice continually thwarts his efforts. Instead he belittles him and keeps him on a short leash."

"And that upsets you?"

"No one likes to see the man one chose as the symbol of masculinity and married being made sport of."

"That's an interesting way of putting your marriage."

"I have my pride, Lieutenant. Nelson may not have always lived up to my expectations, but he is my husband, and it doesn't suit me to have him held up to ridicule."

"Maurice went that far?"

"Not in obvious ways, but he knew how to pick at his manhood."

"I see. And did you suffer personally at Maurice's hands, or did he only get at you through your husband?"

"More often the latter. He knew I am guilty of the sin of pride. I know he was often watching my reaction while he was needling Nelson."

"Why would he want to hurt you, Mrs. Hargreave? Kae, I mean."

"Nothing personal, I'm sure. It was just his way."

"And you're saying that 'his way' got him murdered?"

"I can't imagine any other motive."

"So every Hargreave would have one?"

She nodded.

"And Mark Fitzgerald? Did he also come under this umbrella of abuse by Maurice Hargreave?"

Hank detected that Kae hesitated just a second or so, but he couldn't be clear exactly what he saw. She had quickly brought under control what was going to be a spontaneous reaction to the mention of the lawyer's name.

"I'm sure Mark must have had his moments with Maurice. I am not in the office, so I didn't see their day-to-day relationship." She paused and added, "You'll have to ask him."

"I will."

The rest of the interview consisted of setting out the details of Kae's day in downtown Newport. To Hank, she seemed purposely vague on times and places. Yes, she had visited several antique shops. No, she didn't remember any particular names. They all stretched along the antiques' district of the city, and she just went from one to the next. She remembered her long walk on Broadway, but wasn't certain now of the name of the store. She had the number, and that was what she had been looking for. The number itself? It had already gone from her mind.

She had no regrets about missing her lunch date with Donna.

"Did you buy anything?" Hank asked congenially.

"Oh, I picked up a few trinkets. Nothing big. I didn't see any furniture, but I found a vase I liked and also a small framed print. Prices are good here, compared to Boston. I'd like to look again. I guess I'll have the time now."

Hank raised his eyebrows.

"We can't leave on Sunday, can we? I'll have some time on my hands."

"Yes, I will want you all to stay on until we do some checking and clean up some details of our investigation."

"So we're all suspects?"

"I don't have any hard evidence yet. When we check the alibis, we'll be able to eliminate some people." For the first time, Hank was sure he was looking at uneasiness on this otherwise self-assured woman's face. "I'm afraid you are one of the people who seems to have a very sketchy alibi for the murder time."

"Yes," she said pensively. "I know. I hope that's not going to present a problem."

Hank waited for an appeal to his masculine good nature, but it didn't come. Instead, Kae sat lost in her own thoughts, and Hank could only observe her. She was troubled by something, and in due course, he would know what it was.

CHAPTER TWELVE

After the last of the Hargreaves' questioning was over, Hank sent Ben to the kitchen to make notes on the recollections of Mattie and Jan. Hank thought it farfetched that either of them had shot Maurice Hargreave. Louise Kent had indicated that she and Mattie were in each other's company during the period when the murder most likely took place. And Jan had been turning out the bedroom being readied for Mark Fitzgerald during the same time. Ben would enjoy questioning them.

After his sergeant had left on this commission, Hank began to stretch and walk about the room. His attention inevitably was drawn back to the Kent family photographs, and it was while he was examining one, that he heard a light rap on the door. Before he could react to it, he saw Caroline standing in the open doorway.

"Excuse me," she said. Had she seen him looking at the photographs? She gave no indication. "Sgt. Davies said you were alone, and I could talk to you."

"Come in, come in. How is Mrs. Kent?"

"Fine," Caroline said. Her voice sounded puzzled.

"I wondered if she was suffering any ill effects from having a murder committed in her home."

"My mother-in-law is a strong woman."

"That was my impression," he said, "but you never know." It felt as if he was sparring with her, and he didn't want that. "How are you?" He smiled his best smile at Caroline and noticed for the first time that her eyes were green. The light seemed to flash in them, which he found pleasant to watch.

"I'm very tired, if you honestly want to know. I feel as if I have been awake for at least a week."

"I'm guessing that you had been doing a lot of running around this morning, anxious over your guests. Discovering a dead body in the middle of that was not in your plans for today. And despite what you said, you are very worried about your mother-in-law. One can see you care about her a great deal, and you are anxious over her welfare."

He could see her softening toward him. They had gotten off on the wrong foot; his official abruptness earlier had offended her. He wanted to put that straight.

"While you're doing your analysis," Caroline said, "you had better add that as a new businesswoman I'm scared to death that this murder will harm my chances of succeeding in making this place into a going concern."

"I hadn't thought of that one."

"I have, and I can't think of who would want to spend a luxurious weekend in the Inn at Kenwood Court where murder is one of the features of the stay."

"Quite the contrary, I'm going to argue. In my business, I've learned people are drawn to this kind of thing like moths to a flame. I'd say it will put your place on the map, and you will have to beat the hordes back."

Hank was trying to be upbeat, but Caroline reacted fiercely to his supposition.

"I don't want *the hordes* coming to Kenwood."

"That's fair," he said apologetically.

"There's something else I must ask you." He waited expectantly. "Nelson Hargreave has asked if his family can stay on a few more days."

"Is that a problem?"

"Well," she began. "I want you to tell me. Is it safe?"

"Safe? Oh, I see what you mean."

"It still seems surreal to me, but someone has died here by violent means. And someone else committed the crime. Is that person staying in my house? I have responsibility for my mother-in-law and the servants. I can't jeopardize their safety."

"No, no. You can't. The only thing I can say is that Mr. Hargreave was killed for reasons which appear to me to have nothing to do with you and this house."

"I'm sure you're right."

"You could elect to close the inn and dispose of your guests that way. I'm sure they could find other accommodation in town."

"I would find it hard from a financial standpoint to close down the inn, Lieutenant. I do have new guests coming at the beginning of next week. That's if all the publicity hasn't driven them away. And I don't have enough rooms for them and all the Hargreaves."

Her voice was overwrought, and Hank took her firmly by the arm and sat her down in the chair. She gave him no resistance.

"When is the last time you ate food?"

"What?"

"Food. You know chicken, peas, apples. Bread and butter. That sort of thing," he said lightly.

"I… guess it was this morning."

"You were too busy to stop for lunch, and now you've had no dinner."

Caroline nodded. She looked up at him and there was a tiny smile that Hank found encouraging.

"Louise tried to get me to drink brandy, but I had enough sense to refuse. I would have been on the floor if I had done that."

"Good. You have got some sense. Now how do you get something to eat around here?"

"You must be hungry yourself, Lieutenant. I was going to tell you that we have put out sandwiches for you and your officers in the kitchen."

"That was very thoughtful of you. I appreciate it." She smiled, and he said, "Now, is there anything else you would like to tell me?"

"Actually, yes. I have been giving a lot of thought to the Hargreaves."

"Have you remembered something important?" Quickly he switched his mind back to his case.

"It's not anything that points directly to the murderer. It's more what I've observed. Louise and I have been talking upstairs. We've both noticed things. There was a lot going on with the family while they were here. I think if we put it all together, it will identify who killed Maurice."

As Hank understood that Caroline was about to play amateur detective, his heart sank. This was the last thing he needed. A sidekick. But, he also knew that among the hypotheses and suppositions that Caroline had already made for herself concerning this crime, there were bound to be a few nuggets he would be happy to hear. He settled back in the desk chair and took his own notebook from his pocket.

"Why don't you tell me what you've got while it's fresh in your mind? And after that we will both go to your kitchen and get some supper."

"I think we should begin at the beginning," she said. "Back to yesterday afternoon when all the Hargreaves first arrived."

He should have asked to have some sandwiches sent into the office before they started on this narrative. Hank had a feeling that this was going to be an epic saga. The one positive aspect was the relaxation he felt being in Caroline Kent's company. Despite his sensual reaction to Kae Hargreave's subtle eroticism, he liked the owner of Kenwood, with her luminous green eyes and unaffected enthusiasm to help him solve his case, à hell of a lot more. What was the story behind that wedding picture? How should he ask?

"I noticed it right away," Caroline was recounting. "And, of course, Mattie kept talking about it. They didn't all like each other. The Hargreaves, I mean. I suppose if any of them had ended up dead, there would be more than enough suspects." She paused and looked earnestly at Hank. "Do you follow me?"

"Yes," Hank said. "By the way," he added, his gaze automatically drifting to the wedding ring on her left hand, "I need to ask you. Where is your husband? Is Mr. Kent normally living here with you and his mother?"

"I assumed you knew, Lieutenant, although how you could I can't now imagine. I'm a widow. My husband is dead."

"I'm sorry. I must have said that very badly. I apologize." Caroline's spirited manner was ebbing. Hank cursed his impatience to know about the wedding photo and the ring.

"I only thought that there might be another member of the household to question. Again, I'm terribly sorry to have asked you."

"You had to. It was a natural question. Don't apologize."

"Thank you." He hoped he had been pardoned. "Now. What about the Hargreaves? It sounds as if you have made a study of them, and I would like to hear your observations. I think they will be very useful." Caroline was staring off into space. He waited several seconds before continuing. "Why did you say earlier that you liked Maurice?" She turned back to look at him, and he saw that she was composed.

"At first I thought he was just one of those autocratic men who like to ride roughshod over his family," she began slowly. "But then I thought, no, there's more to him. He had depth, you see. He was real. Does that make any sense to you?" Hank nodded. "There was a lot going on with him. Maybe I didn't like him as much as I was interested to observe him." She paused as if she had some flash of understanding.

"I think that must be the key to it, don't you? What I said about something going on... something that Maurice was planning... that was suddenly a threat to someone." Her green eyes were bright with excitement.

"And that person killed him?" Hank remembered the papers Mark Fitzgerald had been called to see in person.

"Yes. Now what we have to figure out is what was Maurice up to? What had he put in motion that had to be stopped?"

Hank was writing on his note pad. Amateur or no, the woman had hit on what might be a key. Had Maurice indeed been up to something? She is going to help, he decided with some amusement. It was a very welcome thought, and it took away that burning sensation he had almost gotten used to feeling across his shoulders and down the back of his neck.

Brian Hargreave had now had several of the vodka drinks he had come to depend on in his young life. There was no denying he was drinking too much these days, and this stay at the Inn at Kenwood Court only presented more opportunity than usual for indulgence. He reached in his pocket and took out the packet of aspirin he carried with him and picked out two of the tablets. Their taste in his mouth was chalky and sweet and he washed them down with the smart taste of the vodka remaining in his glass. He shuddered and sat down in one of the big armchairs. He felt like hell.

"Shouldn't take aspirin on an empty stomach. Destroy that along with my liver. And, why not? Who's to care anyway?" He stood up and went to the cabinet to pour himself another vodka. Sipping his drink he picked out the shadow of a man in the doorway of the room.

"Hello, Father," Brian said. "Can I get you a drink? You must be ready for one." Automatically he began to mix his father's usual.

"Your mother finally fell into a deep sleep, and I thought it would be better if I left her."

Lionel came into the room, and Brian handed him his drink.

"Mother seems very upset by Maurice's death," Brian said.

After several seconds passed, it seemed that his father did not intend to answer, and Brian wondered if his father, too, wanted to be left undisturbed. He knew little of his father's moods and found it difficult now to read his thoughts.

"Is Mother thinking at all about the anniversary party?" He tried to make the question sound uncomplicated. "It seems unfair of Maurice to get himself murdered in the middle of our plans to celebrate."

"Do you think Maurice had any control over that?"

"Oh, no," Brian said quickly. "I didn't mean it that way."

"That's the way it came out."

"I'm sorry, Father. I don't want to upset you. I was only concerned about Mother. I would like to see her." His eyes, now accustomed to the dimness of the room, watched his father.

"The best thing for your mother now would be for me to take her home."

"The police won't allow that. We'll have to stay on for a few days until they finish up with us."

"What else do they want to know? We've all told them everything about today."

"They have to check our alibis," Brian said.

"Alibis? Your mother doesn't need an alibi. She should be in her own home at a time like this."

"I'm sure we will be able to go home by Monday or Tuesday. Can I see Mother when she wakes up?"

Lionel put his empty glass down on the table.

"I should go back upstairs."

"Wait. We ought to talk. I want to help."

He was surprised to see his father look at him as if he were a stranger. There was no affection in his steel gray eyes. As Brian stood motionless his father pushed past him and left the room. Now the son stood, silhouetted in the shadows by the window, staring grimly out into the faint moonlight.

After Caroline and Hank finished their talk, they came out of the office to see that one of the police officers, whose face Caroline was beginning to find familiar, had arrived with the gun found next to Maurice Hargreave's body. It was now sealed in an evidence bag, and both officer and gun were being followed down the hallway by an agitated Harold Hargreave.

"Yes, Jarvis?" Hank inquired, looking at both the newcomers.

"This man wants to say something, Lieutenant. He insisted on coming with me. He saw the gun and says he recognizes it."

Hank turned sharply to Harold, who seemed bursting.

"What can you tell me about this gun, Mr. Hargreave?"

"Maurice was shot with grandfather's gun!" He sounded gleeful, thrilled to be part of this new development in the case.

"You can definitely identify it as the weapon which belonged to your grandfather? Joseph Hargreave, I believe was his name."

"How did it get here?" Harold reached to grab at the gun, which Jarvis was holding back. "I don't understand," he said suddenly. "Who would have brought it with them?"

Hank looked first at Harold and then at the gun.

"Mr. Hargreave, do you recognize this gun?"

"Of course. It belonged to my grandfather."

"Who owns it now?"

"Who owns it? Legally? I'm not sure."

"When was the last time you saw it?"

"Oh, I couldn't be sure. Maybe as long as a year ago. I can't remember for sure."

"But you know that it belonged to your grandfather who has been dead... for many years, I would imagine."

"Since 1988."

"But where has the gun been kept? Who has had it?" Caroline saw that Hank was getting exasperated at trying to make sense of the situation.

"It was in the office. The big office at Hargreave Industries. My grandfather's office. Maurice has it now."

"So it was Maurice's gun?"

"I guess you could say that. My grandfather bought it to keep in the factory when it was first built. He thought there might be a robbery, or something like that. The payroll was kept in cash and paid out every week. There was a good reason for having a gun on hand."

"And the gun was always in the office? Even up to the present time?"

"Well, you could ask... well, you can't ask Maurice, of course, but well, there is my father. His office is connected to

Maurice's. He was back and forth." Harold paused and nodded his head thoughtfully. "Maurice still kept the gun around. I'm sure."

"But it was never used."

"Oh, not for protection anymore. We've got a security service now at the plant. We don't worry about armed robbery, things like that. Besides, everything's electronic. We don't keep money lying about like the old days."

"Where in the office?"

Harold didn't appear to understand the question, and Hank repeated it. "Where exactly was this gun kept at Hargreave Industries? The last time you saw it."

"In Maurice's desk drawer. That's where I always saw it. If he opened that top side drawer, you could see it."

"Several people would know the gun was there? Your father, for example?"

"Oh, I'm sure. And Tina," he added brightly.

"Tina Hargreave?"

"She didn't like having the gun there. I know she would have preferred that Maurice not have it in his desk, but, to tell you the truth, I think it amused him to frighten her. Once he laughed and said his father had put it there and there it would stay."

"What would stay?" Now it was Nelson coming to see what the commotion was about. He had appeared from the direction of the billiard room.

"Mr. Hargreave," Hank began, "we seem to have identified what we believe to be the murder weapon." He allowed Nelson a close inspection of the old Colt .32.

"Grandfather's gun," Nelson said. "Of course. It would be done with that."

"You can positively identify that gun as belonging to your grandfather, and now your uncle, Maurice Hargreave?"

"It belongs at Hargreave Industries as far as I'm aware, and yes, it appears to be the same gun. We've all seen it at one time or another. Every time Maurice opened that drawer, there it was."

"Was the desk ever locked?"

"Perhaps at night. Tina should know about that. I doubt that Maurice kept the gun loaded. That would have been an irresponsible thing to do, and Maurice was not irresponsible."

"Would your uncle have brought it with him to Newport?"

"Oh, I doubt it," Nelson said. "I've never known him to take it with him when he traveled. Wouldn't that be illegal, Lieutenant?"

"It wouldn't be wise, but it depends on the permit. Can you tell me the last time you remember seeing this gun? At the office… in the drawer?"

Nelson shook his head.

"I honestly can't say. I don't remember. I wasn't in Maurice's office that often." He looked at his brother.

"Don't look at me," Harold howled. "Everybody knows I tried to stay clear of Maurice."

Caroline was watching Harold as he spoke. She detected something in the way he was now smiling that suggested he knew more about the subject of the gun than he was letting on. She was remembering Louise's pronouncement that Harold was fond of snooping and wondered what information he might have and how he might have gained it.

"Ben," Hank said, interrupting Caroline's train of thoughts, "find Mr. Lionel Hargreave. Let's see what he knows about this gun. In fact, I think we ought to get all the Hargreaves to tell us what they know about it."

"Yes, Lieutenant," Ben said.

The gun had been traced to the Hargreave family, and Harold's first question had been a good one. Who had brought it with them when they came to celebrate a family anniversary?

CHAPTER THIRTEEN

Hank Nightingale lived in one of the two ground floor apartments housed in an old pink Victorian villa located in a quiet street, a block behind the Redwood Library. When he had first taken the place, he had done so without much thought. It was a temporary move that had stretched into a permanent one. The place was home now, with its tall old-fashioned windows that let in the winter drafts and its high ceilings which sucked the heat skyward. There was a tiny bathroom tucked into a corner of what had once been part of the dining room and next to it, a small kitchenette. Hank had furnished the place with a combination of family cast-offs and casual furniture picked up at discount stores. He often thought he'd like to give the place more of his personality, but there never seemed a time when he felt like doing anything tangible in that direction. Instead he had settled his books and music and pictures, expanding comfortably about the three rooms, in such a way that he knew where everything was, and that was enough to feel the place was his.

In his living room, which he had decided must have been the original morning room in the house because it caught the sunrise, he had installed his father's old mahogany desk and worn leather chair. From this operations' base, he kept track of his personal life and spread out whatever office paperwork he chose to bring home. As a detective, there were times when a quiet evening with a drink and his shoes off allowed him to progress further with a case than the days and nights spent amid the clamor and interruptions at the station house. Now he was sitting at the familiar desk, facing the pile of papers he had removed from Maurice Hargreave's brief case.

The organized quality of the files showed a precise, focused owner. Most were tagged with the initials *H.I.*, and clearly related to Hargreave Industries. Several folders held the third quarter results of the company. Hank was no accountant, but a quick look at the sales, earnings and profit figures appeared to indicate the business was healthy. There were also computer print-outs tracking inventory and purchasing. As Tina had said, Maurice seemed to keep an eye on everything, even travel expenses. Mark Fitzgerald had indicated that Maurice had a special document he wanted him to see. Was it contained in one of these files? Hank sifted through the files, looking for anything out of the ordinary, but all appeared in order.

After looking through all the *H.I.* files, Hank came to three files without the familiar initials. The first was thick and marked *Townsend Crest*. Hank opened this with some curiosity. Lionel Hargreave had casually mentioned that his brother had begun talking about a merger, but examination of the file's several documents painted a far different picture. Maurice Hargreave was not exploring merging the family business with its competitor, the Townsend Crest Corporation, but rather selling the company outright.

The sum to be paid by Townsend Crest was $52.8 million.

There was a flow of correspondence and one agreement which indicated that the deal was set to go through on the following Friday at exactly 2 p.m. in the afternoon. All the correspondence was addressed to Maurice Hargreave, but the response letters had been sent back over the signature of Mark Fitzgerald, acting as counsel for the company. The agreement to sell contained only the name and line for the signature of one owner, Maurice Hargreave. Hank thought hard. It had been a long day, but he was sure that he had understood that the business was owned jointly by the two brothers, Maurice and Lionel. Scowling he began to read each letter in its entirety. He learned that Mark Fitzgerald was the executive at Hargreave Industries in charge of the negotiations to sell.

"Well, well, well," thought Hank. "It will be a pleasure to interview the company's counsel again. I wonder what he will tell me as to why he didn't feel it important to share this information with me earlier today." Carefully Hank placed all the papers back into the *Townsend Crest* file and closed it.

Now there were only two more files left, both of them light in weight. One was blank and the other marked *Pemberton*. Hank hesitated only a second or two before opening the unmarked folder first. In it he found the memo of understanding, which Lionel Hargreave had signed earlier that day. A quick scan of the paragraphs told him exactly why Maurice could proceed with the deal to sell his family's company. According to the paper in Hank's hand, Lionel had agreed in principle to sell his share of ownership in the company to his brother Maurice for the sum of $16.4 million, to be paid out in quarterly installments of $820,000 over the next five years. Hank repeated the sum out loud. "Sixteen, point four million dollars."

"That is a lot of money." Hank referred back to the printed page. The document obligated Maurice himself to pay out the money, not Hargreave Industries or the Townsend Crest Corporation.

Hank stood up. There was a difficulty with all this, and he wasn't sure he was seeing exactly what it was. There was the sale to his brother of Lionel's share in the company, coming before the sale of the company itself. Lionel would get over sixteen million dollars for himself. And, presumably, his wife would share that sum. What about their three sons? Two were employed in the company. What was their financial future? Did the sixteen million take care of it?

Hank did some mental calculations. Four quarterly payments a year. Three sons and Lionel and Emily. How was Lionel planning to divide the yearly sum of $3,280,000? If, thought Hank grimly, he was planning to share at all.

But, more importantly, what was the reason why no one had mentioned that the company was to be sold to Townsend Crest? Hank was sure the answer must be that not everyone knew. Lionel had dismissed the merger as something Maurice was only considering. Was Lionel telling the truth? He had told the police that he would be opposed to a merger with their rival. Had he voiced this opinion to his brother and been rebuffed?

Who would be in Maurice's confidence in addition to Mark? His devoted daughter-in-law Tina had been an extremely cool customer under interrogation. 'A sounding board for Maurice,' she had called herself. Did Maurice confer with her on this decision? Or did she avail herself, as Hank was now doing, of a search through Maurice's private files, to which her close working relationship would give her easy access.

Hank went into the kitchen and fixed himself a drink. He had resisted having any alcohol when he first came home. He planned to be up early in the morning and wanted his head clear. But, this new development in the case was unclear. It didn't fit with any of the interviews he'd had with members of the Hargreave family.

Sipping the scotch, Hank suddenly remembered what Mark Fitzgerald had told him about the will which Maurice had made after his son died. His share of the company would revert to his brother Lionel, if he outlived Maurice. So did Lionel own everything again? Despite what he had said, did Lionel know he would own the company if his brother died?

Why had Lionel agreed to the sum of $16.4 million? It was certainly much less than half of the value Maurice was getting from Townsend Crest. Of course, there could be company debt and other financial obligations which must be settled from the $52.8 million. Did Lionel think he was getting a good deal by selling out to his brother? Furthermore, did Lionel know what Maurice had been planning to do next Friday? If he did, did he care?

What had Caroline Kent said earlier? 'Something that Maurice was planning.' He could visualize the concentration which had materialized in the frown creasing her forehead. Could she have heard some details of this proposed sale and not understood what they meant? Hank eyed the telephone. Was it too late to call her? That her mother-in-law might be disturbed by the ringing of the telephone this late was finally Hank's rationale for not calling Caroline. Whatever he had would keep until tomorrow. Instead he went back to his desk and picked up the file marked *Pemberton*. As he began to open it, he felt sure this had to be the mysterious document Mark had been summoned to see. To his surprise, he found the file contained nothing.

If Hank had decided, despite the late hour, in favor of calling Caroline, it would have been difficult for her to have answered her own telephone. For at that moment, she was holding a flashlight and inspecting the contents of the bureau drawers in the darkened bedroom of Maurice Hargreave's suite at the Inn at Kenwood Court. Earlier that evening, after completing his examination of Maurice's rooms, Hank had asked her to lock the door and keep the key in her possession. Nothing unusual had been found among Maurice's possessions, and Caroline had been disappointed to learn that the search had yielded up no clues. Hank had not indicated that the room was off-limits to the house's owner, so at midnight, after she had made a round of the second floor hallways and satisfied herself that everything was quiet, Caroline had silently turned the key to unlock Maurice's door and crept in.

Once inside the suite, she had to admit she felt a bit foolish furtively entering a room in her own home. Her heart was beating with a rapid throbbing, and she had to take a few deep breaths to settle it down. But after her eyes had adjusted to the darkness in the room, she felt it a thrill to begin systematically examining the possessions of its now deceased occupant.

The problem was, like the police, she couldn't find anything unusual among the clothes, shoes and toiletries of the late Maurice Hargreave. Whatever important exists, she sighed, must be in that brief case. She had checked pockets and dumped out the hamper of dirty clothes. She had lifted chair cushions and even the mattress of the bed to run her hands deep into the furniture's crevices. There were no hiding places in the suite, no secret panels, no loose floor boards. Feeling now the absurdity of her desire to look for clues in a room already fine tooth-combed by the police, Caroline was preparing to leave when she felt her heart again begin to beat in fast rhythmic thumps. Someone was gently turning the handle of the door from the hallway.

Quickly Caroline crossed the sitting area and slipped into the bathroom. She turned off her flashlight and closed the door almost to the jamb, leaving a small slit through which she hoped to see what would happen next. She heard the visitor move easily through the sitting area and make for the sleeping alcove. This new person was not using a flashlight and seemed familiar with the lay-out of the suite. Caroline touched the bathroom door lightly with her fingertip. She heard the drawer of the bedside table pulled open. Caroline stretched the door gap as large as she dared and saw the back of the figure bending over the table. The build of the mysterious intruder, wrapped in a long bathrobe, was slender. The robe appeared in the darkness to be of a soft, feminine drape.

While she was certain the person wasn't Donna, it might be Tina or Emily, or even Kae. It could also be Brian, whose stature so resembled that of his mother. The invader now closed the drawer, almost with a slam, and a soft whisper of "damn" escaped from the lips.

Caroline still found it impossible to see enough of the room through her small aperture to discern the identity of the person who was now moving back across the room toward the hall door. From her poor vantage point in the bathroom, she could not be sure that she was alone in the room until she heard the door close and even then she felt it required that she wait a few seconds before coming out of her hiding place. Finally she emerged and peered out into the hallway.

There were always night lights burning for the guests. Caroline paused outside Maurice's door looking first to the left at the main staircase, and next to the right, at the corridor which led first past Tina's room, and then Brian's. The two bedroom doors were closed, and Caroline walked cautiously and looked down the stairs. She could hear or see nothing. The big linen closets stood nearby at the top of the stairs and, with her heart pounding, Caroline opened their door and turned her flashlight's beam around the interior. Again, nothing. The only unexplored area was the hallway further along, which turned and ran down the length of the west wing. If Kae or Emily had been Maurice's midnight caller, either would surely have had time to return to her room by now. Determinedly, however, Caroline continued her search, making the circuit past the three double guest rooms occupied by the Hargreave married couples and now stepping out onto the gallery which allowed her to play the flashlight down into the grand hall below. There seemed to be nothing out of the ordinary.

A left turn around the gallery would have brought her back to her own living quarters in the east wing. Once again she was feeling a bit ridiculous should she be caught sneaking about her own home in the middle of the night. She was about to call it a night when she suddenly remembered that Mark Fitzgerald was now ensconced in one of the small bedrooms in the recess at the back of the west wing.

Mark Fitzgerald was not a tall man, but his muscular shoulders, in Caroline's estimation, did not make him a candidate for the form whose identity she was hoping to discover. Therefore it was on a last impulse that she decided to complete her inspection of the upstairs by creeping softly along the hallway where Mark's room was located.

She was virtually to the closed door before she picked up the drift of voices coming from within the room. Caroline edged as near to the door as she dared. Several feet to her left was another door which opened onto the loggia, and Caroline mentally planned her escape route through it if it became necessary. Meanwhile she settled her nerves down and strained to hear what was being said inside Mark Fitzgerald's room.

At first the voices were difficult to distinguish. Gradually Caroline became sure of Mark's being one of the participants. She picked up the thread of the dialogue as the sound of Mark's voice spoke reassuringly to the second person in the room.

"The worst thing" and "panic" were some of the words she thought she heard. Then, something... something... "so far." Caroline listened keenly for the response. A woman's voice. That was definite. "If Nelson finds out—" Suddenly the elegant voice was raised and Caroline knew at once to whom it belonged. "Where I was today, I won't get a penny from him." Caroline heard the passion in Kae's voice.

Mark's response was swift. "I'll have enough Hargreave money for both of us when," and then his tone softened. Caroline thought he must have said "when this is over," but it may have been what she expected him to say. His companion did not respond, and Caroline could only guess what was happening within the room. At least a whole minute must have passed without any more conversation. Caroline listened closely and had an idea that the two people in the room were engaged in activity which did not need verbal communication to take place. A fledgling detective she might be, but not a voyeur. If Mark and Kae desired a romantic interlude, even in the middle of the murder investigation, she would leave them alone.

Softly she went into the loggia and hurried through the cold night air to the door at the opposite end which led into the east wing. Her thoughts were spinning inside her head as she tried to hold tight to everything she had heard and seen on her adventures during the last hour. Her mind told her that she ought to make some notes. After a night of sleep how much would remain fixed as fact, and how much might be suggested by her dreams? There was her pad and a pen next to the telephone in her bedroom, and Caroline sat down in the arm chair and began to write all her impressions and questions in quick scribbling.

Who were candidates for being the person inside Maurice's room with her tonight? How long had Kae and Mark been having an affair? And what did Mark Fitzgerald mean when he said he would have 'enough Hargreave money?' If only Hank would share with her what he was sure to learn about Maurice's business activities and the future of Hargreave Industries. The family's wealth had to be at the root of this crime, and Caroline now believed that the motive for the murder must trace back to money. Maurice had said to Kae only yesterday, "No good comes of being greedy." The murdered man had urged his nephew's wife not to give in to that temptation. Had she? Did she find it impossible to wait for Mark to make good on his promises to take care of her?

And what did her husband Nelson know about his wife's infidelities? Caroline had met Nelson first of all the Hargreaves. From the beginning he had seemed the simplest of all the family to understand. Was he as colorless and uninspiring as he appeared? How would this seemingly uncomplicated man react if his wife were unfaithful to him? Nelson had been gone for most of the afternoon, long after his Newport tour would have ended. Had he followed the clandestine pair? Where had Kae and Mark been all afternoon?

Caroline's eyes were closing as she tried to continue to focus on her note pad. Still, the solution to the mystery of who had murdered Maurice continued to elude her. All she had discovered was another mystery to investigate: the triangle of Nelson, Kae and Mark. Did it have a connection to the crime? The money... greed... love... passion... she was leaning back now against the cushions of the chair. The pen had eased out of her hand, and she was fast tumbling into a not unwelcome sleep.

CHAPTER FOURTEEN

The following morning was one of the few occasions since they had returned to Kenwood when Louise was awake before her daughter-in-law. Caroline's usual energy had been sapped by the murder, Louise decided while she dressing. Louise repressed a smile as she thought of Mattie's face when she saw her mistress up and taking Caroline's place in the usual morning routine.

As Louise unlocked the big front door, she was surprised to see Nelson Hargreave, dressed in sweat clothes, jogging up the front drive. Then she remembered that Caroline gave all the guests a key to the house. Most used it, she suspected, for returning late in the evening.

"Good morning, Mr. Hargreave," she said. "It looks like it will rain today. You were wise to get your exercise in early."

He stopped his slow run and walked purposefully in a wide crescent toward her. Louise saw as he came nearer that while he was perspiring, he was breathing evenly and with little effort.

"That's all right, Mrs. Kent," he said, gesturing toward the open door. "I'll walk around a bit to cool down before I come in." He continued making his way toward the side of the house. She ought to have asked him about Harold and whether his brother did take daily walks to aid his 'constitution.'

The next Hargreave Louise saw was Emily. She was standing at the top of the main staircase, looking intently down.

"Good morning, Mrs. Hargreave," Louise said as she reached the top of the stairs. "I hope you are feeling better this morning."

Emily turned slightly.

"I couldn't sleep last night," she said, "and in the middle of the night I went down to the library for a book. I love the library; it's so dark and snug."

Louise nodded. "I've spent many happy afternoons there, reading and thinking."

"My husband said I shouldn't go wandering about late at night, but Mrs. Kent said the whole house was at our disposal, that we were to be at home here."

"Oh, yes," Louise answered as Emily resumed staring down at the grand hall below them.

"I stood right here last night," Emily said, "and I felt as if I could see the house as it must have been when they had the great balls with everyone in their wonderful clothes."

She looked up at the gilded chandelier hovering overhead.

"Last night I could hear the orchestra playing, and even the sounds of the guests. People were talking and laughing."

Louise frowned. "Why don't you come down for breakfast?" she coaxed. "I know you had a shock yesterday, but you ought to eat something hearty. You don't want to get rundown—"

"This morning I was thinking of the day that I was married. That was forty years ago today. Lionel was tall, and of course he was so good-looking. And he had such a brilliant future ahead of him. Everyone thought I was lucky to marry him."

Louise heard the bracket of disappointment around her voice, and with a sudden jolt she thought of Frederick. Everyone had thought she had made such a good match.

"Now he says he wants to retire." Emily looked at Louise, her blue eyes pleading. "I wanted him to have his chance. You can understand that."

"Mrs. Hargreave, I think perhaps I ought to take you back to your room. I'll have Jan make you up a tray."

Emily took one last look at the grand hall before she yielded to Louise's gentle pressure on her arm. "He didn't have his chance," she said softly, "and that's all I ever really wanted."

As the two women came to the door of Emily and Lionel's room, Louise saw that Brian was waiting for his mother.

"Oh, Mr. Hargreave," Louise said. "I'm glad you're here. I think your mother ought to have her breakfast in bed." She gave a signal with her eyes, which she hoped the young man understood. She had taken a dislike to Brian, and she found it awkward now to enlist his aid. His dark eyes were unreadable.

"Come, Mother," he said with more tenderness than she would have thought him capable. "You didn't need to get up so early. Where is Father?"

"Lionel…" Emily said, looking around.

"Is he out for a walk?" He turned to Louise and explained that his father was habitually an early riser and often walked before breakfast.

"Maurice," Emily said to her son, "is dead."

"Yes, Mother," Brian said quickly. Now he looked to Louise for help. "We'll get you some tea. Would you like that? And some toast and maybe even a soft-boiled egg. Remember when I was little, and you used to give me that when I was home sick from school?"

Emily stared at him as he eased her into the big high bed. With some finesse he slipped off her shoes and settled her against the pillows, covering her with the quilt.

"Maurice," Emily repeated.

"Maurice," Brian said, his voice a soothing sing-song, "was a pompous little man who made useless trinkets. You've got to stop thinking about him, Mother. You're making yourself ill." He turned to Louise. "Isn't she, Mrs. Kent? Tell her what Maurice had wasn't worth anything, and you don't want her to think about him anymore."

"I'll go and see about her breakfast," Louise said. She had decided they needed their privacy. As she closed the door, she took

170

one last look at the son's face as he comforted his mother. He was angry, despite his affectionate tone of voice. It was strange, she thought, how Maurice Hargreave's presence still haunted his family. Louise supposed it would remain so until his murderer was caught.

"It can't be Emily," she sighed as she went down the stairs. "I hope that with all my heart." But could it be the son who wanted her peace of mind so desperately? Could he have believed that Maurice's death would give that to her?

The Newport police station was located on Broadway in an unassuming, modern brick building. Hank's office was a drab cubicle on the second floor with a window view of the parking lot. When he arrived at 8:30 later that morning, Ben Davies was already at his desk in the squad room which surrounded Hank's own space.

"Fingerprint report is on your desk, Lieutenant," was Ben's greeting to his superior. The smile around the edges of the sergeant's mouth told Hank there was news in it. "The medical report will be up later on."

Hank put down the half empty cup of coffee he had picked up on his way to work and began reading the report on his desk. Ben came into the office to await the direction he was expecting to be given.

"Get on her alibi immediately," Hank said without looking up from the report.

171

"I called the restaurant first thing. There's a front desk man on duty because there are rooms to let in the upstairs. The waitress stationed on the terrace when Emily and Lionel Hargreave were supposed to be having lunch there yesterday is a woman named Betty Malone. Lives in Middletown. She comes in at eleven today."

Middletown was the town north of Newport on Aquidneck Island.

"Do you have a home telephone number?" Ben nodded. "Call her and tell her to sit tight until you get there. I want a complete statement."

Hank stared out into the squad room while Ben made his telephone call. Emily Hargreave's prints had been clearly identified on the gun which had killed Maurice Hargreave. That meant she was in the gazebo and handled the murder weapon at some time yesterday before Caroline had discovered the body. If Emily had been, according to her statement, lunching at a restaurant one half hour's walk away from the crime scene at the time of the murder, well, that was a real puzzler. If she wasn't, well, it seems they had a suspect. Did it fit? Emily Hargreave as the murderer? Yesterday he would have placed his money on the husband, but you never know in this business. He had long ago stopped believing that some people were incapable of crime. As far as he was able to see, anybody was capable of anything.

"She's home, Lieutenant, and I'm going out there. Want to come along?"

"I wish I could, but I want to follow up something with another of our cast of characters."

Ben seemed pleased to be going off on his own, and he started toward the stairs.

"Check with me at the inn when you have something," Hank called after Ben's retreating figure. "I'm going out there after I check on the progress with the post mortem."

As Hank was about to reach for his telephone receiver, the instrument began to sound. He picked it up before the first ring was ended.

"Nightingale," he said. He was impatient for news of the autopsy.

"Lieutenant...," the voice was tentative. "It's Caroline Kent."

"Ah," Hank said into the receiver. "You can answer me a question."

"What is it?"

"Pemberton. The word *Pemberton*. Have you ever heard it before?"

"What is it?"

"If I knew that I wouldn't be asking you." Hank spaced out the words of his next sentence. "In connection with the Hargreaves this weekend, have you ever heard one of them use it? Especially Maurice."

"I don't think so," Caroline answered. He suppressed his disappointment.

173

"Try to remember. Think hard," he said.

After a short silence, she repeated that she was unfamiliar with the word and asked again if Hank had any clue to what it might mean. Hank hesitated only slightly before deciding to explain how he came to know of Pemberton by the title of the empty file.

"You say there are no papers in the file?" Caroline's voice took on an edge of excitement after he finished.

"I said it was empty."

"Then that's what they were looking for in Maurice's room last night. The missing file. And someone has already taken it!" The last was said with such emphasis that Hank wished with all his might that he had gone straight from home to Kenwood this morning. He hated getting information like this over the telephone. Caroline was rattling on about the mysterious figure at midnight, and hiding in the bathroom... Maurice's talking about money and greed, and how ridiculous she had felt about prowling around the house... but, of course, when she heard Kae in Mark's room, she—and at this point, Hank began to bellow at the telephone.

"Stop talking. I can't follow a thing you are saying."

"Well," Caroline said from the other end of the line, "I thought you would be interested in what happened here last night. I made notes afterwards. About the murder. You're still investigating our murder, aren't you?"

174

"Of course I'm still in charge," Hank said. "I'm planning to come over there in half an hour. Can all this wait until I can get there?"

"Of course," Caroline said evenly. "I just thought it was important, and you would want to know right away." Hank heard the new tone, and he knew he had offended her.

"Look," he said easily. There's some new evidence I have in the case. I'm sorry if I was abrupt, but I didn't get much sleep last night."

"I understand," she said, her voice now quiet. "I'll wait for you in my office. I have some calls to make to arrange things for the new guests coming next week. I've found them other accommodation."

"That sounds like the right thing to do. Are the Hargreaves staying on with you?"

"For the time being, yes."

"Good. We'll have officers in and out of the house for the next few days."

"One more thing," she said. "Monday is the regular day for the service to do the heavy cleaning. Is there any reason why they can't come in the house?"

"We've dusted for all the fingerprints we need and sealed off the gazebo. We think we've got the murder weapon. I don't see a problem. I suppose you could tell your service to keep an eye out for anything unusual, but I don't know what it could be."

175

After he and Caroline had finished their conversation, Hank went back to the fingerprint report on his desk. Besides the information on the gun, there was another sheet on the identity of the prints found on surfaces in Maurice's suite. Hank was very interested to learn who beside the dead man and Jan, who cleaned the room, had been inside the room. Only one other set of fingerprints was found. Tina Hargreave had touched several of the room's surfaces, including, Hank was interested to note, Maurice's bedside table.

CHAPTER FIFTEEN

Breakfast found the three Hargreave brothers the only occupants of the vast dining room. Mattie had set out chafing dishes of oatmeal, scrambled eggs and sausages. Harold ate heartily from his full plate while Nelson contented himself with toast and coffee. Brian chewed pensively on a sausage he had stuffed into a croissant. Nelson periodically eyed him with annoyance.

"Must you hold that in your hand like that?" Nelson asked finally.

"Are you talking to me?" Brian asked. He had been fully aware of the looks his older brother had been giving him across the table.

"Your manners are terrible," Nelson said.

Brian put down his food on the plate in front of him and pushed it away toward the center of the table.

"See what I mean? You are more at home in a diner than a proper home."

"What has he done wrong?" Harold asked, now finished with his food. He put out his hand as if to push his plate back from his place, but hesitated. "Is this the wrong thing to do with your plate when you are finished eating?"

"Of course," Nelson snapped. "It's good form to leave the plate in front of you until it's collected."

"By the servants," finished Brian. "I see. Well, thanks for the tip, big brother. That's a good thing to know whenever I'm invited out in high society."

"I don't have to worry about that," Harold said.

Brian stood up.

"Wait a minute," Nelson said. "I want to talk to you."

"What about?"

"I need to talk to you." Nelson turned to Harold. "And you, also."

"This sounds ominous," Harold said.

"I've spoken to Father," Nelson began, "but he was difficult to reach."

"He's concerned about Mother," Brian said. "Anyone can see it. She's terribly upset."

"Yes," Nelson said, "so it's up to us to make the plans. Hargreave Industries—"

"Oh, the company," Brian interrupted. "I'm not interested. You and Harold work this out." He wanted to take a walk and sort out the problems on his mind.

"Me?" Harold's voice was dubious. "Nelson, you have the head for all of this. It's your show."

"Will you allow me to take charge of the company now that Maurice is dead, Harold? Do you have any problems with that?"

"I've just said," Harold answered. "It's your show. I'll continue in my humble job. Just keep giving me a paycheck. With a nice raise, of course."

"It's Fitzgerald who's going to be the problem," Nelson continued. "Do I have your support against him?"

"Do you think he'll stick around now that Maurice is gone? I don't see that he has much future in the company without him. And despite what she said for Maurice's benefit, Tina hates the arrogant son of a bitch's guts."

"What has Tina to do with it?" Brian asked. His curiosity held him at the table now.

"I only suppose that Maurice has left that little bit of goods his share of the company," Harold said. "Maury's share."

"Father owns the company now." Nelson waited for the effect his announcement would have.

"He does?" Harold was clearly surprised. "How? Does Tina know?"

"How do you know?" Brian asked.

"Father told me this morning. I met him outside after my run. He's talked to Mark who knows the terms of the will. Maurice changed it after Maury's death in favor of Father. It's clear Father

179

doesn't want to run the company, and I'm asking you two to support me to head things."

"It's Father's decision apparently. Talk to him."

"Father doesn't seem to want to talk about that for some reason. I thought if you and Brian were to tell him it's important for things to stay in the family, he would agree. I just can't stand the idea of Mark Fitzgerald getting his hand in the till. In fact, I'd like your help to get him out of things completely. He's not a Hargreave, and he doesn't deserve any of our money."

"But do we?" Brian asked. He looked at both his brothers in turn.

"Don't be ridiculous," Harold said. He turned to Nelson. "Little brother wants to go to Italy to study next year. That's the price of his coming in on this."

"Certainly," Nelson said, waving his hand as if the request was so insignificant as to be equal to nothing. "That's fine."

"Thank you, Harold," Brian said. He was impressed with Harold's imagination; he himself hadn't thought of the ploy at all. "I'm happy to find myself in the position of being able to help you."

Harold's smile was as wide as his broad face. Then, as if to punctuate his statement, he belched, making no effort to cover the barking sound with his hand.

In the kitchen Louise was finding Mattie to be very trying on her nerves. She had come into the kitchen to make up a tray for Emily and stayed to help Mattie in the kitchen with breakfast. After Jan had taken Emily her tray, the maid reported that Kae, Tina, and Donna were all wanting to be served in their rooms. Mattie grumbled her continual disapproval of the family as Jan went back and forth with the trays.

"I don't know why Mrs. Caroline lets them Hargreaves stay when one of them is a murderer," Mattie declared with an especially unpleasant glare.

"The police are here, Mattie. We are being protected."

"I couldn't sleep at all last night."

"You don't have to sleep alone on the third floor. Caroline and I could make you up a bed in our sitting room." When they had first come back to Kenwood, Mattie had gloried in choosing several of the rooms in the old servants' attic to set up as her living quarters.

"I sat up with my light on and had my bureau pushed against my bedroom door."

"I'm surprised you didn't have a poker from the fireplace handy," Louise said.

"I didn't think of it. I'll take one for tonight."

"You ought to feel safe then."

"I knew no good would come from making the place into a hotel. Don't know what type is going to turn up. Mrs. Caroline never should have—"

"Mattie!" Louise's sharp voice surprised even her. "That's enough. You have work to do."

The startled expression on the old cook's face told Louise she would speak no more. Louise nodded and turned to give her attention to the view from the kitchen window. She had enough affection for Mattie to let her recover herself without being watched.

Through the glass Louise could see the gazebo and the officer on guard to keep out curiosity seekers. She knew that two more police officers had been stationed at the front gate to keep out more onlookers and the press. How much longer they could remain under siege in their own home was a worry. Caroline had already received telephone calls from several media outlets for interviews. Her response of "No comment" was not going to hold off the publicity barrage for very long. The Boston and Providence morning papers already had the story. Louise began to share her daughter-in-law's worries that this murder was going to be very bad for business.

It was while she was thinking about Maurice and the unfair way in which his murder was going to affect Caroline that she saw the steady gait of a familiar figure coming toward the back door. She had forgotten. It was Saturday, one of the two days George Anderson came to work on the grounds. Dressed in his gardener's clothes and carrying a worn canvas satchel with his hand tools, George had reported for work. Louise went outside to meet him.

"Morning, Mrs. Kent," George said in his familiar wooden voice. "See you got yourself some trouble."

"Yes, we have. I suppose you read about it in the papers."

"Never read the papers. Heard it on the radio in my truck."

"Goodness. I'm surprised you decided to come today."

"Last Tuesday when I was here I told the young Missus that I would come to cut the path back today. The one down to the Cliff Walk. Thought she was counting on me to do that. She was very particular the other day that I do it next time when I come. Said it was all overgrown and the guests needed to get through it to walk on the Cliff Walk."

"Of course. She did think it was important."

George continued in his slow monotone. "Said one of the guests complained about them seed pods getting stuck to their clothes."

"Yes, I know. I had the same experience the other day. I had to pick them off my trousers." She had cleaned her gardening clothes before putting them in her hamper. Louise was sure that if Mattie saw them, she would use the pods as another reason to admonish her former mistress over doing chores.

"Well, then I'll just get to it."

George turned and ambled back down the path. He stopped near the gazebo and talked to the police officer on duty. The officer inspected the satchel and seemed satisfied with its contents. With an official motion of his hand he waved the gardener toward the Cliff Walk path. George nodded and got to his work.

When Hank arrived at Kenwood Court after speaking with Caroline on the telephone he went straight to her office. She was working with such diligence at her desk that she didn't hear his knock. He eased open the door and looked in at her. Her soft brown hair shone in the morning light, and he stared at the top of her head for several contented seconds before speaking.

"Hello." Caroline jumped. "Sorry," Hank said. "I didn't mean to startle you."

"It's all right," she said, putting down her pen. "The telephone has been ringing all morning with people from the press. I'm a bit on edge. I'm waiting for the Hargreaves to decide if they want to issue some kind of a statement."

"If I were one of those media people I would be getting out my checkbook now in preparation to buy your story." He was looking at the calculator on the desk. Caroline turned it off and put it in her desk along with some bills.

"I'm going to do without that kind of income." She frowned, and he wondered if he had overstepped the bounds of their new acquaintance by commenting on her finances.

"I did hear you have a story to tell me," he said.

"I know I must have sounded silly on the telephone this morning, Lieutenant, but I do have some really important things to tell you."

"Oh, I'm sure you do," Hank said, taking out his notebook. "Let me get them all down for the record."

"I think they're significant to your case," she said.

"Go on."

184

Caroline sat up straight in her chair, opened her notes, and slowly began to recount everything she had written down during the night. He was a professional policeman now as he listened attentively, interrupting with a question from time to time to guide her statement.

When Caroline had finished telling him everything, he smiled, and she was pleased.

"What do you think it all means?" Her voice could not contain her excitement. "Do you think whoever was in Maurice's room was looking for the Pemberton papers?"

"It's possible," Hank said. There was a hint of doubt in his voice. "We know from the fingerprints taken yesterday from Maurice's suite that Tina has been in the room already."

"Have you asked her about Pemberton?"

"I haven't asked anyone yet. I rather think my first interview is with Mark Fitzgerald. If anyone should know what Pemberton refers to, I think it's him. Fitzgerald seems to be the person who was most in Maurice Hargreave's confidence."

"Not Tina?"

Hank shook his head. They both sat in silence until the telephone's ring roused them. Caroline answered it and handed the receiver across to Hank.

"Hello. Nightingale." Grabbing his book, Hank began to write. Caroline waited impatiently as Hank wrote, said "right" and "O.K." a few times, asked if the statement had been signed, and after a long pause, gave a final "Yes, bring it to me here." When the call was completed, he handed back the telephone receiver.

Caroline looked at him expectantly.

Hank hesitated. "There's something else important you don't know yet."

"Can you tell me?"

"Inasmuch as it's going to cause me to make an arrest, I suppose I can."

"An arrest?" He thought she looked both sad and happy at once. She was just beginning to think she was going to help him solve the crime. "You know who did it?" Her eyes were wide.

"We have evidence which points in a certain direction." Caroline swallowed. He saw she looked frightened now. "This morning," Hank said, "I saw the results of the fingerprint tests on the .32 found next to Maurice Hargreave's body. The gun which we are sure now is the murder weapon and was kept in the victim's own desk and generally accessible to all the suspects here."

"Was it one of the Hargreaves?" Her voice was taut.

"The fingerprints found on this gun match those of Mrs. Emily Hargreave." Caroline drew in her breath with a loud, astonished noise.

"It can't be."

Hank held up his hand to continue. "I had Sgt. Davies interview the woman who waited on Emily and Lionel yesterday at lunch." Caroline was shaking her head in disbelief. "The waitress,

Betty Malone, had an interesting story to tell. Her statement," and here Hank looked at his notes, "is that Lionel and Emily began to quarrel not long after they were seated."

"I don't believe it. It can't be Emily."

"Ms. Malone remembers hearing the name 'Maurice' mentioned several times. Her recollection is that she had brought the drinks and the soup course, then watched Emily, who was crying, get up from the table and leave the restaurant. It was early in the lunch service. She remembers there were only patrons at two other tables on the terrace, so she's pretty sure of the time being early, ten minutes perhaps past noon."

"But would Emily have had the time to get back here in time to shoot Maurice? It takes at least a half an hour to walk back here. And she's not a young woman. If she were upset—"

"She took a cab."

"What?"

Again Hank checked his book before proceeding with his details.

"The hostess in the restaurant says that an older woman matching Emily Hargreave's description came in from the terrace and asked her to call a cab. She did, and the cab arrived almost immediately. The driver had just dropped someone off near Memorial Boulevard in the neighborhood around the beach. The taxi log says the fare was picked up at the restaurant at 12:17 and brought to this address at approximately 12:35. Just at the right time to get down to the gazebo and shoot Maurice. The medical examiners evidence is that Maurice was killed between 12:30 p.m. and one."

"Why didn't anyone see her? If the cab left her off in the front drive she would have passed around the house, or even come through the first floor to go out to the back." Before he could offer an answer, she continued in a strained voice. "Had she taken the gun to the restaurant with her? If she hadn't she would have had to go to where presumably she had hidden it, her room most likely. No one saw her in the house." Caroline was grasping at the disjointed elements in her scenario. "It doesn't make any sense, Lieutenant. Anyway, I can't believe Emily killed Maurice. What would have been her reason?"

"Pemberton. Remember Pemberton. Something Maurice was doing that made someone want to end his life. You said that yourself yesterday. Emily has a husband and two sons in her brother-in-law's business. Maurice's plans could have been a danger to any or all of those three men. No, I think she killed to protect her family."

"And you're going to arrest her?"

"Ben is getting the warrant now."

"And what about the alibis of the rest of the family? What about Kae and Mark's little affair? They could have conspired to kill Maurice over this Pemberton business. Are you going to check where they were at lunchtime? Did you check with the office at Hargreave Industries to see what time Mark Fitzgerald left yesterday for Newport? And Donna? And Nelson? Do you know for sure they were shopping and sightseeing? Who saw them? I think Nelson was up to something yesterday."

Hank put on his best professional manner and tried to calm Caroline. He liked her and he didn't enjoy seeing her upset.

"All the alibis are in the process of being checked right now. I have other officers besides Ben Davies, and they are all making the calls and checking with the bus tour company, the restaurant where Donna said she was waiting for Kae, and every antique shop in Newport. Believe me, if my case against Emily goes forward, it will be airtight."

"It can't be true. That woman couldn't possibly have murdered anyone, not even to protect her family. Everything has to be wrong. There must be an explanation of the fingerprints."

"We'll see what Emily Hargreave has to say."

"Yes," Caroline said in a tired voice. "I see you are being thorough. There's only one thing. About Emily Hargreave. I know you're wrong."

"I know what you are thinking," Hank answered kindly. "You have gotten to know Emily Hargreave. You like her, and you can't believe someone you know could actually commit murder."

"What if you're wrong? What if the murderer is someone else?" Hank absorbed the question without replying. He had no desire to argue with her that solid police procedure generally led to accurate conclusions.

CHAPTER SIXTEEN

Caroline's certainty that Emily was not the murderer of Maurice Hargreave had not convinced Hank that he was on the wrong track in his pursuit of the solution to his case. He sat at Caroline's desk, alone now in the office, the empty Pemberton file his hand. "Damn it," he said to himself. "I've got the evidence. The woman's fingerprints on the gun, the cab driver's log that she was here at 12:35, the waitress saying she had been angry and Maurice's name was mentioned. What more do I need to convince her?" Her. That was the problem. Caroline.

He had brought Maurice's files, along with the statements he had collected yesterday, to the inn, and while he went through everything again, checking for any loose threads, Caroline remained in the back of his thoughts. She had left him in her office with a look of disappointment in him on her face. He had wanted her to see the merits of his case, to accept that his professional work had solved the mystery. It was suddenly very important for Caroline Kent to recognize that Hank Nightingale was good at his job.

What else he would learn about himself and his growing interest in Caroline was interrupted by the opening of the door. Ben had arrived with Mark Fitzgerald.

Mark entered the room with less than his former arrogance and took the chair next to the desk. His eyes could not help but fall on the slim folder which Hank had left for his observation.

"Pemberton," Hank said slowly. "I'm sure you've heard of it." When Mark failed to reply, Hank waited patiently. Several seconds passed while Hank feigned passive indifference toward the company counsel.

Finally Mark spoke with the simple syllable, "Yes."

"Good. That's good. We're getting somewhere."

"How much do you know?" Mark asked.

"Not enough. So why don't we get on with it. You're beginning to obstruct justice, counselor, by not cooperating with my investigation."

Mark squirmed slightly in his chair and crossed his right leg over his left. Hank wondered if the man were a smoker and the cigarette would come out next.

"What do you want to know?" Mark tried to make the question sound offhanded.

"I know Maurice Hargreave signed an agreement to buy out his brother's share of the family company before he died. Yesterday, in fact. I also know that he was preparing to sell the entire Hargreave company next Friday." Mark nodded, and Hank added, "Quick work, don't you think?"

"These negotiations have been ongoing for some time."

"Yes, I saw your name all over the correspondence to sell the company to the Townsend Crest Corporation. We won't take the time to discuss why you kept me in the dark about it yesterday."

"I'm very sorry about that, but at the time I felt I had to."

Hank waved his apology aside with an offhanded gesture of his own.

"As I've said, that was yesterday. I always feel like each day of an investigation, we start anew. Keeps me getting out of bed each morning. I imagine you feel the same way about your job."

"Well, I suppose," Mark started, now affecting an amiable manner, but Hank cut him off again. He could see the lawyer in the courtroom now, pulling out all the tricks of his trade.

"And a nice fee for yourself for negotiating the sale of the company, I imagine. Isn't that how these things work? How many people know about these plans besides yourself?"

"Lionel Hargreave signed over his share. He knew about that."

"Obviously," Hank said. "But did he know what his brother was planning to do with the entire control of Hargreave Industries? That there was to be no merger, as Maurice had suggested and everyone had been led to believe?"

Mark hesitated before carefully replying that he didn't think so. When Hank took his time absorbing this, Mark added in a tone that was critical, if not quite disrespectful, that he was sure that Maurice's plans would have made no difference to Lionel.

"Was Maurice Hargreave planning to retire?" Hank tried a new line, and the look of astonishment on the other man's face gave him his answer.

"So no one else knew about Maurice Hargreave's plans," Hank asked, "not even Tina?"

"Maurice didn't tell her. If she snooped and found it out on her own I can't say. She liked to pry into Maurice's affairs more than was good for her. I often advised him to be more careful with documents around her, but he dangled them in front of her like a ball of string for a kitten."

"I see. And what about her job? And the rest of the employees? Were they to be kept on by the new owners?"

"We knew that some would, some wouldn't. It would depend on overlapping responsibilities. Townsend Crest planned to keep the factory running for the present time. I know that."

"But not the office staff?"

"That's the new management's decision. Personally I would expect them to keep Nelson. He has the sales contacts. As far as Tina goes... well, to keep her you would have to need an overbearing, irritating executive assistant, now wouldn't you? And as for that other weak link in the family chain, Harold, I'm not sure what he would be

194

good for. Keeping the vending machines stocked in the company cafeteria?"

"You don't pull any punches, do you, Mr. Fitzgerald?"

"Why should I? They're not my relatives."

"And Mrs. Hargreave?"

"I said Lionel—"

"Mrs. Nelson Hargreave… Kae Hargreave," Hank said easily. "Surely you're interested in her future plans."

The effect on Mark of Hank's reference to Kae was electrifying. Mark sputtered, uncrossed his legs, and shot up out of his chair, all the while his face turning a brilliant shade of red.

"How dare you!" he shouted.

Hank waved him back to his seat. Now the lawyer's hand reached into his jacket pocket and extracted a cigarette. Without hesitation, Mark lit it and began to puff vigorously.

"Mr. Fitzgerald, it may surprise you to know I have no desire for information about your bedroom activities with Kae Hargreave. I only want to solve a murder. If your affair has a bearing on this case, I'll know it. So why don't we get back to the original question I asked." Mark sat down slowly. "Tell me about Pemberton."

"Pemberton," Mark repeated. "It's simple, really."

"Good," Hank responded. "I hate when things are complicated."

"You asked me before about Maurice's retiring. If you knew him, you would know his whole life was business. Over the years he had taken the company his father started and tripled it in size. It wasn't just a matter of making money with Maurice. It was the challenge. Outwitting the competition, gaining an advantage. Maurice loved taking the risk, especially when others wouldn't."

"It sounds as if you admired him, Mr. Fitzgerald."

"I did. He taught me a lot."

"I see."

"Maurice had taken Hargreave Industries about as far as it could go in its market. We could have expanded into Canada, and we did think about it. But, in the end, Maurice wanted something new. A new enterprise not connected to what his father had built up."

"Was Pemberton a new business?"

"Yes. We were going to call ourselves The Pemberton Consulting Company, Inc.. Maurice liked the name, he picked it out."

"You say, 'we.' You were partners in the new deal?" Mark nodded. "Fifty-fifty?"

"Yes. As a matter of fact we were."

"I know where Maurice was getting his money for the venture. Where was yours coming from?"

"I have some capital. And, of course, the fee for brokering the deal between Hargreave and Townsend Crest. I was getting 5% of the sale price as a bonus."

Ben stopped taking notes and did a quick calculation on his pad. Five per cent of $52.8 million was $2,640,000. He turned the paper to let Hank see the figure.

196

"And the new company?" asked Hank, making a quick glance at the number. More than two and a half million dollars.

"The beauty of it was that we wouldn't need much capital."

"Why was that?"

"You must be aware, especially in your business, of the increased emphasis for security preparations in both the private and public sectors these days. Everybody wants to develop an infrastructure to promote safety, but how many experts are there in the field? Not enough, I can assure you. Maurice's idea was to start a consulting company which would offer to provide the information technology needed to set up these systems."

"Computers?"

"Our Pemberton Company would identify the software system needed for the clients' operation, put together the equipment package, arrange for the training on its use."

"I suppose that's lucrative."

"You bet. Think of the possibilities. Aviation, hotel chains, Fortune 500 companies all need information security. The federal government alone is looking for all kinds of contractors to help them set up their systems. It's a limitless market."

"And you would both have enough expertise in this area?"

"It's just a case of managing the operation. We would hire all the tech people we need to provide us with the guts of the packages we would offer. Maurice would have been the point man with potential customers, and I would handle drawing up the contracts and the financial agreements. We'll do leasing as well, and that would be my portfolio."

Hank shook his head. The workings of the business world and high finance always amazed him. Pemberton. To his policeman's mind it didn't sound like a real company, just a scheme to make money. He looked across the desk. Mark Fitzgerald was clearly happy with the idea from which he no doubt stood to make more money than Hank would ever see in his municipal paychecks.

"Do you understand, Lieutenant?"

"Oh, yes. Yes, I do," Hank said frowning. "The Hargreaves, except for Maurice, were to be cut loose so that you both could make a lot of money." Mark started to object to his plans being so starkly summarized, but Hank did not give him the opportunity. "Sounds to me like a motive for murder."

"Murder," Mark said. "You think that's why Maurice was killed? Because of the Pemberton venture?" Hank nodded. "Well, I guess that lets me out as a suspect."

"Let me ask you this, Mr. Fitzgerald. Is there any reason why Pemberton can't proceed without Maurice? Then you could have all the profits."

"There would be no need for me to dispose of Maurice, I assure you, Lt. Nightingale. I needed his shrewdness. Believe me, I'm not happy to lose him as a partner."

"But, do you intend to proceed with the new venture?"

"I haven't thought it all through yet. But, I am keeping it as an option, if I can find the right partner. The idea is sound."

"You are not planning to continue with Hargreave Industries under their new management?"

"You mean Lionel Hargreave? No thanks."

"That *is* the motive, Ben. I'm sure of it." Hank's voice sounded relieved.

"But, Lionel Hargreave sold his interest, Lieutenant. Why would he and his wife be unhappy that they were going to get all that money for his share? Over $16 million, you said."

"As I see it there would be a few reasons why Emily would kill Maurice. One, the first, is that she thinks he cheated her husband out of the fair value of the company. And, second, that Maurice didn't let Lionel in on this Pemberton business."

"What did you make of that? I'm not sure I understand what that security consulting stuff is all about."

"Just understand the dollar signs."

"And what about the two sons? Nelson and Harold. And Tina, too, I suppose. Nobody seems to be caring if the younger generation in that family had that company sold out from under them."

"Yes," Hank said, "and that's actually what I think Emily Hargreave realized. She knew, more than her husband did apparently, that Maurice Hargreave couldn't be trusted to take care of her sons' future."

"And she took matters into her own hands?"

"She brought the gun with her. Harold said his father's office had a connecting door to Maurice's. If she visited her husband at work, she could have taken the opportunity to help herself to the gun, which everyone seemed to know was kept in the desk drawer."

"It does seem to add up."

"And now let's go find her."

The shock of Hank's announcement that he planned to arrest Emily for murder had taken some time to pass through Caroline's body. After leaving Hank in her office, she went upstairs and sat for a time on the loggia. The day was gray with chilly air to match. By evening, rain was expected.

Caroline had brought her notebook with her, and she forced herself now to concentrate on the many strands of the case and to what they might be linked. To whom, she amended her thought. She sat in silence, conjuring up the faces of the Hargreaves, trying to get a message, a meaning to the mystery.

"And then," she said aloud, "there is Mark Fitzgerald." His was the piece that wouldn't fit, and she stood up with determination. "I've got to know. And I don't see why I can't find some of these things out for myself."

Taking her book, she went back into the house by way of the gallery, which overlooked the grand hall. Below her was the scene she least wanted to see. Hank Nightingale and Ben Davies were standing, facing Lionel who had his arm around Emily. All four were grim-faced, and Caroline strained to hear the words coming from Hank's stern lips.

"I have the warrant here for your arrest, Emily Hargreave, for the willful murder of Maurice Hargreave. I have the duty to inform you that you have the right to remain silent. Anything you say can—"

Caroline rushed down the stairs and reached the hall in time to hear Hank finish reciting the warning. Emily, always pale, appeared ashen as she stared in front of her.

"There is a grave mistake being made, Lieutenant," Lionel said. "My wife didn't kill my brother. It's madness to think she would do that. She couldn't do that."

"Mr. Hargreave," Hank answered, "I think you should know we have strong evidence against your wife."

"I know what you think you have, but it's circumstantial."

"Fingerprints are not circumstantial."

"She only picked up the gun after Maurice was dead."

"How do you know that?" Hank asked. "Were you there?"

"No, no, of course not. She told me."

"Yes, well you did make a statement to me that you may wish to change if you want to avoid an accessory charge."

The front door flew open and Brian came in, followed by Nelson and Harold.

"Father!" Brian's black eyes were blazing. "What is going on? Harold said they are arresting Mother for Maurice's murder."

201

Lionel turned away from his sons. The expressions on the faces of those standing near the foyer gave Brian his answer, and he went immediately to his mother's side.

"I told you," he whispered softly to her ear. "You should have told the truth from the beginning."

"What's this?" Ben asked. He was standing close enough to hear. "What truth? What do you know?"

"Tell him, Mother." Brian's voice was supportive.

"I can't," she said weakly.

"Then I will. I saw her," Brian said, turning to Hank.

"The day of the murder?"

"Yes, Lieutenant. I was in my room all day, as you know. The bedroom window overlooks the front drive. I heard the cab pull up on the gravel. She got out."

"What time was this?"

"I looked at my watch because I was surprised to see her back so early from lunch. And my father wasn't with her, of course, and that troubled me. It was just after 12:30."

"Good God, Brian," Nelson said. "Do you realize what you are doing? You are placing Mother at the murder scene at the time when Maurice was killed."

"She didn't do it," Brian explained patiently to his brother.

"How do you know this, Mr. Hargreave?" Ben asked.

"She told me," Brian said. "I asked her about it this morning. She told me everything. She said—"

202

"Mrs. Hargreave," Hank said, interrupting her son, "I think it would be in your best interests to make a new statement before we go any further here. Do you want to call your lawyer? We will have to take care of all of this at the police station."

"Do you want me to get Mark?" Brian asked.

"No." Lionel's voice was emphatic. "Call Anthony Conroy. His number is in my book. It's upstairs on the table next to my bed. Give him all the details and ask him to come to Newport as soon as possible."

Brian nodded and turned to go. Hank saw him lock eyes with Caroline.

"Just a minute, Mr. Hargreave," Hank said to Brian. "Do you have any more information to add to what you have just said? Did you see your mother enter the house after she got out of the cab?" Brian shook his head, and Hank asked the inevitable. "Where did she go?"

"She stood there for a while outside the front door. Staring up at the house. I couldn't see her face that closely, but I thought she was crying. Then I saw her walk around the side of the house."

"Do you remember which way she went? Left or right?"

Brian thought for a few seconds. He seemed to be trying to picture the scene in his mind.

"Right. She was walking slowly, and she went that way." He gestured with his right hand.

"The gazebo is on that side of the house," Ben observed.

"That's right," Hank said, turning to Harold. "Now I wonder if you would like to pick up the story."

Harold appeared dumbfounded. Caroline had never seen him at such a loss for words. Everyone was staring at him, and he was clearly uncomfortable.

"You made a statement that while you were reading on the veranda you saw your mother coming up the path from the Cliff Walk at 1:30 p.m.," Ben said. "You signed that version of events on the day of the murder."

"Yes, well, yes," Harold said uneasily. "Yes, I did."

"Do you want to amend *your* statement?" Hank asked flatly.

"I suppose I'll have to." Hank nodded. "The thing is, well, it's rather an embarrassment. That's all. You see I didn't think that tiny lobster salad sandwich and a plate of rabbit greens for lunch was very filling. I was hoping Mrs. Kent here would offer me another sandwich, but when I came back in the house and took a peek in the kitchen. Well, that vinegar bottle of a cook was there, and I knew she wouldn't give me so much as a carrot stick."

Hank looked incredulously at Harold.

"I knew my wife had a box of chocolates in her bureau drawer. Of course, she didn't know that I knew it was there, and I had only taken out three the day before when I first found it. I'm sure she didn't notice they were missing. After all it was a two-pound box."

"Mr. Hargreave," Hank exclaimed with as much patience as he had left, "get to the point."

"What did you do?" Nelson asked. He was staring at Harold with a disgusted look on his face.

"The point is," Harold said to Hank, as if he were speaking to a child, "I went upstairs to our room and took some more chocolates from my wife's box."

"So you did leave the veranda."

"Of course I did if I went upstairs."

"What time was this?" Hank asked.

"I'm not sure," Harold said. "It was after I ate my sandwich, and if you say my mother was walking around the side of the house there at 12:30 or so, and I didn't see her. Well, I'm no detective, but I would say that it was then."

"How long were you gone from your chair on the veranda?"

"I suppose at least fifteen minutes. First I went to the kitchen, then upstairs for a bit."

"And you didn't see fit to inform me of this little jaunt of yours at the beginning of the investigation?" Hank asked with obvious exasperation.

"I didn't want my wife to know I took the chocolates. She gets very mad when I eat her chocolates."

"Mr. Hargreave," Ben said on behalf of his superior officer who was too furious to speak, "this is a murder inquiry. We are looking for an account of everyone's movements during the key time between 12:30 and 1 p.m. when the medical examiner says the murder took place."

205

"If Mrs. Hargreave picked up the gun in the gazebo, then the crime had to have been committed between 12:30 and the time when she touched the gun." This was Caroline's voice, musing on the rush of new facts being introduced. And now she turned to Emily and asked, "Do you know what time you went into the gazebo?"

"I'm not sure," Emily said shakily. "I got out of the cab and walked around the house. I stood by the gazebo for a while. I don't know how long."

"Think, Mrs. Hargreave, think," Caroline implored. "It's very important."

"You don't understand, my dear," Emily answered. "I'm just not sure now. I can't say any more than that."

And with that she turned to Hank as if to signal she was ready to go.

CHAPTER SEVENTEEN

"That's my case," Hank said. He was standing with Caroline in the foyer after Ben had taken Emily and Lionel to a waiting police car. "Pemberton. The key is Pemberton. You were right, Mrs. Kent. Maurice was planning something, and it was the reason why Emily killed him." Patiently he explained the details of the consulting scheme to Caroline. She absorbed them in silence, her mind racing to see the flaws in the argument as Hank spoke.

"I'm sorry," he said finally. "I know you wanted a different ending."

"There's something still wrong. I know it. Maybe I've seen something, heard something—"

"No, please. Take this arrest as something good. You can get back to running your business now. With any luck, you won't be affected by this. This murder is a Boston affair. It had nothing to do with Newport. People will soon forget it happened here."

Pemberton. Caroline said the word over and over as she worked about the house the rest of the afternoon. Had she heard it? The Hargreaves had been at Kenwood Court less than twenty-four hours before Maurice was murdered. She had talked to each, observed each. Had anyone said 'Pemberton?'

Caroline walked through the house, to the library, the salon, the dining room, all the while picturing the Hargreaves, listening in her mind for the drifting sounds of conversation.

"I'm not getting anywhere," she said as she left the billiard room. "I don't know anything."

The conservatory was beyond the billiard room in the corner of the west wing, and it occurred to Caroline that some time spent with the plants might clear her head. Despite her indifference to outdoor gardening, she had often found an irrational comfort in tidying the potted plants, snipping off yellow leaves and drying stems. Perhaps the solace was in the fact that plants in containers were just that: contained. The foliage in the expansive outside grounds was too uninhibited for her to control.

The room had been much favored by Frederick Kent's mother, Alicia. She had a passion for playing bridge, and during the summers of the family's residence she could often be found there with other society women indulging in her favorite pastime. Now, amid the tall ferns and thick greenery of the conservatory, Caroline found Harold Hargreave. He was stretched indolently on a chaise longue, paperback book in hand, his eyes riveted to the page. Caroline saw that he was about a third through the volume.

"Oh, Mr. Hargreave," she said. "I didn't know anyone was in here. I came to check if it was time to water the palms. They don't need much, and sometimes I forget to do it at all. I didn't mean to disturb you."

"That's all right. I'm having a hard time concentrating on my book." He closed it and laid it on the table beside the chair. This one was a John Grisham. He must have finished the Tom Clancy. "I'm so upset about my mother. The police must be crazy to think she murdered Maurice."

"Oh, I know," Caroline said with feeling. "There has to be a mistake."

"I sure hope the police realize it soon. I don't think Mother's going to like jail."

"Mr. Hargreave," Caroline said as she tried to take in the meaning of that thought, "I've been thinking. When you came in the house yesterday after lunch to go up to your room—"

"Wasn't that silly of me?" Harold interrupted her with a touch on her arm, which she was careful not to recoil from. "I had to confess like a schoolboy."

"Did you see anyone in the house?"

"What?" He wasn't following her.

"Don't you see? If someone who was inside the house was on his... or her way to the gazebo, you might have seen them. You might have seen the murderer."

"I see. I see," he said thoughtfully. "Yes, I see what you're getting at. The murderer. I could know a clue."

"An important one. *Did* you see anyone?"

She waited. Should she prompt him? "Tina was working in the house while Maurice was in the gazebo yesterday. Did you happen to see her?"

"Tina, of course." His small eyes were bright. "That would make it a nice ending if we could pin this crime on Tina. Wouldn't Nelson be pleased to be rid of her."

Caroline held back from answering. She wanted to give him time. When he finally spoke, he was frowning.

"Can't be done on my word. Sorry. I didn't see Tina. Wish I had. Didn't see anybody, in fact. Sorry."

"Well," Caroline said. "I thought perhaps you might have forgotten."

"No." His hand reached for his book. When Caroline didn't leave, he stopped his fingers from picking it up. "I'm sorry," he repeated, looking directly at her, "but I can't help you."

"Pemberton," she said, still watching his face.

"What did you say?" He looked surprised.

"Pemberton. What does that name mean to you?"

"I don't know anybody by that name. Is that what you mean? A person connected to the murder?"

"I was told it's a company name."

"What kind of company?"

"Computers, I think."

He shook his head. "I don't know much about that. We have computers at the office, of course. All our records are on them, and I can use the damned things, but I don't like them. Too much can go wrong. Erase a whole bunch of data. I've done that a few times. Give me the old-fashioned file any day."

Mentioning Pemberton to Harold had not drawn any information, and Caroline wondered on whom next to try out the word. She had returned to her office where she was opening the bills which had come in the day's mail. The knock at the door was a welcome distraction, and she got up from her desk to open it. Nelson Hargreave stood waiting in the hallway, his tall frame looking weary and defenseless.

"May I come in, Mrs. Kent?"

"Yes," she said, stepping aside. She closed the door as soon as he was inside and motioned for him to sit down. "You must be shocked, Mr. Hargreave. I know I am."

"My mother, you mean. I don't understand why the police could think she killed Maurice. I'm sure she didn't."

"She's innocent. The police will realize that and re-open the investigation."

"Why don't they investigate Mark Fitzgerald?" He asked the question sharply and stared directly into her eyes. His looked fierce, and their gray color was suddenly deep and intense. "Why don't they find out where he was all yesterday afternoon? I know he wasn't at the office."

"Have you told this to the police?" Caroline asked. It was an intriguing piece of news.

"They're 'checking people's alibis.' That's what I was told."

"I'm sorry they weren't more helpful. I know there isn't anything I can really do, but I—"

"Oh, you've been good to let us stay on," he said. "That has been a help, and now that Mother is... well, Father and I will have to stay on longer, of course. That is, if we can."

"Yes. I thought under the circumstances that the guests I was expecting on Tuesday shouldn't come. The police wanted to finish their investigation, and I didn't think... well, I didn't think I ought to have guests come right after..." She struggled not to say 'the murder,' but couldn't think of another word.

"I should apologize, Mrs. Kent. This all hasn't been good for your inn and its reputation, has it?"

"You mustn't think of that. Your mother's well-being should be what you are concerned for."

"That's so kind of you. To think it was only a short time ago that I came here to see your inn, and we talked of my parents' anniversary party, and all the arrangements seemed so perfect. And now..." He looked at her and shook his head sadly. "And now, look how it's all turned out. Today is their anniversary, you know."

"Your family must be a great comfort to you."

"I suppose so." Nelson remained dispirited.

"Will your wife be staying on with you?"

"I beg your pardon."

"You said a minute ago that you and your father would be staying on. What about Mrs. Hargreave?"

"Kae? Why, I don't think so. No, she ought to go back home. This is nothing to do with her." He was firm.

"And Mr. Fitzgerald? Do you think he might want to stay on?"

"Mark? Why would he stay? What has he got to do with our family affairs?"

"Oh, naturally. Somebody's got to be in charge at Hargreave Industries now that..." She let her voice trail off again as she watched his reaction.

"Oh, no." Again he was firm. "Mark won't have to be back at the office. That's all over."

Caroline felt a churning in her chest. "You mean Hargreave Industries is all over? The company is no longer in business?"

"No," he said, surprised. "I mean Mark Fitzgerald will no longer be employed at Hargreave Industries."

"He's working for The Pemberton Company, is that it?"

"I don't know where he's going to work, but I know it's not with my family's company. Not at Hargreave Industries. No. I'll be in charge from now on."

The rain had started to fall, and the damp sky seemed to darken around them as Hank watched the Hargreaves arrive at the station house. Emily, supported by her husband, hesitated in the doorway and trembled.

Hank left Lionel in a waiting area and directed Ben to complete the necessary paperwork on the arrest. Emily could wait in an interrogation room. It was always better that way, Hank believed. That the suspect should understand the finality of incarceration was usually helpful when the time came to get down to getting at the truth of the crime. And Emily, Hank was convinced, was a perfect candidate for spending time in the solitary atmosphere of the bare, gray room used for questioning suspects.

In the meantime, Hank would compose his own approach to the interrogation, deciding on his strategy for making Emily reveal what he needed to know to complete his case. It was only a matter of time before she would confess. It was a pity that a woman, who had otherwise been a pillar of respectability, had resorted to murder to avenge what she had judged to be crimes against her family, but she had. There it was. Hank could only do his duty and give the prosecutors what they needed to convict her in a court of law.

Sitting at his desk, making some notes, his eyes strayed to the stack of neat reports just completed by his officers on the alibis of the guests at the Inn at Kenwood Court. May as well examine them all, he thought, picking up the first document from the top. This was Timothy Jarvis's report, and he had taken the downtown business district. As Hank had suspected, the information on Kae Hargreave's movements was extremely sketchy. Two antique dealers remembered her coming in before lunch. She had made purchases in both establishments. After these stops, there seemed to be no confirmation that she had done any further browsing. Her whereabouts after twelve noon were at this point unknown.

As for Donna Hargreave, a waitress at the restaurant where she had claimed to have had her lunch did remember her. She had been an enthusiastic customer, happy to chat each time the waitress had come by the table. As far as time, the waitress believed that Donna had come in shortly after noon and stayed for more than half an hour.

The second report was filed by Keisha McAndrews, who had checked out Nelson Hargreave's activities. The first stop had been the tour bus depot. The clerk at the counter had no recollection of selling the ticket, but some waiting around the depot had led to the finding of the bus driver of the tour Nelson had taken. Yes, of course, he had remembered Nelson. A tall man, gangly. Kept bumping his head getting on and off the bus. McAndrews's notes indicated that the driver had taken to looking out for his passenger and reminding him to watch his head.

"Well," Hank thought, "that's interesting. Almost as if he wanted to be remembered. Let's check the times."

According to the report, the bus had left the depot at 11 a.m., with an itinerary which included traveling through the various historical parts of the city and two stops, one at Hunter House, the Preservation Society's eighteenth century colonial-era house, and the second at The Breakers, representing the late nineteenth century 'summer cottage' period. The tour was finished at 1:45, and, yes, the driver remembered Nelson's last exit from the bus when he was thanked by his passenger for his several considerate warnings on the low height of the exit door.

McAndrews, who was on the list to take the next exam for sergeant, had also found Sylvie Becker, Nelson's seat mate, at the bed and breakfast where she was staying. Nice work, Hank thought, by the ambitious officer. He liked working with the women officers. They were good at getting the details and generally had more patience than their male counterparts in interviews.

Sylvie Becker had no trouble remembering Nelson Hargreave. "A very nice man," she offered. "I'll bet," Hank said, wishing he could have watched the German woman's face during the interview. One of the disadvantages of rank, he knew, was that legwork out in the streets was no longer looked upon as worthy of his time.

The summary of Sylvie's information was that she and Nelson had sat next to one another on the bus during every segment of the tour. Afterwards they had lunched together at a restaurant next to the depot and lingered over their coffee, talking. Nelson had encouraged her to visit Boston and had given her his telephone number (at the office, McAndrews had gone to the trouble to find out) so that they might get together when Sylvie visited the city. Their lunch had come to an end at around three when the waiter seemed to be showing his irritation at their claiming the table without any further ordering. Needless to say, the waiter remembered them and confirmed the lateness of the hour with Officer McAndrews.

So they hadn't returned to her room, Hank noted with some interest. Well, that might be a move being saved for the Boston rendez-vous. A man like Nelson Hargreave might take his time and await his opportunity. At any rate, it didn't seem to matter to his murder case. The times he was interested in were between 12:30 and 1 p.m., and the report in his hand indicated that during that time Nelson would have been on his house tour of The Breakers.

The last check was on Tina Hargreave and Mark Fitzgerald.

Toby Erickson had gone up to the Hargreave Industries office, where he had obtained copies of the faxes Tina claimed to have sent to several of the company's departments from Caroline's office after she had been left alone there on the day of the murder. The date/ time setting of the Boston fax machines showed that Tina had indeed sent them from the inn during the time that she had sworn.

217

Interviews with several members of the office staff concerning Mark's movements on Friday, however, were not favorable to his alibi. His secretary remembered that Mark said he planned to leave for Newport around two, but she had been sent out of the office on an errand to the factory at about 11 o'clock and afterwards had gone on her lunch break. When she returned at two, the lawyer was definitely gone.

Hank was pleased to see that she had been asked who directed her to go to the plant, and it was, not surprisingly, her boss. Further conversations with others in the office could find no one who remembered seeing Mark after approximately ten after eleven. He could have left the office anytime after that and been in Newport in less than two hours. Did he go directly to Kenwood Court? No one saw him or his car. Had he had set up a meeting with Kae Hargreave in Newport sometime shortly after one? It would be worth putting McAndrews on the inns and hotels in town to see if the couple checked in for a few hours. Hank made a note of it.

While Emily Hargreave waited alone, to feel her isolation and to ponder what might lie in store for her, Hank called for Ben to bring her husband into his office. As Lionel entered, it was clear that he also was feeling the strain of being in a foreign territory, detached from the safety of his known environment. Hank always wished for the power to read minds, not for the obvious reason of obtaining information, but for the more subtle one of learning how people were

218

feeling inside. Were they terrified? Sad? Confident, or tense? It wasn't always that easy to tell, although like most detectives, Hank felt he had a better sense of emotions than most. Now as he studied the man in front of him, he thought he recognized guilt.

"Sit down, Mr. Hargreave," Hank said, indicating a chair and nodding to Ben to take notes. "Let's make this as easy as possible."

"Thank you, Lt. Nightingale," Lionel said as he sat down. His movements were awkward, and he favored his back as he eased his tall frame down onto the chair.

"Do you have any idea when your attorney will arrive?"

"I talked to my son a few minutes ago. Mr. Conroy was leaving immediately and should be here in two hours. I expect my wife should wait for him before making any further statement."

"That's fine," Hank said. "I would like to take a new statement from you."

"I've been thinking of that while I've been waiting, and I realize now I made a mistake yesterday. I should have told you the truth. Brian," he looked at Hank, and his eyes had a distinct brightness as he mentioned his son's name, "has just been chastising me on the telephone, and he is right. I've put my wife in jeopardy." He looked straight at Hank, and Hank found himself feeling empathy toward this tired aging man, who had lived for so long under the thumb of his younger brother.

"I'd like you to tell me again about your lunch with your wife, Mr. Hargreave. Start from when you left the Inn at Kenwood Court."

219

Lionel began, his words spoken in a voice that was hollow and fatigued. He described their walk to the restaurant, adding in his perception of his wife's happiness over the day and the coming celebration. Once at the beach near the restaurant, they had walked to the ocean's edge and he was reminded of their honeymoon forty years ago, when they had cruised the Greek Islands, and Emily had childishly delighted in seeing the dazzling blue waters of the Mediterranean for the first time.

"It started out a wonderful day. Emily was so happy, happier than I had seen her in a long time."

"And then what happened?" Hank asked.

"You must understand that I thought she would be pleased with my decision. Over the years she had been so unhappy with my position in the company."

"Because of your brother?"

"Yes," Lionel said, lowering his head. "She had pride, and she thought my place in the company, always taking orders from Maurice, was humiliating. I disliked the business, but my father had never allowed me to train for anything but going into the company, so I felt I had no choice."

"Until now when you signed over your share of the company to your brother."

"You know about that?" Hank nodded. "It was time for me to retire. I wanted to travel with Emily, have our own lives separate from Maurice."

220

"But, why did she become so angry at lunch? What did you argue about?"

"Because that's when I told her, Lieutenant."

"Told her what?"

"That I had sold my half of Hargreave Industries to Maurice."

"You hadn't discussed this decision with her prior to your agreement with Maurice, prior to yesterday?"

"No, I hadn't."

"I'm afraid I find that hard to believe, Mr. Hargreave."

"It's true."

"You made a major decision on your retirement and future plans and did not take your wife of forty years into your confidence? Come on, I want the truth. No more lies." Lionel frowned, and now Hank grew angry. "I'll tell you what I think. Your wife has known about this plan for some time and has built on her hatred toward your brother for not only pushing you out of the business, but your sons, as well. So much so, that she decided to kill her brother-in-law in revenge."

"My sons!" Lionel's expression was incredulous. "What have my sons to do with this? Maurice gave me his word that their status at the company would not change because I left."

"Mr. Hargreave, after next Friday there will not be a Hargreave Industries."

"What on earth are you talking about? Next Friday. What in God's name do you mean?" A look of puzzlement spread over Lionel's face.

"Mr. Hargreave, do you know what The Pemberton Company is?"

"Pemberton? Is that what you said?"

"Yes. It's a consulting company."

"Consulting? We don't use consultants at Hargreave Industries. Maurice never believed they knew more than he did."

"Pemberton is a new company," Hank said. "It doesn't actually exist yet."

"Then I suppose that's why I've never heard of it," Lionel answered.

CHAPTER EIGHTEEN

"Is Lionel Hargreave telling us the truth this time? That's the question," Ben said when he and Hank were alone in the office.

"I don't know," Hank said. "I've got to sort this out some more."

"As I see it," Ben offered, "the whole case hinges on who brought the gun from the office to Kenwood Court. Our murderer had to know before he, or she, left that the killing would take place while the family was on vacation. And if Emily—"

"I know, I know," Hank said with vexation. "If Emily Hargreave didn't yet know of her husband's plans to sell out and retire, why would she have planned the murder in advance, which bringing the gun to Newport would signify?"

"Suppose somebody else had planned the murder, brought the gun and all, and then Emily used it before this murderer had his chance."

"No. Two murderers is one too many." Hank ran his fingers through his thick black hair and shrugged. "No, the key is did Emily know in advance? Just because her husband didn't tell her, does that mean someone else did?"

"Like Mark Fitzgerald? He knew."

"And I bet Tina did, too."

"Why would she tell Emily of all people?"

"Good question, Ben. And the answer is it doesn't make any sense that Tina would take Emily into her confidence. How about Nelson? Or Harold? Mrs. Kent said he was a snooper. Maybe he's the one who told his mother."

"I like that for a theory."

"We'll have our opportunity to test it when we talk to our suspect." Hank looked at his watch. "Her attorney should be here within the hour. Why don't we take a break for something to eat? I don't know about you, but I didn't get lunch, and I could do with some food. I'm buying."

"Thanks."

As the two men headed down the stairs, Ben shared a thought he had tucked into the back of his mind. "Why do you suppose Emily Hargreave went straight to the gazebo when she returned to the house? Had she taken the gun to the restaurant?"

"You're full of good questions today, Ben. And the answer is, I don't know. She may have been carrying it in her purse for the entire trip for fear her husband might discover it if it were in their bedroom. I think that's one of the questions we should ask her."

After she dressed the next morning, Caroline walked noiselessly through the private family apartment on the second floor in the rear of the east wing which she shared with Louise.

Both Kent women had a bedroom suite in the wing, their individual privacy maintained by the sitting room which separated them. The large space in the east wing had originally belonged to the second Mrs. Henry Kent who used it not only for her sleeping quarters and to house her large wardrobe, but also to entertain ladies at afternoon tea. The old walls held many secrets of old Newport enthusiastically shared by the women who once ruled society in the city. In whispering confidences and knowing smiles everyone who was anyone was scrutinized, disassembled and judgment was passed, all over pots of Darjeeling, lacy sandwiches and plates of cream cakes.

Now Caroline slowly turned the knob of Louise's bedroom door and looked in.

"Come in, dear," said a clear voice.

Caroline came into the room and went over to the bed where Louise was sitting, propped up against a mound of ivory, embroidery-trimmed pillows. Caroline tenderly kissed her mother-in-law on the cheek.

"Good morning, Louise. How are you feeling?"

225

"Fine," Louise replied in a firm tone. Her lively blue eyes were rested and bright.

"Do you want your morning tea?"

"No, Caroline, I've been in this bed much too long." She pushed back the heavy quilt in preparation to get up.

"Louise, you had a busy day yesterday. Perhaps you shouldn't come down just yet. After all, it is Sunday, and Mattie said she was afraid you are—"

"Overdoing it," Louise said, finishing the sentence. "Well, I'm not."

"I'm sure you know how much you can do."

"Of course I do, and it's a lot more than Mattie Simpson thinks I'm capable of. Why that woman would have me in a chair with my feet up all day long!"

Caroline smiled and sat down on the bed. She took Louise's small pink hand. Her slender fingers were well-defined, sculpted. The old gray diamonds of her engagement and wedding rings in their platinum settings looked cold as ice in the light. In response to Caroline's grasp, Louise rested her other hand on top of her daughter-in-law's larger one.

"You've been doing so much work on the grounds, and yesterday you were up and about before me. Now, Louise, you know you don't have to do so much."

"I want to help, Caroline," Louise said. "Please let me."

Why this should make Caroline begin to cry was something she couldn't define, but it happened, and Louise was hugging her and soothing her as if she were a small child again.

"Oh, Caroline, it's all right. You have a good cry, dear. I've been wondering when you would."

Caroline sniffed in her damp tears and looked up into the older woman's kind eyes. "What do you mean?" she asked.

"This murder… and this inn business, it's too much for you."

"No," Caroline said, her voice full of determination, "no, it isn't." She pulled back from Louise's embrace and met her eyes. "No," she repeated. "Everything's going to work out."

"You can sell the house. It won't bother me."

"Louise, of course, it would. This is your home. You love it here!"

"I do," Louise said softly, "but I could bear it if I had to leave now."

"But, Reed is here, don't you feel it? I do." Caroline's voice was strong now, and Louise squeezed her hand. "And you must feel that Frederick is here, too."

"Of course, I do, dear, but I've learned that the dead are always where you are if you still have love for them."

Now Caroline turned her eyes away from the penetrating gaze of the other woman.

"Caroline?" There was no answer. "Caroline, you must promise me that you won't be too headstrong about keeping the house as an inn. You must accept when it's time to give it up."

"You think I'm going to have to give up on it?" Caroline looked back at Louise. "You think I'm being foolish?"

"Perhaps it was I who was foolish for encouraging you."

"My money won't last forever, Louise, but I'm going to work as hard as I can to make Kenwood Court profitable. I expect things to be tight through the winter, but in the spring and summer we'll make a bundle. Right now Maurice Hargreave's death here seems awful, but I know we can go beyond it... people will forget that it happened here—"

Caroline's sentence was cut short by a light rapping on the door, which now opened, accompanied by the sound of the clatter of the breakfast tray.

"Your breakfast's ready," Mattie's voice announced. "There's a nice omelet and bacon, toast and marmalade, and a big glass of orange juice."

Mattie's hard stare pushed Caroline into a standing position, and the tray was put in front of Louise. While she held the tray firm above her thighs, Mattie settled the bed covering back into an orderly arrangement. Louise looked at her food uneasily.

"Some of them Hargreaves is already in the dining room, Mrs. Caroline. Today is Jan's day off, I don't have to remind you."

"All right, Mattie," Caroline said. "I'll see to them."

228

"None of them talks polite to one another. I don't like that. Their own family, mind you, and not polite."

"I said I'll go down, Mattie. Is their food cooking?"

"Eggs and bacon, same as for the Missus, and some oatmeal for those that don't want that. All in due time."

Caroline was in the doorway now, and she took a last look at Louise, who was obediently beginning to eat under Mattie's watchful guard.

"Mattie," Louise said, "why don't you go with Caroline and help her?"

"As soon as I see that you've eaten a proper meal and gotten you settled in your bath."

"Mattie, I'll turn into a duck if you make me take one more bath. As soon as I eat I'm going to get dressed and help with the guests."

As Caroline shut the door she heard Mattie's scolding tone. "And don't you think you'll be doing any gardening today."

The Sunday newspapers were full of the arrest of Emily Hargreave for her brother-in-law's murder. Hank sipped his morning coffee and looked for a long, thoughtful time at the front page of the *Boston Globe* with its color photo of Emily's face as it stared blankly out of the window of the black and white police car. In the background of the picture was the leafy autumn backdrop of

229

Kenwood Court, the house a blurry gray mass amid the thick trunks of the beech wood trees.

The arrival last night of the lawyer from Boston, Anthony Conroy, had not brought clarity to his case against Emily. She had continued to maintain, under Hank's steady questioning and her attorney's worried gaze, that she could not say positively what she did or didn't do on Friday after she had left the Newport Cab Company's taxi in the front drive of the inn and arrived at the summerhouse at the back of the estate grounds. That she was or was not carrying the Colt .32 in her purse was a fact about which Emily was also uncertain.

The bail hearing was set for tomorrow at 10 a.m., and Hank walked over to the window which looked out into the back yard. He was wondering what he could say to Emily later today to make her give him some facts.

All traces of the previous night's rain were gone. His neighbor's cat was sunning herself on the fence behind the house where he lived. The sleek black animal was sitting on the rail, her thick glossy fur absorbing the sun's rays. Her half-closed eyes displayed her feeling of independence.

Hank looked at the clock and shook off the feeling of envy for the cat's free and simple life. The morning was almost over. He would have to spend some time this afternoon at the station with Emily, trying to get her to admit that she had killed a man. Then it might be a good use of his time to return to the inn and talk to Tina Hargreave. It had become his strong feeling that she knew about

Pemberton. Could he get Emily to tell him that it was Tina who had given her the information that became the motive for the crime? Tina was sharp, Hank was convinced of that. And he was sure there wasn't much that happened at Hargreave Industries that she didn't know about.

The Sunday newspapers had also arrived at the Inn at Kenwood Court. Caroline had a standing order for several copies for the guests, and now they sat on the writing desk in the morning room, ready for the Hargreaves should they desire to see the family's name in their headlines. Caroline wavered as to whether she should hide them, but in the end decided that it was not her decision.

One thing Caroline had done was to keep the telephone calls away from the murdered man's family. The phone had rung steadily as reporters pursued the Hargreaves, first for statements about Maurice's death, and then about Emily's arrest. Nelson had conferred with his father, who Caroline was interested to note was the one who talked to Mark Fitzgerald, and the family had finally issued a statement. Caroline had duplicated it, and Mark offered it to the members of the press. It said little beyond the facts of Maurice's death having occurred and the family's belief in Emily's innocence. It satisfied no journalists in pursuit of their story. None of the Hargreaves cared about the media's needs in covering the news, and Caroline was tiring of being the person caught in the middle.

"I'm housebound," she said to herself, as she looked down at the newspapers. She forced herself not to dwell on the somber image of Emily's face. Instead, looking at the bright orange and yellow autumn leaves made Caroline think of the outdoors.

"I haven't been out even to run errands since the murder on Friday. I wonder. Is there some excuse I could find to get out of the house today?"

Looking at the desk in the morning room reminded her of Tina's computer which had stood on it so recently. How long would it have taken her to go out to the gazebo and kill Maurice had been a question of Caroline's from the beginning of the investigation. On the day of the murder Tina had been in the house and acted strangely, and Caroline continued to look for the hole in Tina's alibi.

Caroline had worked out some of the times in her notebook, and she thought she could personally account for Tina's whereabouts until around 12:40. Harold said he had been upstairs eating chocolates. Could Tina have shot Maurice and gotten back to the house before Harold resumed his reading on the veranda? Emily had gone to the gazebo about the same time and picked up the gun. The time available for Tina's getting down to the gazebo was very narrow. Had Emily seen Maurice's daughter-in-law out on the grounds?

Tina continued to perplex her, and Caroline suddenly decided to re-create her walking to the gazebo from the morning room. She had surmised that Tina would walk, albeit it quickly, rather than run. If anyone had seen her, there would have been nothing unusual about seeing Tina on her way to or from the gazebo to see Maurice on some business matter. But, running on the day of the murder would be out of character and also memorable.

"Caroline! Wait a minute."

Brian Hargreave caught up with Caroline as she walked passed the veranda on her way to the gazebo.

"I'm just going down to the gazebo," Caroline called as she tried to keep her pace.

"I thought the police wanted it sealed. Can we go inside?"

Caroline looked at her watch. She had been gone from the morning room for a minute and seventeen seconds. When they reached the gazebo, she looked to see the time again. Less than three minutes. Dare she pretend to visualize the murder in her head and Tina's imagined movements? Looking at Brian, she realized the futility of enacting the crime now. Resigned, she looked into his curious eyes.

"I was thinking of taking a walk on the Cliff Walk. Do you want to join me?" she proposed.

Brian's pleasurable surprise in the suggestion was evident as he followed her through the pathway and out onto the Cliff Walk. Caroline paused to look at the work George had done on the previous morning to clear the path and noted the gardener's usual precise handiwork. She and Brian walked easily through the space, the trimmed shrubbery giving ample room for their arms and legs to pass unencumbered.

The sun was shining, and the Cliff Walk was busy with people moving in both directions. Most were walking leisurely, tourists pausing to look at whatever caught their eye among the sights of the ocean and on the land. Others, with the gait of exercisers, moved more purposefully. Several runners braved the crowded scene, weaving in and out of the steady flow of people, dogs, and the occasional baby stroller.

Brian was silent. Caroline supposed he was thinking of his mother's arrest. He had been primarily gazing out at the water, but looked from time to time back at the lawns sweeping up to the grand houses above the Walk. They had passed The Breakers, and Brian had given the house a long scrutiny, shaking his head.

Caroline liked his features. He resembled Maurice, although his young frame was slighter than his uncle's had been. Neither man could be called handsome, but each had an intensity that she found attractive.

"My family are idiots." Brian said suddenly, and it took Caroline several seconds to process his opinion.

"I see," she only said. If one of the Hargreaves had planned the murder, that one couldn't be such a simpleton.

"Take Maurice," Brian continued. "Everyone thought he was so smart, but what did he do but go ahead and get himself murdered."

"He couldn't have known that."

"This trip to Newport was a mistake. The Hargreaves don't belong here." He nodded up at the house they were passing. It was the massive stone and turreted form of Ochre Court. "My family wouldn't have been accepted in places like that in the old days. We were in trade."

"The Kent family's money first came from the China trade."

"That was different. Sailing ships and willow ware are a long way from what my family did to make their money."

"I didn't think there was anything wrong with making china. Isn't that how the business got started?"

"My grandfather had the misfortune to start up as the Depression hit. He was saved by the war. The army needed military-grade tableware for the training camps. Old Joseph got the contract for the tableware for the officers' mess. Honestly, you may ask? I hardly think so."

"But you can't be sure."

"The war made us rich. That made my grandfather what is commonly known as a war profiteer."

They had reached the Forty Steps and Brian stopped to lean against the wall and look down at the stone steps which led to the sea's edge. Caroline waited, enjoying the fresh air and her own thoughts. At last he turned, and they started walking back to Kenwood.

"What is that monstrous thing?" Brian asked suddenly. He was staring across the green lawn at Ochre Court again. "Is that meant to be Gothic?"

"Yes, I think so," Caroline said with a laugh.

"Who's responsible for that indignation?"

"The house was designed by Richard Morris Hunt at the direction of the original owner. He wanted to make an impression."

"That's an understatement."

"Now it's the part of the university here in Newport. Salve Regina."

Brian expelled a long breath. "Egos," he complained. "It's a bad thing to mix egos and money."

They were passing The Breakers again, and Caroline couldn't resist asking Brian what he thought of that house, another of Hunt's creations.

"You're joking," he said. "All these houses are too much. Yours is tolerable because it is restrained, but you must know it is too big for one family to live in."

"That's why I can rent most of it to other people."

Now it was Brian's turn to laugh. "Could you live in The Breakers?" he asked. "Be honest."

"It really is too much. They all pretty much are, I agree."

"So you wouldn't live there?"

"The downstairs interior of The Breakers is out of scale to my eye. It's dominated by the Great Hall, and the space is just too big for it to feel like a real house. I've felt overpowered standing there. The statuary and the fountain—"

"That's unusual," he said. "Tina said almost the same thing."

"The same thing? What do you mean?"

"She mentioned the fountain and statues."

"At The Breakers? When?"

"The first night at dinner, on Thursday. Mother was talking about going to the mansions that afternoon with my father and how much she had loved The Breakers. Tina said The Breakers was, let me see... 'full of crap,' I believe her exact words were. 'Just a big waste of space'."

"It does have seventy rooms."

"She and Maury built one of those modern houses with all the latest doodads in it... media room, exercise room, bathrooms with Jacuzzis and God knows what else. Anyway, Tina laughed at The Breakers because of the stuff in that big hall you mentioned. I guess she didn't know that those kinds of things were the Sub-Zero refrigerators and Viking stoves of the nineteenth century."

They had reached the pathway to the inn, and Caroline led the way up to the house.

"Why don't you have that rain check drink you promised me now? We can talk some more."

"Perhaps, but it will have to be later," Caroline answered. "Let me see what my time is like. It's my maid's day off."

"Then let me book you for tomorrow night," Brian answered, a slight flippancy creeping into his voice. "If that isn't her day off, also."

"Actually, it is." Caroline tried to ignore his acid tone. "Jan has off Sundays and Mondays."

"I see. Well, get back to me when you are free."

They had reached the gazebo, and Brian paused at the doorway. He seemed riveted to the path. The air around them was still, and Caroline was reminded of the day that she had found Maurice. Closing her eyes she could see his body, limp with death. She tried to picture him alive, but she couldn't. Whenever she tried to get her mind to concentrate on Maurice's face, she realized it was Brian's that she kept seeing.

CHAPTER NINETEEN

Hank's second interview with Emily Hargreave had not been satisfactory. She told him nothing new. His insistence that she reveal to him what she knew about the new company called Pemberton which her brother-in-law was forming was met with a stony silence. Anthony Conroy had pursed his lips and tried to meet his client's eyes, but Emily had seemed not to care. Finally Hank had given up. She needed to spend more time in custody he believed. Emily wasn't frightened yet, and he felt that she would not talk until she was scared enough to do so.

Now, facing Tina Hargreave across the desk in Caroline's office at the Inn at Kenwood Court, Hank began again on his quest to discover how Emily and Pemberton and the murder of Maurice could be connected. He had come to the house late Sunday afternoon and summoned a surprised Tina to meet with him.

"Is there some new development in the case?" She looked uncomfortable sitting in the chair. For the first time Hank noticed how muscular her body was. Her shoulders hunched awkwardly forward, and she looked stiff from lack of exercise. "Lieutenant?" She was waiting for his answer.

"You could say that," he said.

"But Emily is still in jail, isn't she?"

"Yes." Did he see a slight relaxing of her back muscles? "I'm trying to fill in some blanks I have about the business side of Hargreave Industries. My sense was that you were the one to talk to."

"Of course. How can I help you?"

"The Townsend Crest... merger. I understand that was what Maurice let everyone believe was the plan he had for Hargreave Industries. In actual fact, he was planning to sell the family company to the Townsend Crest Corporation. Were you aware that was his plan?"

Tina hesitated. "I had wondered about it. Maurice was awfully cagey about the Townsend Crest deal, Lieutenant. More so than was his usual manner. He kept telling me not to involve myself, that it was mostly a legal matter, and I couldn't help with it."

"And that was unusual?"

"Oh, yes. Normally he told me everything."

"But I would think, as his executive assistant, you would have had access to all his papers?"

Tina looked down and grasped her right hand with her left. Hank saw the gleam of the huge blue sapphire in her engagement ring. "One of the terrible things that has happened... along with

240

Maurice's death, of course… is my realizing that I wasn't in Maurice's confidence as much as I thought I was, Lieutenant. I've been very hurt to find this out." She looked up, and her almond-shaped brown eyes were wet and unhappy.

"I see."

"After my husband died… Maury… died," she sniffed, "I wanted to continue to be a Hargreave. I don't have much family myself. Both my parents are dead, and I'm an only child. Maurice was like a father to me at first, after Maury died. Then he seemed to change." She looked amazed. "He grew tired of having me around."

"I can see that would hurt you."

"Yes, I didn't know what to do, and—"

"You were left out of the Townsend Crest sale." He cut her off impatiently. They were getting far off the track of where he had wanted to go. "And you knew nothing about the new venture Maurice was planning?" Tina shook her head violently. "Pemberton. The new consulting company?" Again she shook her head, this time in a slow, sad movement. "You saw no documents relating to the new company?"

"I never knew Maurice had the slightest interest in that sort of thing, computers and security. I always thought he was fascinated by the manufacturing process. I wouldn't have believed that he would want to do something like that."

"Would you have believed that he wanted to make more money? More than manufacturing could produce?"

241

"I don't know. Honestly, I don't know. I never thought Maurice was just out to make money."

"I see," Hank said. "That's a very interesting viewpoint."

Tina's final comment about Maurice stayed with Hank for a long time after she had left the room. *Was* it out of character for Maurice to have formed the consulting company? Why had he done it? And why had he chosen to call the new firm by something other than the family name which, Hank was sure, would be prominently displayed on the front of the building which now housed Hargreave Industries. Only one person, Hank realized, could give him that answer and he went in search of Mark Fitzgerald.

He found the company counsel sitting in the morning room, sharing a companionable silence with Kae Hargreave. Both were engrossed in reading the newspapers. Kae looked up first as Hank stood in the doorway. She smiled at him. It was a forthright, welcoming look, and Hank felt the smile he offered in return was an awkward one.

"Come in, Lieutenant," Kae said.

"I'd like to talk to Mr. Fitzgerald."

"Not me?" Kae asked. She smiled again and got up. She was wearing an olive green dress which draped agreeably on her body. "I can sense when I'm not wanted. I'll wait for you in the hall, Mark. I do want to take that walk around the grounds you promised me." She turned to Hank. "My husband never walks, only runs for his exercise.

242

He thinks walking is for the weak." She looked over her shoulder. "Sorry, Mark, but that's what he says."

Before the lawyer could reply, she was gone. Hank wondered where her husband was. "She's an uncommon woman," he observed.

"Yes, Lieutenant. I'm sure you know that I know that."

Hank sat down, and Mark waited.

"I have a question or two for you, Mr. Fitzgerald, about the late Mr. Maurice Hargreave."

"What do you want to know?"

"Why was Mr. Hargreave not using the Hargreave name for the new consulting company?"

"Townsend Crest wanted the rights to it. In some markets it's the brand distributors know."

"I see. No other reason? I've never heard of Hargreave products. Couldn't Townsend Crest have put its own brand on everything?"

Mark shrugged. "I suppose they could have. But they didn't want to."

"And that was all right with Maurice?"

"Yes. I think you're attaching too much importance to this detail, Lieutenant. Maurice's son was dead. He would have no one to carry on the name."

"What about his brother's sons? He might expect they would have children one day."

"Maurice didn't care about his brother's sons. I'm sorry, Lieutenant, but that's the way things were with him. You may find that shocking, but that's the truth."

"On the contrary, Mr. Fitzgerald. What I find shocking is murder. And I want to know the truth about that."

"I thought you did. You believe Emily Hargreave killed Maurice because of what I just said. He didn't care about her husband or her sons. Emily resented Maurice terribly. Everybody in the family knew that. Lionel had the titles of president and chief operating officer, but that was window dressing. Maurice made all the decisions. Lionel had an M.B.A. from Harvard, you know, but Maurice had the instinctive cleverness and genius for running a business. He was a college drop-out, by the way. He was proud of it. Early on I was told he often teased his brother about being a Harvard man, called him pointy headed, that kind of thing."

"Not a particularly nice side of Maurice Hargreave's character."

"No, but I think as time went on, he mellowed. Probably realized he could have made more use of Lionel's business school education, but of course he would never admit it."

Hank could well understand why Emily Hargreave resented her husband's brother. "Did Emily know about Maurice's plan for Pemberton, Mr. Fitzgerald? Did you tell her?"

"Why on earth would I tell her? I hardly ever spoke to her."

"I think she knew about it. How did she know?" Mark shrugged.

"Her husband, on the other hand, seems to have been in the dark about the plans for the new company."

"I'll repeat myself," Mark said. He looked at the doorway, perhaps to assure himself that Kae was still in the vicinity. "I didn't tell her. My suggestion is that you should be asking Tina these questions."

Mark looked at the door again, and Hank nodded for him to go.

"I've already asked Tina," Hank said to himself when he was alone, "and I don't think she did tell Emily about Pemberton. So that means I'm back to square one."

Refusing Brian's invitation to have a drink nagged at Caroline as she worked alone in the kitchen to get the Hargreaves' supper ready. Something in the look in his eyes as he stood in front of the gazebo's door had stayed with her. What did he know? What was he keeping inside? Perhaps she could have learned something about the mystery. But she still had a business to run, and the work didn't get done unless you did it. And that took so much of her time.

She debated all this with herself as she assembled the ingredients for a green salad. The Sunday evening meal at Kenwood had always been, by Kent family tradition, a cold buffet. So far the inn's guests had not complained.

Mattie had cooked earlier that afternoon and was taking the rest of the day off. Mattie's concept of a day off was bewildering to Caroline. The woman worked as if there was no such thing as leisure time. She had no friends or family she visited, no outside activities she pursued, no religion she practiced. Now, with some free time forced on her, she was upstairs in her third floor hideaway watching television. Caroline didn't know which were her favorite programs, only that she liked the set's volume turned to loud, and the sounds of muffled laughter coming from it could be heard outside Mattie's closed sitting room door.

Early in their return to Kenwood, Louise had quieted Caroline's fears that Mattie was being overworked.

"She enjoys what she does," Louise explained. "She likes to cook and fuss at you. She tested me when I was new to the family. The best thing you can do is to give her the room to do what makes her happy... which too often is to try your patience."

Caroline had thanked Louise for the advice, but she still found it difficult to follow. Mattie's ability to get under her skin was something Caroline realized she often allowed the cook to do. She had to learn to ignore Mattie's tirades and to appreciate her skills.

"A penny for your thoughts."

"Do you know all you like to talk to me about is money?" she asked as she turned toward the sound of Hank's voice. "Is it obvious to you I'm always thinking about it?" He had come close to her, and she caught the hint of his cologne. It was a soft, clean fragrance.

"You weren't thinking about money just now."

"How can you be so sure?"

"I am a detective."

"That's right." Hank had a reason for being in her kitchen. "How is Emily Hargreave? Am I allowed to ask?"

"Of course. And the answer is that she is the same as when she left here yesterday."

"She hasn't confessed?"

"No, nothing as convenient as that."

"But she still is your main suspect?"

"Nothing's changed about that. The evidence is strong against her."

"But—"

"Please, let's not rehash things. You believe what you want, but I've got to look at—"

Now Caroline interrupted him with a vehement "You're wrong. I know it."

Caroline had been chopping vegetables for a salad, and now she gave a last blow with the knife which sent the end of a cucumber flying across the counter. It took a bounce and landed on the floor. Hank bent down to pick it up. She took it from him and tossed it in the sink scrap bin.

"Look," he said, smiling tenderly at her. "Let's not argue." She thought she must look very angry if he was humoring her. "I've actually come with an altogether different suggestion than talking about the case."

"What?" Was that her voice sounding so suspicious?

"I wondered if you might be hungry."

"First you think I'm broke, now hungry. What an impression I've made on you."

"The first day I came here we started sparring like this, and I thought it was my fault. Now I'm not so sure. Why do you like to argue with me?"

"Me? I don't argue with anybody. Ask Mattie."

"Would you like to come for some dinner with me or not?"

The effect of this question on Caroline was unexpected. She felt weak in the knees, and she wanted to run.

"I have to get the Hargreaves their dinner."

"Where is Mattie? And Jan?"

"They have the time off."

"And Mrs. Kent?"

"She's in the dining room, laying out the plates and silverware. We take care of the guests' meal together on Sunday evening."

"I see," Hank said. He looked stymied.

"Would you like to have supper here? With us?" Her legs felt stronger now, and she was surprised at the warmth in her voice. "After we serve the Hargreave party."

After the Hargreaves' meal was over Louise declined Caroline's offer to join her and Hank upstairs for supper with the excuse that there was a program on the television she "always watched." Caroline had never known her mother-in-law to have a favorite TV show, and she wondered what her gesture of refusal meant. Did she not want to be in Hank's company because she didn't like him? Or was she indicating that she thought the two young people ought to be alone?

Whatever her reasons were, and she wasn't giving them away by word or look, Louise made up her tray and took it up to the third floor to share with Mattie. Caroline heard the slice of the sounds of canned laughter as Mattie's door was opened and then closed. What a surprise Louise's entrance must have been to her cook. Caroline wished she could have seen the look on her astonished face.

"Did you cook all this yourself?" Hank asked as he filled his plate with smoked salmon, cold roast beef and potato salad.

"Mattie did this morning. Have some green salad, too."

"I don't think I have room for it." He looked sheepishly at the mound of food on his plate.

"Here." She handed him another smaller plate.

"I know you made this with your own two hands. I saw you." Caroline watched as he served himself a liberal plate of the salad.

"When's the last time you had a decent meal?" she asked.

He stopped and his face reddened. "I came to take you out for dinner because I was worried about you not taking proper care of yourself. I'm used to skipping meals in my business. I can handle it."

"Obviously," she said, nodding at his tray. "You never know when you may eat again. Do you want bread?"

"All I can say is that you had better fill up your dish. I want to see you eat everything on your plate." He added the bread to his tray.

Caroline nodded obediently and took generous portions of the food. When she was done she took a bottle of red wine and two glasses.

"Come on," she said to Hank. "Our sitting room is on the second floor. We can go up the back stairs."

CHAPTER TWENTY

News of the Hargreave murder case had been relegated to the inside pages of Monday's newspapers. There was nothing new, as Hank was so well aware, and he supposed he was glad that the papers didn't try to keep the story on the front page by manufacturing information. If Emily had been a young woman, and the crime could be conjectured one of passion, there might have been prurient *speculation*. As it was the newspapers accepted the killing as an old family quarrel which had finally been settled. Somehow, seeing the motive picked up by the press caused Hank to have doubts of his own reasoning. Could he and some jerk of a reporter be thinking alike?

Certainly Caroline was having none of it. Last night, once their dinner had been consumed, she had returned to the case. Wine had made him agreeable, and he had listened to her thoughts once again.

"I think Tina could have done it, Hank. She could have gone down to the gazebo, run back before Harold got back to the veranda."

251

"The times aren't right. I've given that scenario the same once over. Harold was in his room during the time Tina was with you. He would have come back outside too soon. Tina wouldn't have gotten back to the house without being seen. Emily would have been there, too."

"What about Mark?"

"I would pin this on him if I could," he said. The alcohol had loosened his tongue. "I don't like him."

"He and Kae—"

"Caroline," he remembered saying. "Can we please talk about something else?"

And they had. Hank had been happy to learn something about her private life. She spoke easily about her own family. She had an older sister, unmarried, who lived in Chicago and worked in the financial sector.

"Definite Type A personality," Caroline had added. Her parents lived in a retirement community in Arizona. Hank hadn't gotten the impression the Weldons were a close family, spread out as they were on three points of the compass. Rather it was to her mother-in-law that Caroline appeared to be closest.

He had asked more about herself, always a good move, and she had chosen to tell him about her youthful acting aspirations, the lead parts in school productions, her college years, coming to New York and the later roles off-Broadway. "Off *off*-Broadway, mostly," she had laughed.

252

"And what happened? Why did you give it up to become an innkeeper?"

"I didn't have what it takes to survive in that business. You need passion and single-mindedness."

"Qualities I've noticed you possess."

She looked surprised, and he had stared at her reflective oval face for a long, long time. There was a fire burning in the room, and he had been able to watch her as the light outlined her head. He saw a proud woman.

"Why did you give up acting? Was it because of... when your husband died?"

"It would be easy to say it was," Caroline said. She looked around the room, at anything but his eyes. "At the time I thought I was too sad to think about work. But, I'll tell you something honestly." Now she looked straight at him. "I haven't missed it once since I've come to Newport. Now what do you think that means?"

"It wasn't important to you after all."

"Yes. That was the part of my life that didn't mean a lot to me."

But her husband had. That was obvious. There were photographs around the sitting room of the blond, blue-eyed Reed Kent, some when he was young, with his father and mother; others with Caroline when he was older. They were casual snapshots, and they showed a man of spirit and substance. Hank was used to

253

summing people up, and he summed up Caroline's husband as a person to be reckoned with, even in death.

"What am I getting myself in to?" he asked aloud as he put Monday's newspaper down on the kitchen table and picked up his coffee cup. The aloof black cat was sunning herself again this morning on the familiar railing, and Hank shook his head as he watched her sleeping in the warmth of the early morning sunshine. "I don't get involved, remember," he reminded himself. "I don't need that kind of entanglement. Police work and relationships don't mix." He had seen too many examples of that in his time on the force.

Yet Caroline's face in the firelight was in his mind, and when the telephone rang, he didn't completely displace it as he picked up the portable handset.

"Nightingale."

Keisha McAndrews, who was on duty at the station, breathed a sigh of relief. "Lieutenant. I'm glad I caught you."

She began speaking rapidly, and as he held the phone tightly against his ear, listening to Keisha's information, his thoughts were running.

"What do you mean she confessed?" His impatience at not being there on the scene came out in his voice. "Confessed to who?"

"Well, I'm not sure exactly." Keisha's voice was reflecting her absorption of Hank's mood. "When we took in her food this morning, she said she wanted to confess to the murder. Lt. Howard was here so he went in and she just started talking, I think."

"Wait a minute. Howard took her statement?" Hank's question was full of anger. "What kind of procedure is that?"

"No, no, Lieutenant, it's all right. Mrs. Hargreave said she killed Maurice Hargreave. She apparently kept saying that over and over. 'I did it, I did it.' Like that. Lt. Howard told me to call you. He hasn't done anything." There was a long pause on Hank's end. "Sir?" Keisha asked.

"Is Mrs. Hargreave still in her cell?" The question in Hank's mind was a nagging *why*.

"Yes, sir."

"All right. Have her moved back to one of the interrogation rooms. I'll be there in about twenty minutes. In the meantime, call the lawyer. Conroy. He's staying at the Marriott in the harbor. Tell him to come right away. Oh, and you better get Ben Davies out of bed and tell him to come in, also."

If Hank had thought things would be clearer after he took charge of the situation at the station, he was in for an unaccustomed surprise. Emily Hargreave still displayed all the vagueness of the previous day, now to which was added her absolute determination to state, "I killed Maurice." Her lawyer's request to meet alone with his client and the subsequent consultation between them did not shake the confession. "I did it," was Emily's greeting as Hank entered the interrogation room with Ben. Anthony Conroy could only shake his head. It was one of those rare occasions when Hank felt sorry for a legal adversary. The silver-haired lawyer was well-dressed in an expensive conservative fashion. His dark blue suit, navy tie and starched white shirt looked more at home in federal court than the halls of the Newport police station. His soft white skin was shaved closely, and there was a slight hint in the air of the smell of barber's talc. Hank mused on what prior business might have caused Emily's husband to consult with him.

Hank nodded to Ben to begin the tape recorder.

Ben spoke the opening vocal tag for the tape into the machine.

"On the day of the murder you took a taxi from the restaurant back to the Inn at Kenwood Court after you left lunch early because you had argued with your husband. Is that correct, Mrs. Hargreave?"

Emily nodded, and Hank commanded that she answer his question for the record.

"Yes," she said in a shaky voice.

"What was the argument about?"

"What does it matter? I killed Maurice. Isn't that enough for you to know?"

"I'm afraid not, Mrs. Hargreave. I need the details."

"I shot him."

"Where did you get the gun?"

"I, I... can't remember."

"Did you have it with you at the restaurant?"

"I don't know... yes, I must have."

"Why did you shoot your brother-in-law?"

"I hated him. I've always hated him. I'm glad he's dead." And after a moment, she added, "I'm glad I shot him."

With that statement, Anthony Conroy became paler in color, if that was possible.

The news that Emily had confessed to the murder quickly made its way to her family at Kenwood Court. Caroline was in the kitchen, cleaning out the coffee urn when Brian came to the doorway.

"Oh, Mr. Hargreave—" She saw him frown. "Brian. Good morning."

"Mother's confessed."

Caroline was astounded. Her thoughts raced. Was it possible?

"Why?" she finally asked.

"You still don't believe she did it?"

"No," she said sincerely. "I can't."

"She didn't. I'm sure of it."

"Then why—"

"You don't understand my mother." His lips seemed unable to form any more words, as if the muscles of his mouth had lost their control. Once again Caroline had the sensation that he was keeping something back.

"There has to be a mistake," she said gently.

"Father is changing his clothes," he said slowly. "I'm going to drive him to the police station."

"Lt. Nightingale is a fair man," Caroline said.

"I'd better go," Brian said suddenly. "Father may be waiting."

Caroline stood for several seconds before following him out of the room. Her heart was beating rapidly. She caught up with him in the foyer where his father was standing alone. Lionel looked drained, defeated. She stood and watched as the two men silently left the house.

"There is something terribly wrong," she said to herself. "If I could only guess at what it might be." She turned back from the door to see Tina coming out of the dining room.

"Good morning, Mrs. Hargreave," Caroline said.

"Oh… Mrs. Kent," Tina said absently. As she came nearer, Caroline could see that the woman was upset. While at first it appeared a natural reaction to Emily's confession, on second thought this struck Caroline as unnatural. Why would Tina appear distressed on Emily's behalf?

"I've just heard the news," Caroline said, watching Tina closely. "About Mrs. Emily Hargreave." When the other woman nodded, Caroline offered her sympathy in the situation.

"Yes, well, she's got her lawyer."

This choice of words occurred to Caroline to be a curious one. She was looking for a way to prolong the conversation when she became conscious of Tina's eyes moving sideways, focusing on the distinctive shape of Harold Hargreave as he came through the dining room door. Caroline watched as Tina ran hurriedly up the stairs.

If Harold was aware of the reason for Tina's irritability, he took no notice of her as he entered the foyer.

"I don't know what I'm going to do after we leave your home, Mrs. Kent. I'm going to miss your cook unbearably. She makes the best blueberry waffles this side of heaven. I suppose I could ask for the recipe, but inasmuch as my wife is a terrible cook herself, there wouldn't be much point. Instead I shall have to daydream about them and bemoan my never having them touch my lips again."

"You could come back for another stay, Mr. Hargreave. Then you could have them again."

"I'm sorry to disappoint you, but this chateau is too expensive for my tastes, Mrs. Kent. You know what they say... champagne tastes, beer budget. Or is it beer barrel budget? I'm never sure."

If Harold was affected by his mother's current predicament, he was putting on an awfully good front, mused Caroline.

"I'm very sorry about your mother. I still think she must be innocent."

"Oh, I agree," Harold answered without much thought. "The picture of my mother getting a gun and putting it to Maurice's head is one I can't conjure up."

"But somebody did," Caroline pressed, watching his face.

"Of course somebody did. What are we having for dinner?"

"I beg your pardon," Caroline said, even though she had heard him exactly. "I really don't know yet."

259

"Would it be possible to have some sort of lamb dish? I'm very partial to a roast lamb, but my wife dislikes it, so we never have it at home."

"Lamb," Caroline said coolly.

"Yes. Donna claims she can't stand the thought of those little fluffy lambs cavorting in the meadow one day and gracing our dinner table the next."

"Lamb," she repeated.

"Would that be possible?" Harold looked hopeful, as a child might when asking for a special treat. Caroline could only nod dumbly.

"I'll speak to my cook," she said brusquely.

Harold, however, did not catch the implication in her voice. He was too busy looking pleased with himself and did not seem to notice when Caroline took her leave of him without further comment and made her way to the kitchen.

Louise knew the cleaning service was generally finished at 3 p.m. on Mondays. They were paid by the job, and as soon as they arrived in the morning, they began sprinting energetically through the hallways and up the stairs with mops and polish in a mad dash of cleansing efficiency. The frenzy of their movements always had a disconcerting effect on Louise, and this morning she felt their impact on the already tense atmosphere in the house more than usual. Guests were cris-crossing cleaners as they worked, while the cleaners, focused on their self-imposed timetable, were uninterested in the comings and goings of Hargreaves. The garden was always Louise's refuge at times of unrest, and today was no exception. Care of the shrubbery, which had overgrown in huge proportions during the years of the tenants' inhabitancy, provided endless opportunity for work. Louise had a good eye for symmetry, and she enjoyed clipping and trimming, pausing to step back and see the effects of her work. It was also a labor which allowed her mind to examine other things.

The first thing she wanted to sort out was the invitation Caroline had extended to Hank the previous evening. Louise had not been surprised that Caroline had offered the hospitality; it was obvious she had wanted to talk to the detective about the case. The murder must be cleared up quickly for the good of the business.

But, what about Hank's intentions? What was his real reason for staying to dinner? That he might be interested in Caroline as a woman was, Louise knew, very possible. And that was something that Louise was not prepared for, although her conscience told her it would soon have to be.

Meanwhile, Hank would continue to be around until the case was wrapped up even though Emily had confessed.

"Although that woman wouldn't kill a squirrel, let alone a bear of a man like Maurice," Louise said to herself as she stepped back and scrutinized a clematis vine that was threatening to overtake a neighboring shrub. She knew Emily didn't like her brother-in-law. But, Louise agreed with Caroline. Emily was not the killer.

Louise had come to the view that it was Tina. How she had looked at Maurice in the gazebo that first day remained vivid in Louise's memory. But, Tina had an alibi that seemed strong, and she and Caroline had helped to give it to her. Therefore it stood to reason that it had to be someone else.

Who else was there? She began to clip back the vine.

That morning she and Caroline had gone over the suspects again, and she could see that Caroline was leaning away from Tina toward Mark Fitzgerald as being the guilty party. "She has no proof, though," Louise thought.

Louise had watched Kae and Mark carefully that morning at breakfast. Now that she knew of their relationship, Louise looked for them to make a slip. They had barely spoken at the table, and Kae had made what turned out to be a futile effort to engage her own husband in conversation. As usual, Nelson Hargreave had been preoccupied. Mark had left the house right after breakfast. Why was he anxious to be alone?

"Caroline doesn't like Mark, just as I don't like Tina. But is that a good enough reason to suspect someone of murder?"

CHAPTER TWENTY ONE

While Louise worked in the garden to avoid the chaos indoors, Caroline was in the middle of it. On Jan's days off, Caroline assumed the duties of seeing that the guests' bedrooms were tidied. Hiring another maid to come in on those days was a goal she hoped she could soon reach.

Kae Hargreave was in her room when Caroline knocked. As Caroline entered the room, her eyes went to the bed, which had already been made.

"Oh," Caroline said. "I've come in to make up the bed."

Kae looked vaguely at the bed. Her face looked stale as if she had not taken her usual care with her make-up.

"And I've done it myself. I expect you think that's odd."

"Oh, no," Caroline said quickly. She wanted not to offend.

"I don't know what's the matter with me today," Kae said. "I feel so restless. I couldn't read." She gestured toward a book by the bed. "Nelson was so upset about his mother."

263

"Yes, I'm sure he was."

"Of course his father didn't help by asking Brian to go with him to the police station."

"I think Brian suggested it."

"I finally had to insist that Nelson go on after them." Her hands made fluttering gestures as she spoke. Caroline had never seen Kae lack for control. She seemed uncharacteristically unnerved. Kae went to a chair and picked up a pair of her husband's pajamas and began to refold them. Her hand smoothed the fabric slowly, and she made a neat rectangle of the clothing. "These ought to be laundered," she said.

"I don't usually offer the service, but under the circumstances I'd be happy to do some laundry for you, Mrs. Hargreave."

"We only packed for the weekend."

Caroline left the room, and in a minute she was back again with a large brown wicker basket from the hall linen closet.

"Here, Mrs. Hargreave," she said. "We can fill this up and I'll take it for you."

Kae took the basket and began to put clothes in it. Caroline noticed they seemed mostly to be athletic clothes belonging to Nelson Hargreave. Her own lingerie would probably need hand-washing, Caroline presumed. When Kae was almost finished, she held up a man's white sock.

"What do you suppose this is?" she asked. Her expression was puzzled. She sorted through other socks and examined another. "There is something on this one, too."

Caroline took the pair of socks and saw the familiar sticky seed pods. She pulled one off and held it between her fingertips for Kae's inspection.

"It's just a seed pod. They pull off."

Kae was wrinkling up her nose as though the tiny balls represented some peril. "Be careful. I don't want them sticking to my clothes." Her voice suggested she had a genuine grievance.

"All right," Caroline said. She made an effort to be understanding of Kae's antagonism toward such harmless by-products of Mother Nature. "They're just seed pods. We've gotten them on our own clothes from the pathway to the Cliff Walk. As a matter of fact, I just had the gardener cut that path back on Saturday. It won't happen if anyone walks through there now."

Kae frowned again, and Caroline took the basket out of the room and carried the dirty laundry and the offending seed pods down the back stairs. The laundry room was in the basement, and Caroline would have gone there had not the front door bell rang. Hastily she deposited the basket in the pantry and went to answer the door.

The mailman stood on the doorstep with a package, and she took it. It was Louise's latest selection from the Mystery Book Club.

"How appropriate," she thought as she thanked the mail carrier and closed the door again. She was standing in the foyer when for the second time that day she saw Tina coming her way. She appeared not to have lost her black mood of the morning.

"I'm going out for a walk," Tina said tersely.

"The sky is getting cloudy," Caroline said in an attempt to be pleasant. "It looks like it might rain again."

"I don't care. I need some exercise. Being cooped up in this family is beginning to drive me crazy."

"Yes, I'm sure it is," Caroline replied. To herself, she voiced the opinion that the Hargreaves were beginning to get on her nerves as well.

As the rain began to fall shortly after four o'clock, Hank was staring out of his grimy office window down onto the parking lot. He watched as the drops of water hit the panes of glass and dribbled down through the dirty path they made to the wooden sill. There was no doubt in his mind. Hank Nightingale could think better on a sunny day.

He had been sitting, contemplating his case, and asking himself why he wasn't satisfied with it. He had his confession, true, but a nagging that had started in his mind that morning had only grown stronger as the events of the day unfolded.

In some ways it all fit together. 'Something Maurice was planning.' Early on Caroline Kent had said that was the motive for the murder, and if you accepted Emily's confession, then the impending sale of the company had to have driven her to her final act of

266

desperation. She couldn't bear to see the business of Hargreave Industries disappear. Not when she had her sons standing ready for a new generation of management. Emily's whole life had been her family. Add to that the obvious vacillation of her husband concerning his role in the company over the years and you could understand her state of mind. And, finally, there was Lionel's decision to sell out and leave his sons' fate to the mercurial Maurice.

Well, it was all there. Hank found himself beginning to convince himself that he was worrying over nothing. This was his case. He knew the motive. Emily had the opportunity. As for the gun, Toby Erickson had talked to Lionel's secretary to see if his wife was in the habit of visiting him at the office. She did come on occasion, came back the report, the last time being the week before the family's Newport trip.

The jingling of the telephone on his desk broke abruptly into his thoughts.

"Nightingale."

"Oh, Hank, I'm glad it's you." Caroline's unsteady voice was almost unrecognizable. "Please come. Hurry. It's happened again."

"What has happened?"

"It's Harold Hargreave. I—" Her voice trailed off.

"What's happened to Harold Hargreave?"

"Oh, Hank, it was awful. His head. I found him."

As Hank listened to the words, his stomach began to churn as he spoke. "He's dead?"

"Oh, Hank who is doing this?"

Another Hargreave was dead, and Hank knew he had no answer to Caroline's horrified question.

It had all been part of a routine Caroline carried out each Monday afternoon as soon as the cleaners left. She went from room to room, putting crooked pictures straight, chairs evenly back, and table tops full of bric-a-brac to rights. Oftentimes there were lights left on in empty rooms and even the occasional cleaning cloth or polish bottle left behind by the rapidly moving workers. Today she set about the familiar task with no thought of finding anything out of the normal ordinary.

The conservatory, at the extreme corner of the back of the house beyond the library, was the last room she visited on the first floor. The cleaners had a habit of leaving the lights on in this room, and Caroline was momentarily surprised to find that the conservatory was dark. There wasn't much that could be put out of order in this room. The cleaners didn't move the plants and flowers from their established spaces, and the Bentwood furniture only required a light dusting. It was rare that Caroline needed to do more than turn out the lights. So it was that as she was about to turn from the darkened conservatory doorway she found herself reaching for the light switch in an involuntary action to assure herself that the room was as she wished it. A quick look around the space, and she would move on to check the second floor.

Harold's body was practically in the exact center of the room. He had fallen forward, and Caroline could see immediately that the back of his head had an unusual shape to it, as if there was something attached to it. At first she stood immobilized, feeling nauseously averse to examining her second corpse in four days. The first murder scene had presented a curious attraction, and she had studied Maurice's corpse with interested detachment. Now the originality of violent death was lacking for her, and she wished with all her being that someone else had found this body.

Yet, after a minute of standing with her eyes closed as she tried to wash away the sight, she forced herself to look again. Except for Harold's lifeless figure, the room appeared much the same as it always did, a cool, green space for lounging and repose.

She came closer to the body, her eyes irresistibly focused on the back of its head. The irregular contour she could now see was caused by the matter from his brain which was horribly loose on the back of his scalp. He had been struck by a heavy object, and the room was full of heavy objects. Whoever had been Harold's assailant had unlimited choice of his or her murder weapon among the numerous ornamented pots and tubs. It must have been done spontaneously, thought Caroline. Two people came into the room. They argued. One struck the other. Was it done in anger? Or in fear?

Caroline was finally able to stop staring at the sight of the head wound. She looked carefully at the rest of the body. When Harold had fallen, his left hand had caught under his chest. The right hand, however, was stretched out across the tiled flooring. Caroline looked closer at the closed right hand. Was there something white visible in the fleshy fist?

Caroline's heart beat rapidly. She was sure there was a ragged piece of paper trailing from Harold's hand. Dare she try to see what it was? She looked back to the empty doorway. The house was quiet. Quickly she bent down and carefully put her face as close to the pale hand as she could get without touching it. There was writing on the paper, and Caroline took her fingernail and pushed at the scrap's fold to force it open. Harold's fingers had already begun to stiffen, but the paper loosened from its fragile berth. It popped out of the fist and rolled onto the floor.

Caroline jumped back in horror. Her first impulse was to run as fast as she could from the room before her curiosity, like that of the cat, was the cause of her demise. But she stood motionless and the impulse passed. She knew she shouldn't touch the paper because there might be fingerprints, but she had to see what the writing was. What could she do to open the paper without touching it and leaving her own prints?

A stack of lacquered cardboard coasters was on one of the end tables. She took one and centered it over the crucial clue and pressed gently. The paper, a torn right triangle about two inches wide on one side and an inch on the other, gave way. Lifting the coaster, Caroline stared at the writing. The top lines were torn and incomplete, but the bottom seemed more comprehensible.

The full printed message said:

trude BR

er loggia

20 guest BR

3:23 gallery

6 Gladys's BR

Caroline studied the words and numbers. It was hopeless to try to find their meaning now, so she closed her eyes and forced herself to memorize them. As soon as she went to her office to telephone the police, she could write them down. Meanwhile, she wondered if she should try to re-crumple the piece of paper or leave it as she had moved it. She finally decided that it wouldn't matter how it was found and left the room without disturbing the paper any further.

Another murder investigation would begin. It was if she was about to see a play for the second time that she hadn't wanted to see the first time.

Driving with Ben to the scene of the second Hargreave murder, Hank was tight-lipped and grim. Neither man spoke.

Emily Hargreave was still safely tucked in a jail cell, her bail hearing having been postponed after her confession. Her husband and their two sons had visited her earlier at the station. Right now he knew that the three men were at the Marriott, discussing Emily's defense with the lawyer Conroy. A call to the Marriott had confirmed they were there and that they had all gone together, directly from the police station. This new family tragedy would bring them back to the inn.

Hank inventoried the rest of his suspects. Left were the three Hargreave daughters-in-law, who were at Kenwood Court, and the company counsel Fitzgerald, whose whereabouts, out of the house, were unknown. The circle was narrowing.

When they arrived at the house Hank instructed Ben to assemble everyone, except for Caroline, into the morning room to wait for their questioning. First he wanted to view the body and the murder scene with the person who had discovered the crime.

The group of gathered suspects, as compared to the aftermath of Maurice's killing, was a diminished one. Louise was directed, along with Mattie, to the morning room. Mattie's reaction to the second murder was one of genuine terror, and Louise had felt her hand grasped tightly by the trembling cook as they walked through the house accompanied by Officer Jarvis. Another murder, and this one inside the house.

In the morning room, they found Kae, Tina and Donna sitting, separated from each other as if they were complete strangers. Donna was sitting alone on the sofa, crying and wiping her eyes. Her hair was hanging disheveled about her face, and a clump had attached itself to her wet cheek. Neither Kae nor Tina made any move to comfort her. Louise settled Mattie on a chair and went to Donna. She offered her sympathy.

"I know who killed him," Donna sobbed to Louise. "I know who did it."

The abruptness of her declaration startled Louise, who could only murmur, "Yes, of course, dear. You'll have plenty of time to tell the police all about it."

"No, no, I mean it." Donna raised her voice and jerked violently toward Kae. She pointed to her and cried, "It was Nelson. He killed my precious Harold."

Kae looked coolly back across the room and shook her head. Her voice had its usual polish as she spoke. "You're mad."

"Mad! Oh, I don't think so." Louise put an arm out to quiet Donna, but the woman shook her off. "Nelson wants everybody out of his way at that company. First he killed Maurice, and now he's killed Harold. I remember what he said in the car coming down here. He wants to run Hargreave Industries. That's what he said. You were there. You can't deny it!"

"You'd better watch your accusations, Donna," Kae said angrily, "or you could find yourself in trouble. You see, Nelson has been at the police station all day with Lionel and Brian. He couldn't possibly have killed your 'precious Harold,' as you call him."

Donna screamed and heaved herself up from the sofa and made a dive for the chair where Kae was sitting.

"Then you did it! You were here all day."

Kae jumped aside at the last instant, and Donna fell with her full weight onto the chair. At the sound of the scream, Officer Jarvis had come running into the room.

"What's going on here?" he asked, but no one answered, and he could only take in the sight of Donna face down in the armchair.

"You think I did it?" Kae demanded, looking down at Donna. "Well, I think you did it. Any woman in her right mind would have taken a gun to that man years ago. His table manners alone would have driven any normal woman to murder."

When she was finished her diatribe, Kae looked haughtily about the room. If it had not been a police order, Louise was sure she would have swept grandly out of the room, thrilled to have had the last word. As it was, Kae could only step back and allow the startled policeman to help Donna to sit up in the chair.

In the conservatory Hank stood taking in the murder tableau. The room was chilly, and he flexed his back and shoulders to keep from getting the neck cramp he could feel coming on. A few feet away the corpse of the late Harold Hargreave wasn't minding the lack of warmth. There would be no more chocolates purloined from the tempting two-pound box in his wife's bureau. If only they could talk, Hank thought, these victims. One last word from Harold to tell me who is behind this plot to eliminate Hargreaves.

Were there more intended victims? Had Harold's death been part of the original plan?

On the surface, the murder method supported the explanation that Harold was killed for a separate motive. He was a snooper, and his snooping had made him dangerous to the murderer. Hank saw the small, torn bit of paper next to the body, and he realized that this could be an important clue. Yet he disciplined himself, as was his usual method, to ignore it until after he focused himself on the scene and what it suggested to him as a whole.

Were there vibrations he received from the dead? Or waves from the evil left in the room? He could never be sure what it was he sensed. Nevertheless he followed the familiar investigative path, standing amid the scene, sniffing, feeling, absorbing the sensations all around him.

Caroline watched him from the back of the room where she stood and waited. At last, Hank bent over and peered at the piece of paper on the floor.

"Sergeant," he commanded, and Ben Davies handed him a pair of tweezers.

Slowly Hank read over the words and numbers. He showed no sign that he either comprehended them or was baffled by them. He gestured for the evidence bag and the cryptic message was sealed up and put aside.

"Mrs. Kent," Hank said without turning. "I wonder if you could come here. Be careful where you step. Come behind me."

Caroline obeyed the command.

"What time did you enter the room and see the body?"

"It was twelve past four. I checked my watch."

"And did you see anyone in the immediate vicinity of this room when you entered?"

"No." Caroline's voice was subdued. "I came here directly from the library. No one was there, and the hall back here between these two rooms was empty."

"Good. I don't think I need to know any more from you now, Mrs. Kent. You may go. When I take your full statement later I shall ask you to remember the last time you saw everyone in the house and the approximate times. Before discovering Mr. Hargreave, that is."

"Hank," she began, "I've got to know who is doing this."

"Oh, and do you suppose I don't?" he snapped.

He saw her face redden. She had been hurt by his retort. But, he couldn't stop to apologize for any pain the curtness of his manner had caused. Looking away from her at the room's exterior door which led out to the veranda, he spoke to Sgt. Davies.

"We'll have to post some guards about the place. We can't be too careful now."

"Yes," Caroline said carefully, mirroring his thoughts. "I realize there's still a murderer here in the house. I think—"

He spun back to her. "You are not to think anything. I don't want you to interfere. Sgt. Davies will escort you back to where the others are waiting in the morning room. You must all stay there."

And with that, Caroline was dismissed.

Later that evening, after the questioning had been finished and the police search of the house and grounds had just begun, the man and the woman were the last of the guests to leave the dining room after the service of a very quiet meal. As the rest moved ahead of them, the two deliberately slowed their steps and lingered back in the room. The man shut the door.

"I had to do it," the woman said before his accusing eyes could stop her speech. "He had the notebook. The fool found the notebook."

"Always so damned nosey!" The man's voice was a hiss.

"He didn't know what it was, but he knew he had something. I couldn't be blackmailed. Not now. Not when we're almost free."

"Free, you say. I thought we could leave soon. But now, with the police everywhere—"

"Don't lose your nerve."

"Don't worry about me. I've held up my part of the bargain." The woman glared, but he paid her no attention. "What did you do with the notebook?"

"I burned it. I took it out of the house to do it. No one will ever know what it is now."

There was a sound from the opposite side of the room. Someone was coming from the kitchen to clear the table. The woman quickly turned the knob near her hand and went into the hall. Behind her the man watched the back of her head and wondered.

CHAPTER TWENTY TWO

The burned ashes of the notebook were found in the old gate house early the next morning. What they had been was not immediately recognizable, but the ashes still retained some heat and the officer knew she had found something important.

Staying up all night to lead the investigation had not brought Hank Nightingale any reward, and he stood now, having been summoned to inspect the find.

"It looks like paper, sir," its discoverer Lucy Estrada, her eyes bright with excitement, said. "And something thicker."

Hank took his pen and separated some of the charred remains.

"A small book, I think, Officer. This looks like some of the cover material."

"Do you think it's important, sir?" Lucy's words were undisguised as making her very hopeful it was.

"No doubt it is. Have it sent to the lab right away." Hank turned to go. His step was dragging. "Thank you, by the way," he said, turning back to Estrada. He tried to acknowledge everyone's contribution to the quest.

"Good work, Estrada." Hank hadn't worked with her before, but he had observed her name on her uniform. "See that it gets on its way. Take it yourself."

"Yes, sir," Lucy said smartly.

The sun was barely visible in the morning sky as Caroline sat up in her bed. Her room was colored in shades of pale blue and cream, and she adjusted her eyes to the faint light which the room absorbed into its airy filminess. It was a space that soothed and reassured. For a time she considered sliding back into the comforting cocoon of the bed linen.

She looked at the clock. It was only a few minutes before six. Sleep had come intermittently throughout the night. Each time she had wakened, she had picked up the threads of the puzzle. Twice she had put on the light and studied the copy she had made of the fragment of paper she had found in Harold Hargreave's hand. There was something familiar about the pattern of the numbers and letters, but she had not tried to force reaching for it. Rather she had continued to let her thoughts come and go, waiting for the elusive segment to find its fit, letting the self-selection of her impressions happen naturally.

She was staring at the picture of Reed, wondering what he would have made of all that happened, when the door opened and

Louise came in from the sitting room. She was wearing her robe and carrying two cups of tea.

"I thought you'd be awake," she said, handing one cup to her daughter-in-law's outstretched hand.

"Oh, thank you, darling. Have you been down to the kitchen already?"

"I wish I could sound hardy and say that I had, but Mattie checked up on me a few minutes ago. I suppose she wanted to make sure I wasn't murdered in my bed."

"Oh, Louise!"

"Well, of course, I'm alive, as you can see, and she asked if she could do anything. And I asked for tea."

"The comfort of a routine," Caroline said, sipping from the hot cup. "Mattie's tea. It always tastes the same."

"That's because she uses half a pound of tea to brew each pot. It's liquid strength."

"I never complain."

"Caroline, dear, have you had any more ideas? Since we talked last night."

The two women had sat up in the sitting room in front of the fire until after midnight.

"I've had so many thoughts, I'm exhausted."

"And the result?"

"I think I know how it was done."

"You do?" Louise sat down on the bed next to Caroline. She looked at her daughter-in-law in undisguised amazement.

"Maurice's murder, I mean. That's the tricky one."

"And do you think you know who did it, too?"

"Yes. I'm fairly certain of the murderer's plan."

"Do you know why Maurice Hargreave was killed?"

"For the reason he himself may not have suspected he was vulnerable. Greed. And yet, I heard him say while he was alive, 'No good comes of being greedy'."

"And was Maurice the greedy one?"

"I don't think he looked at what he did that way. He wanted new excitement and challenges. The money was secondary."

"What are you going to do now that you think you know?"

"I'm going out later this morning to test my theory."

"By yourself?"

"I'll be all right. But I want you to be careful in the house."

"Why? Surely no one is concerned with me."

"No, but if I'm right, there is more than one person involved in these murders, and right now I don't know for sure who the second one is."

"Two murderers? Oh, Caroline. Two."

"Yes," she said, reaching over to take Louise's hand. "You'd better stay in the kitchen with Mattie while I'm gone. You two will keep an eye on each other."

"All right, dear. Will you hurry, though? I'll be worried about you until I see you safely back home."

"I'll hurry as much as I can, but there is a timetable to which I'll have to keep."

If the meaning of that remark was unclear to Louise, she didn't question it. Instead, she grasped Caroline's hand and squeezed it hard. Looking into her mother-in-law's eyes, Caroline saw how much she wanted an end to the crimes that threatened to corrupt and stain her treasured family home.

Caroline had one piece of business to do before she left the house later that morning. There was one bit of information she needed, and Hank held it. She would have to ask him if he would let her back into the case, if only briefly, to answer her question. Despite his sharpness with her on the previous day, she hoped he would be cordial today.

Ben Davies was in the kitchen when Caroline came in after clearing the breakfast dishes out of the dining room. Mattie had offered him coffee and a plate full of her banana muffins and homemade strawberry jam as an inducement to keep his police presence nearby, and he was happily taking the bribe.

"Oh, Sgt. Davies," Caroline said pleasantly when she saw him. "I was looking for the lieutenant. Is he in my office?"

"He's out on the grounds, Mrs. Kent. I'm not sure exactly where."

"Thanks, I'll look for him."

"Would you tell him to come in and eat something? He hasn't had anything since yesterday's lunch that I know of. He'll love these banana muffins here." Ben beamed a look up at Mattie, and she returned his look of appreciation with one of her rare smiles.

Caroline went out through the back door and scanned the open vista for a sign of Hank. She joined him on the veranda where she saw he was close to the chair Harold Hargreave had occupied on the day of the murder.

"Do you think he saw the murderer from that chair?" Hank's voice was calm.

"I'm not sure, Lieutenant."

"I thought after Sunday night that I was 'Hank'."

"I believe you were the one who called me 'Mrs. Kent' yesterday in the conservatory."

"I had to do that in front of my investigative team. It would never do to have them see me relax in a scene-of-the-crime setting. I couldn't be so familiar with a witness. Caroline."

"No, I understand." She appreciated his attempt at friendliness, although she continued to feel the brittle tenseness in his manner. He looked exhausted. "You can get some breakfast in the kitchen. Your sergeant asked especially that you come up for some."

"Thanks. I think I will." He looked at Caroline, and she smiled back. She saw that he was thinking, worrying. Did he believe she was in danger?

"What are you doing today?" He nodded at her outdoor jacket. "Are you going out?"

"As a matter of fact, I am," she said, trying to sound as nonchalant as was possible. She saw Hank smile approvingly that she would be away from his inquiry. "I wonder," she began and studied his face closely as she framed her request. "There is something I would like to know. I hope you can tell it to me."

Hank listened to the question. His expression told her that he couldn't see the reason for its asking. He gave the answer, and Caroline thanked him. Another blank space was filled in the puzzle. She hoped he wouldn't be too upset when he realized its significance to his case.

The tourists were out in force in Newport that Tuesday, and Caroline plunged into the middle of them. She looked at their many and varied faces. Men and women, young and old... some serious, others laughing. The Hargreaves had been part of this stream of people who came to the city for a day, a weekend, sometimes a longer stay, to connect with the past, to feel as if it was truly *yesterday* in the Gilded Age. Caroline followed their footsteps through the city, hoping to see and absorb it through their eyes.

"The Breakers was only used for twelve weeks during the summer months," said the tour guide. Twelve weeks. A small slice out of the year. Yet, the legacy left by those wealthy society families' twelve weeks of residence in Newport remained.

Throughout the day, Caroline considered the lives of the upper class women of the late nineteenth century. How different were their lives from those lived by the women in the Hargreave family? She reflected on Alva Vanderbilt. In 1895 she had moved out of Marble House, the splendid classical manor house her husband William had spent $11 million to build for her as a 39th birthday present. Alva would divorce Vanderbilt to marry her neighbor, Oliver Hazard Perry Belmont, who lived down the road in Belcourt Castle, a mansion he had designed to resemble a French hunting lodge.

For despite all their worldly goods, these wealthy women had been held in so many soft cages. The men fought the hard campaigns in the real world that made them their enormous wealth. In response to the limitations placed on them by society, the wives were left to play-act on a stage. Their days were occupied with the dramatizing of their scandals and indiscretions, petty snubs and social cuts. Those were the activities that put the breath into the female world, so narrow and confining for all its wealth and treasures.

What did their lives matter now, at the beginning of the twenty-first century? These women's stories would have been forgotten had they not left behind the houses that were the settings for their legendary machinations, the famous summer cottages that the tourists came to Newport to visit.

And herein lay the key to the murder in the gazebo and the solution of the mystery at the Inn at Kenwood Court. And with the unlocking of the secret, Caroline knew, would come the knowledge of who Harold Hargreave had been unlucky enough to meet yesterday afternoon amid the treacherous flower pots in the Kents' conservatory.

Absence of sleep was beginning to take its toll on Hank. Ben looked as tired, if not more, than his superior when the two met in Caroline's office that same afternoon.

"I suppose you don't have any clever ideas, Ben," Hank said, his voice lacking any real belief that Ben did.

"They aren't clever, that's for sure. We've got the three women on premise and the activities of that Mark Fitzgerald as vague as they could be."

"We can check the places he said he'd been. Someone might remember him."

"The movies, walking, stopped to eat." Ben ran down the list without consulting his notes. "It doesn't mean anything."

"We need a murder time. Right now the medical examiner is saying between 1:15 and 2:30. That's a long stretch."

"The cleaners think they were done with the conservatory around 1:30. But they don't seem to know for sure. I wouldn't put much faith in their memories."

"Who saw Harold Hargreave last?"

"The wife. Says he came in the library with her after lunch. She was watching the TV in there, but he complained about her choice of programs, so he left. Says she thinks he said he was going out to walk off his lunch."

"He never struck me as the type who exercised."

"Nor me, sir."

Hank was thoughtful. "And no one saw him after he left the library. What was the time?"

"I cross-checked the program Mrs. Donna Hargreave says she started to watch with the TV listings." Ben flipped open his notebook and ran his finger down a page. "The movie started at 1:30. She says they saw it from the beginning. Murdered man left about five minutes after it began. 1:35."

"Did anyone see her in the library after 1:35?"

Ben looked at his book again. "That is a big unclear, sir. Mrs. Tina Hargreave said she had looked into the room after lunch to see if she could find, in her words, "some peace and quiet." She saw Donna in there and chose not to join her. She says she went for a walk instead."

"And the time?"

"Tina didn't look at her watch, but thinks it was around two o'clock. She saw Mrs. Caroline Kent, by the way, when she was going out the front door."

"And can Caroline Kent confirm the time?"

"Not really, sir." Ben ruffled some pages and continued. "Says she was in the middle of directing the cleaning people, and Mrs. Kae Hargreave had given her some laundry she wanted done. The mailman came to the door. Sounds like a zoo. No one was paying any attention to the exact time."

"Someone was, if they executed a murder in the middle of it all."

"Yes. That is true, Lieutenant."

Hank decided to go home to get some sleep, and Ben, for his part, had been happy to do the same. Sleep was a long time coming for Hank, as he couldn't shake the mental lock the second murder had on his mind. Without bothering to undress, he had stretched across the bed, thinking he would nap easily after the rigors of the past twenty hours, but he only found himself shifting first his legs, then his arms, and finally deciding his pillows were piled too high and aggravating his always aching neck.

Lying now on his back, a pillow cradling his problematic neck, he stared at the ceiling. Regular exercise, he was now thinking. "I've got to get regular exercise." When he was younger he had been a runner, but now his schedule didn't permit him to run regularly. And his maturing knees told him that when he did, they didn't enjoy it.

"I'm falling apart," he said. "Ever since I turned thirty." That had been six years ago, and Hank only thought this way when he was overtired and feeling sorry for himself.

What other personal misery he could call up at this time was put aside when he heard his doorbell ringing.

"Who the hell is bothering me now?" he complained peevishly as he stood up.

Without stopping to put on his shoes, he padded in his stockinged feet to the front door of his apartment and opened it. Caroline was standing in the doorway.

"You," he said without thinking. "What are you doing here?" In a reflexive action, his hand went to smooth his hair. Damn, he thought, never do this. Never go to the door dressed like you just got out of bed.

"Hello, yourself," Caroline said, eyeing him. "If I woke you, I'm sorry, but I had to see you right away."

"How did you know I was home?" Hank was still standing dumbly on the inside of the apartment and Caroline on the outside.

"You weren't at the station. I called. I took a chance that you would be here."

"How did you know where 'here' was?"

"Did you forget you're in the telephone book?"

"I keep meaning to have my phone unlisted, but I never get around to it."

"I won't ask how long, but I will ask you if I can come in."

"Oh, oh, yeah," Hank said stumbling over his own feet to step back from the door. "I'm sorry. Come in. Can I get you something?"

Caroline came inside and looked around the room. He suffered what he suspected was a hard, appraising examination of his living quarters.

"I didn't come for a social call," she said. "I've come to talk about the murders."

"Yes, well, I don't have any news for you. I'm sorry. I was trying to get a little sleep before I started back on the case later tonight. We think we have the flower pot that bashed in the back of Harold Hargreave's head. It has some ornamental ironwork on it, and it would cause the wound he received. There may be prints on that scrap of paper we found that could tell us something. And we're checking the whereabouts of everyone concerned in the case. You do know you've got police protection at the inn. Are you afraid to stay there? I think you would be within your rights to get all the Hargreaves and Mark Fitzgerald out of the inn anyway. I mean, two people killed since they arrived. You are a hotel, you know, not an asylum. We'll get whoever is responsible for this eventually, but I don't think you are obligated to harbor the guilty person while we're looking for him. Or her."

Hank had been speaking rapidly, non-stop, and Caroline had not tried to speak until he was finished.

"You don't understand. I know all that. The thing is..." She swallowed hard and plowed ahead. "The thing I came to tell you is," and here she paused again to set her jaw firmly so that she would be ready for the rebuttal she was expecting from him, "that I know who killed Maurice Hargreave. I'm sure I know now how it was done. I think I even have some evidence."

Hank's felt his lips trying to move. The response to Caroline's statement, forming in his head, wasn't coming out of his mouth, which opened and closed without speaking a word.

"I think you ought to sit down," Caroline said solicitously.

CHAPTER TWENTY THREE

The last act of the drama in which Caroline now found herself to be taking the starring role was to take place that evening at Kenwood Court. The charges against Emily Hargreave had been dropped, and all who remained in the cast were now getting ready to play out their parts.

The salon was not one of Caroline's favorite places in the house. It was all yellow and gold and had been designed for lavish parties and featured a large open space in the middle of the room for dancing or musical programs. The furniture was placed around the chamber's perimeter and the pieces, including several long benches, were of hard upholstery and an uninviting ornate design. Tall rectangular mirrors heavy with gilt studded the walls. Two enormous chandeliers, laden with the bodies of several chubby cherubs, hung from the painted ceilings. On a bad day, after having watched the cleaners struggle to dust the immeasurable surfaces of ornamentation which clogged the room, Caroline felt she hated it. She had often wished she had the money to re-do the room and make it into a more modern, homelike living space.

Now she and Mattie were arranging some of the chairs in a cluster in front of the imposing fireplace.

"Is the police going to be everywhere when we get these Hargreaves in here together?" Mattie asked suspiciously. "One of them's a murderer."

"Lt. Nightingale will handle everything, Mattie," Caroline said. "We will all be safe."

"I don't think the Missus should be here. All this activity isn't good for her heart."

"Mattie," Caroline said, "there is nothing wrong with Mrs. Kent's heart."

"She ought to go to bed."

"That's ridiculous. She wants to be here, and the police want everyone here."

"If anything happens to her, it will be on your head," Mattie intoned.

"Please. The police will take care of things."

Caroline calculated the seating needs. There would be Hank and Ben. And there would be the people, minus two now deceased, whose coming to the house had started it all. Lionel and Emily Hargreave, their sons Nelson and Brian, Nelson's wife Kae, Harold's widow Donna, Tina, whose relationship with the living Hargreaves was now too cumbersome to describe, and, of course, Mark Fitzgerald.

Caroline counted out seats for thirteen people.

Mattie stood, looking grimly at the chairs. "One of these is for the murderer," she said.

The moment had come for all to assemble. Hank had come with Emily shortly after eight o'clock. The news of her son's death had shaken her. She looked tired and defeated, staring blankly past Caroline's look of concern.

Caroline had met them at the door and felt the stomach flutterings she hadn't experienced since her acting days had ended. Ben had been sent ahead to instruct that everyone was to be on hand, and the atmosphere in the house had become electrified. All the players knew the climax was at hand. They were milling about the foyer and in the grand hall, as if it were backstage on opening night. At 8:20 Hank gave the signal to Ben who moved everyone toward the salon. Caroline hurried ahead, and Louise motioned to Mattie to follow her.

"I trust you know why we are all here tonight," Hank said calmly as the Hargreave party began choosing their seats, Lionel next to Emily, Nelson next to Kae. Caroline saw Hank was surprised when Brian shepherded Donna to a chair. After a slight hesitation, Tina chose the empty seat next to Mark.

"There have been two murders committed here at the Inn at Kenwood Court," Hank began. "One on Friday, and one yesterday... on Monday."

Donna began to whimper, and Brian put his arm around her. She looked gratefully into his face and beamed a crooked smile on him.

"From the beginning, after the first murder of Mr. Maurice Hargreave, the suspicions rested on the members of his family, those present on this vacation trip." Hank added, "And the new guest who arrived the afternoon of the murder, Mr. Fitzgerald." Kae shifted in her seat and looked furtively at Mark's rigid profile.

"The vacation was organized for the family to celebrate the fortieth anniversary of Mr. and Mrs. Lionel Hargreave." Both Emily and Lionel looked down as Hank spoke.

"I'm sorry we ever came," Emily whispered into the air.

"But was that the only purpose of the trip?" Hank paused as the assembled party looked warily at each other. "It seemed that the murder of Maurice Hargreave was planned well before the family ever arrived in Newport. The murder weapon, a Colt .32 which had belonged to Maurice's late father and kept in the office where..." He let his eyes rove across his audience. "Those of you who are here all had access to it. Even I might add, the victim of the second murder, Mr. Harold Hargreave."

"So we might ask," Hank continued, "who planned the trip to Newport? Whose idea was it?"

"We just wanted to have a family party for my parents," broke in Nelson. "I discussed it with my brothers. We didn't even know if Maurice would want to come with us when we planned it."

"Yes," Hank said. "But, he did come. Along with Mrs. Tina Hargreave." He let his gaze settle on Tina, who looked as if she was debating within her mind to speak or remain silent. "Maurice's daughter-in-law... his executive assistant... whose office, like that of Lionel Hargreave, connected to his own."

Tina could hold her tongue no longer. Her face had become an unflattering shade of reddish purple. "Everyone went in Maurice's office." She turned accusingly on the others. "All of you! Bothering him night and day, asking for money, favors, leaning on him. None of you could compare to him." She looked now at the man beside her and glowered. "Especially you. You thought he trusted you. Well, I know he didn't!"

"You're a liar," Mark retorted.

"As I was saying," Hank continued, "the weapon that killed Maurice was brought on the trip for the purpose of killing him at the right opportunity. Now, we know that Maurice became fond of working in the old summerhouse. A suggestion I believe you made, Mrs. Hargreave."

"He needed privacy. You can't make something out of that," Tina responded confidently.

"Perhaps not. As I said, it was certainly a convenience for the murderer to have the victim in that secluded place, away from the main house. But, let's look now for a motive for this killing."

The group stirred. Louise touched Caroline's arm.

"The motive could have been any number of reasons. My interviews showed Maurice was not loved by his family." Tina opened her mouth to speak, but Hank quieted her by saying, "Except perhaps by his daughter-in-law, who described him as a modern-day giant of business." Tina smiled her appreciation. "Was that the extent of your relationship? Business only?"

"Of course," she snapped. "I was his daughter-in-law."

"But others seemed more inclined to hate Maurice Hargreave... or fear him."

"You, Mrs. Hargreave," he said nodding to Donna, "could not conceal your glee when Maurice was dead. Likewise, I remember, your late husband also showed no grief at the time." Donna took to making whimpering sounds again. This time Brian did not offer his arm in comfort.

"The other young Mrs. Hargreave," he now indicated this to be Kae, "exhibited this same lack of sadness over the unexpected death of a family member." Kae shrugged and straightened the collar of the black silk shirt she was wearing. "She had several reasons for reacting this way." Kae raised her head expectantly. "I believe she may have been planning a change in her status as a Hargreave family member, and Maurice—"

"I demand you stop," Nelson exclaimed. "You cannot slander my wife."

"Please, Nelson," Kae said evenly. "This is not the time for histrionics. Let's not wash our dirty linen here in public." To Hank, she said, "It's no bearing on your case. What I may or may not be planning to do about my marriage."

"Are you so sure?" Hank asked. "You need money, Mrs. Hargreave, to live in the style you've become accustomed to, and the person who controlled the money in the family was your husband's uncle, Maurice."

"She wouldn't get any money out of Maurice," Nelson said. His voice had a tinge of bitterness.

"Ah, money. Now we're getting to the motive. Money." He looked at Lionel who was absorbed in his own thoughts.

"Maurice I've been told, by a reliable source, was not interested in money so much as power. Adventure. Risk taking. Success, constant and unadulterated success. That, I'm afraid, was of little concern to the rest of you." And here, he looked from Lionel to Mark and back to Lionel. "You all wanted the money. And I don't think Maurice understood that. At any rate, he was to pay for that oversight with his life."

Emily sucked in her breath and grabbed her husband's hand.

"Mr. Lionel Hargreave," Hank continued, "sold out his share in the company to his brother just this weekend. The deal was completed here at Kenwood Court. But his wife was upset by her husband's actions. She came back here, after having argued with him at lunch. She wanted to confront Maurice about it... at the same time he was murdered, it turns out."

"But she didn't do it," Brian said. His forceful dark eyes challenged Hank.

"No," Hank conceded, "but it also seems that what she... and perhaps most of you ...didn't know was that Maurice had already made another deal. This one was to sell the family company completely out from under all of you. Hargreave Industries was to cease to exist as a trough for the family."

Hank stopped to take a breath.

"Pemberton." Hank said the word softly, and several heads pushed forward to hear it. "You know what it is, Mr. Fitzgerald."

"Yes," Mark said, "I do. And I've told you already. It means for me that I had no motive to kill my partner."

Nelson turned and stared at the lawyer. The look spoke in daggers.

"Maurice and Mr. Fitzgerald were planning to make a lot of money together, and nobody else in this room was in on the arrangement. Unless, of course, you would be included." Hank's finger stretched out in the direction of Kae. Now her husband looked unsurely at her, and she showed some semblance of remorse as she looked away from his pitiful pale eyes.

"Now here's where things get tricky. Remember. Lionel Hargreave had signed his agreement to sell with Maurice on Friday morning. The date to sell Hargreave Industries to the new owners was set to happen a week later. So here's the $64,000 question. Who benefited financially from Maurice's death?"

"Not I," Lionel said firmly. "I was out of things by then."

"But, you weren't," Hank said. "Because you, handily, were Maurice's heir. Even though Maurice owned everything in the morning, you would get the entire business back when he died in the afternoon."

"I didn't know that. Maurice never told me how he had changed his will."

"Mr. Fitzgerald knew. He could have told you... or anyone else for that matter. Your three sons. Their two wives. A lover. We know of one. Conceivably there was another."

Mark was silent as faces turned toward him.

"And there was another possibility. Someone in the family may have read documents he wasn't supposed to. A family snooper, if you will." Donna gasped, and Hank directed himself to her. "I haven't forgotten that you, Mrs. Hargreave, were the last person to see your husband Harold alive."

"I wouldn't kill him. I loved him."

This comment brought a guttural laugh from Tina.

"And, then there was Tina Hargreave, the all-around, helpful executive assistant. You were always on the scene to read any important papers, listen in on any telephone calls, eavesdrop at any doorways."

"Stop these accusations!" Tina was raging now. "I won't sit here and be attacked this way."

"I wouldn't leave if I were you, Mrs. Hargreave. We're just getting to the best part." Hank smiled benignly. "How it was all done."

As Caroline stood and faced her audience in the salon of Kenwood, she could recall no other time during her stage career, even in the smallest of off off-Broadway theaters, when she had felt so physically close to those watching her performance. Slowly she met first Emily's anguished eyes, then her husband's. Emily looked fearful. Lionel's eyes were focused anxiously on Caroline.

"Mrs. Kent has the honor of telling us how it was done," Hank said, "because, I won't be embarrassed to admit, she figured it out."

Caroline steadied herself as she stepped back and felt the hard stone of the fireplace hearth under her feet. "I want you all to know how difficult this is for me."

"Several days ago, a man who came to my house as a guest was murdered. I am not sure that even now I understand fully what that means, but I know I will always remember that moment when I found him. Then, yesterday, I saw another member of the same family dead. It is horrifying to me that two people have died in our home."

Now Louise looked at her, and Caroline saw the face of the woman who had shared her loss of Reed. "Please, oh please,"

Caroline whispered to herself. She could see Reed's face in her mind. "Let me do this, Reed."

"Because I have been here with the Hargreave family, and finally you, Mr. Fitzgerald, I have been a witness to several things, which when accumulated, have shown a pattern. Lt. Nightingale could tell you about it, but he has asked me."

Again, she paused and waited for someone to challenge her authority, but there was only silence and she continued.

"Maurice Hargreave was someone I could see, from the first day he arrived, was a man who was hard and demanding."

"My brother brought all this on himself," Lionel said to no one in particular.

"In a way you are right, Mr. Hargreave," Caroline said. "He had always been difficult, and I suspect you had all managed in your own way to cope with that. But this week he was planning something that would so affect all of your lives that it became imperative to at least one of you that he should die."

Emily began to cry at this point, and Caroline hated what she was about to do to her.

"The end of Hargreave Industries would mean the end of the family's company where Lionel, Tina, Nelson and Harold were all employed."

"Don't forget Mark!" spit out Tina.

303

"No," Caroline said. "He would also lose his job with Hargreave Industries. Although he was to be associated with Maurice in the new Pemberton consulting venture."

"That's only what he says." Tina was relentless in the venom she directed at the man sitting next to her. At her side, Mark only smiled. "And don't forget," Tina added, now a sly look covering her face, "that there were wives to these Hargreaves. They all had the same motive."

"Yes," Caroline conceded, "but to get to know who did kill Maurice, we need to look at who had the opportunity to do so."

"You know my alibi, Mrs. Kent," Tina said. "I was with you and your mother-in-law. Are you going to say I wasn't?"

"No," Caroline said. "And that initially puzzled me a great deal. For you see, almost from the first, I suspected you of being the killer."

"Bitch," swore Tina in a low voice. Caroline shrugged upon hearing the epithet.

"You had the best motive for wanting to keep Hargreave Industries alive inasmuch as it was only your relationship to Maurice's dead son that kept you as part of the company."

"Maurice promised me I always would be a part of the family."

"He had. But, had he recently changed his mind?" Tina frowned. "You had ample opportunity to take the gun kept unlocked in Maurice's desk drawer. And you were the person who managed to get Maurice to work alone in the gazebo on the day of his death, while you made sure you had work to do in the house where you could be seen, first on your computer, then using my fax machine. You even visited in the kitchen."

"But you know I didn't kill Maurice," Tina said with satisfaction.

"No, you're right. I know you didn't kill him."

"Well, then," Tina said, relaxing in her seat, "what's your point?"

"My point is," Caroline said, "and I didn't mean to make it now, but you killed Harold Hargreave."

Tina shot from her seat, and Hank was quick to reach an arm on her. He had quietly moved from the front of the room and had positioned himself to grab her. With another thud, she sat back down. Mark smiled at her again, this time with a satisfied smirk.

"What? What?" Donna was babbling. "She killed my Harold?" She started for Tina but Brian was there to restrain her. A torrent of tears followed.

"Yes, Mrs. Hargreave," Caroline said. "She met him in the conservatory after lunch and quickly killed him by dropping one of the big flower urns down on his head."

"But why?" Donna asked. "Why?" The skin around her eyes was beginning to swell with water.

"Unfortunately because he was what you all knew him to be."

"A busybody," Kae said. "Always listening at doors."

"Yes. I'm afraid so," Caroline agreed. "He had found something Tina had written down that was part of the murder plan. What was it, Mrs. Hargreave?" Tina pursed her lips in silence. "Some notes to help the actual murderer carry out your plan. Why did you keep them?" Tina squirmed as Hank held hard to her arm.

"That was a mistake in what was otherwise an ingenious plan. Because Harold found them. Perhaps even before the murder was committed. Did he know what he had found?" Tina did not answer Caroline, but her look of outrage suggested the affirmative. "He must have recognized your handwriting. Did he try to blackmail you?" Again, Tina's face, and not her words, gave the reply.

"So you did away with him before he could even work out his clue, which you burned in the gate house when you went out for your walk after you had killed him. Remember you passed me that afternoon in the foyer as you were going out? Little did I realize you held at that moment the clue to how it was done."

"When did she do it?" Donna sobbed.

"I expect I saw her right after she had the meeting with your husband in the conservatory. He would have been excited over his find and the prospect of a financial reward for it. He was sitting, off his guard, and it was so simple to take up one of the pots and crash it on the back of his head." Caroline had stepped forward from the fireplace hearth as she made the accusation. "You took the notebook from his hand, but he was holding tight on to it. A piece of one of the pages was torn off in his hand."

"What did it say?" Donna asked.

"There were numbers and some words. At first I couldn't understand what they were. It seemed to be part of a list. A loggia and 20 guest bedrooms, and a gallery. There were also two other mentions of BR's, which of course could mean more bedrooms again. It suggested a house. But I don't know of too many houses, even in Newport, that have 20 guest rooms. It also had one name: *Gladys*, and another part of a word where the paper had been torn off: *trude*. Intrude? *Intrude* into a bedroom? But Maurice was not killed in his bedroom."

Caroline paused before asking in a clear voice, "And who was Gladys? There are no Gladyses in this case. In fact, in this day and age, there aren't many people named Gladys anywhere. That is a name from another era. And 'trude.' That is also part of a name from a time passed. I suggest Gertrude. Gertrude and Gladys. Their bedrooms." Again, the pause for effect before the final answer came. "At The Breakers. Gladys and Gertrude were the two daughters of Alice and Cornelius Vanderbilt, and if you tour The Breakers, you will visit their bedrooms, as well as the upstairs gallery and the upper loggia. Gladys's daughter still retains a family apartment on the third floor of the house, which her mother signed over to the Preservation Society."

"Several of you have visited the house during your stay here. Mr. and Mrs. Lionel Hargreave and Nelson Hargreave have all admitted visiting the house this weekend. Did others of you also go?

307

It seems that Tina was familiar with the details of the interior of the house." Tina looked perplexed. "Remember the first night you arrived? During dinner? You disparaged the house to the family after Emily had said how much she had liked it." Tina expelled a heavy breath. "When did you visit The Breakers, Tina?"

"How do you know I didn't see a picture of the place?"

"I think you went on a tour of The Breakers at some time before the family came to Newport this weekend. You needed to familiarize yourself with the lay-out of the house. Was that before or after you realized how conveniently located my inn here at Kenwood Court was for your purposes?"

"You're out of your mind," Tina said sharply.

"If you have visited The Breakers," Caroline continued, ignoring Tina's exclamation, "you will recognize that the torn paper found in Harold Hargreave's hand after he was murdered was part of a timetable for the house tour, the one starting at 3 p.m.—the one you took when you began planning Maurice's murder."

Now Caroline referred to the copy she had made of the original clue she had seen in the conservatory. "The order on this part of the tour is first Gertrude's bedroom, then the upper loggia. At 3:20, a guest bedroom, at 3:23 the gallery, and then at 3:26, Gladys's bedroom. I know this to be an accurate timetable because I myself took the same tour today and confirmed these time sequences are correct. The tour guides are very practiced at their commentary, and they know they must keep to the tour timetable so that they can move through the house the hundreds of people who arrive each day to see it. All the house tours run the same length."

"What does it mean?" Kae asked. "Why was Harold killed for those notes? Why are they important?"

"Because," Caroline said, "Tina had an accomplice. Her plan was to have someone else kill Maurice while she established a good alibi, one that was dependent on two outsiders, my mother-in-law and myself."

"A man," Kae said with scorn. "She got some man to do her dirty work."

"Yes," Caroline said, "and there were plenty of men in the case who suggested themselves as candidates for the job."

There was silence as heads turned. Caroline looked at Brian. He was watching his mother's face.

Caroline swallowed and continued. "The problem was that whoever killed Maurice for Tina also needed an airtight alibi. What was the good of it all if her accomplice, the killer, was arrested? Her confederate would only name her as an accessory. Tina needed to prepare an especially clever alibi for him during the time of the murder, and these notes confirm the plan that she made."

"The Breakers," Kae began, "but who—" And then the flash of recognition covered her face. She turned to her husband who was sitting next to her and looking ahead. "Nelson," she cried. "You! You were at The Breakers that day. You couldn't have," she cried out again. And then she looked at Tina's malevolent eyes. "And you, you put him up to it." And Kae's singular composure collapsed, and she could speak no more.

CHAPTER TWENTY FOUR

There was another burst of gasping and sobs, which filled the salon. Hank motioned to Ben. They had to be ready.

"Mr. Hargreave," Caroline said to Nelson, who would not meet her gaze, "you've admitted you were at The Breakers during the time of the murder of Maurice Hargreave. This timetable was prepared for you."

"What is your proof?" Nelson asked arrogantly. "A slip of paper. You can't connect me to this insane scheme."

Hank, standing next to Tina, felt her tense. He hoped that she might speak, but she remained rigid.

"But you were on the 12:15 tour?" Caroline prodded.

"Yes, of course I was. And I believe that the bus driver and another person taking the tour have confirmed my alibi. I was in The Breakers when Maurice was killed. You have the statements." Nelson turned toward Hank for confirmation.

"Oh, you were on the tour bus," Caroline agreed. "And I understand that you made especially sure that the driver remembered you. You kept bumping your head as you got on and off the bus."

"I'm tall, six foot four. You can see that. Most doorways and things are made without consideration for someone of my height."

"Yes. And that would also mean that in a group of people you would tend to stand at the back of the group, would it not? And your alibi, as you call Ms. Becker—"

"Sylvie," Nelson said involuntarily. Kae looked shocked when she saw her husband's reaction to the mention of the name.

"Yes, Sylvie Becker," Caroline confirmed. "The woman you chose to sit next to on the bus at the beginning of the tour. She is a foreigner, a student visiting here from Germany, is she not?" Nelson stared at her. He looked astonished. "I'm afraid I talked to her today, also. After I finished my house tour. Lt. Nightingale kindly told me earlier today where I could find her staying."

Hank shook his head as he realized again the significance of the question Caroline had put to him on the veranda that morning.

"She doesn't understand spoken English all that well, does she?" Caroline asked Nelson. "She told me that during the tour, she purposefully stood in the front of the group, as close to the guide as possible, to be able to pick up all her comments. She does remember sitting next to you on the bus very vividly. But, I'm sorry, Mr. Hargreave. She can't actually confirm seeing you in the house during The Breakers tour."

"We went down the steps from the pantry and the kitchen into the gift shop in the basement there. I bought her a book for heaven's sakes. Are you telling me she doesn't remember that I bought her a book about the Vanderbilt houses?"

"Yes, she did say you were thoughtful enough to buy her, a woman you had just met, an architecture book that cost $50. Now why you would do that, unless you wanted her to remember your being together in the house, I don't know. But that incident was at the end of the tour." Now Caroline consulted another paper in her hand.

"By my estimation, you and Ms. Becker would have been leaving the pantry at 1:03. Now your tour started at 12:15. I don't see that you have an alibi for the period between 12:15 and three minutes past one. Exactly the period during which your uncle was murdered. And if we believe that your mother picked up the gun at approximately 12:40, and that the medical examiner says the murder was done no earlier than 12:30, then between 12:30 and 12:40 is the crucial time. Maurice was murdered then, and I say that's when you were in the gazebo and you killed him."

Caroline was aware that Emily had cried out, but she did not shift her attention from Nelson.

"So I just said to everyone else on the tour, 'excuse me, I'll be leaving you all now for'... what did you say, about forty minutes or so... 'so that I can murder somebody.' Come on now, Mrs. Kent," Nelson said assuredly, "that is patently a ridiculous theory. And I'll say again, you have no proof."

313

"On the tour," Caroline said with sureness in her voice, "after beginning in a small waiting room, one passes by the front door again on the way to the Great Hall. It is a very busy spot there with ticket selling going on and with the next tour being taken into the waiting room. My observation today was that it would be simple, as your group moved forward, for you to step backward and blend in with either the next tour or those in line to buy tickets. You could have gone out of the house and, once outside, ran down the side of the house..." And here Caroline paused and inserted in an almost indifferent tone, "Oh, did I mention that Sylvie Becker said you were wearing a sweat suit and running sneakers, not an uncommon outfit for tourists in Newport, but one which I think you'll agree was not the clothing you had on when you left the house that morning after breakfast?"

Here Kae jerked her head, and it was clear she remembered the slacks, sweater, and loafers which had been her husband's apparel that morning at breakfast. "Where did you change your clothes, Mr. Hargreave? I suspect you may have used a rest room in one of the larger hotels. They're right off the lobby, and anyone can use them without being noticed."

"Oh, Nelson," Kae cried.

"Yes, Mrs. Hargreave," Caroline said. "He changed after he left for his bus tour, which he told everyone at breakfast started at ten, but actually started at eleven that morning. Sylvie also remembers the shopping bag you were carrying when you got on the bus. The one that had your own shoes and clothes concealed as new purchases you might have just made at one of the shops."

"You can't prove a word of this. The word of this foreign woman. You just said she could barely speak English."

Nelson's voice was full of confidence. Caroline looked at Tina whose slim, muscular body was strained and tense.

"You left the tour, walked out of the main gate and ran," Caroline repeated, "down the street alongside The Breakers' grounds and onto the Cliff Walk, a five minute jog at the most. On the Cliff Walk a man in athletic clothes running for his daily exercise is a common sight. No one would have paid the least bit of attention to you running past them. The time it would have taken you to reach the pathway to Kenwood Court from The Breakers is less than five minutes. In another minute you could run up our pathway from the Cliff Walk and enter the gazebo. Maurice had just finished his lunch. He was relaxed. You came in; he wouldn't have feared you. At the least he might have been irritated at the interruption. It was a simple task to stand behind him, take out the gun, put in the clip, move to his side and shoot him."

At this climax of the story, Emily began to weep. Caroline forced herself to proceed.

"You dropped the gun beside the body because it could point in any direction among your family or even at someone who worked at Hargreave Industries. It would make them all be suspects." Here Caroline's face darkened. "I wonder if you had any idea it would be

315

your mother who would fall under suspicion because she picked it up when she came into the gazebo and saw Maurice dead."

"And after that it was a simple manner to retrace your steps, running back to The Breakers, and waiting for your opportunity to rejoin the tour as your group passed by the front door again at one o'clock on their way to the breakfast room. Then you would be going into the pantry at 1:03, time to reacquaint yourself with Ms. Becker, to make sure she remembered seeing you inside the house."

"It's all a made-up story with no proof," Nelson retorted. "I've never run on the Cliff Walk. I prefer to run on the road where there are less people to impede my long stride. My whole family knows that. But now that you have suggested that's how it was done, anyone of us who was away from the house that day could have come up that pathway to the gazebo. A man, you said." Boldly he turned and let his accusing eyes meet those of Mark Fitzgerald. "He could have taken the gun from Maurice's drawer at any time."

Mark was quiet. The fullness of the description by Caroline of Nelson's activities needed time to sink into everyone's minds. Hank stood up.

"I'm going to ask you all to remain where you are." Hank moved toward the door and motioned in four unformed officers. When they had secured the perimeter of the group seated on the chairs, Hank went to the fireplace. He put his hand on Caroline's shoulder and indicated she could sit down. Nelson looked straight at Hank and spoke.

"I'll ask you again. Where is your proof?"

Hank reached into his jacket pocket and brought forth a clear evidence bag. The insides were white. Hank held it up and his audience puzzled at its contents.

The bag was opened, and Hank's tweezers extracted one of the socks Kae had given Caroline to launder. In the front row, Lionel squinted down at the sock.

"What is it?" Lionel asked. Hank turned the sock so that a cluster of several seed pods were visible, stuck to the fabric. "What are they?"

"Seed pods," Hank answered. "They appear this time of year on some of the shrubbery that lines the path from the Cliff Walk to Kenwood Court. Anyone who walked, or ran, through there could get them on their clothes. They're sticky." Hank prodded one with a metal rod. "They don't dislodge easily." Hank smiled. "These are your socks, Mr. Nelson Hargreave."

"I don't deny it," Nelson said. "Maybe I did wear them when I may have gone near this path you describe. The one at the edge of the estate, you say?"

"When did you walk through the path?"

"Yesterday." Nelson started to fumble for his words. "I remember now... it was late in the day... yesterday, after Harold was killed. I needed some time to think. I walked to the Cliff Walk. Yes, I remember it now... looking at the water helped me to handle the news of his death."

"Yesterday," Hank said. "You swear that's when you wore these socks."

As Nelson nodded, there came a perplexed voice. "But I gave them to Mrs. Kent yesterday afternoon," Kae said. "Before Harold—"

"Thank you, dear, for backing up my statement," Nelson said bitterly.

"It doesn't matter," Caroline said. "My gardener trimmed the path back on Saturday morning. Only someone who had been on the path before Saturday morning would have gotten the pods on their socks. In fact, the last time would be on Friday, the day of the murder."

"I, I... you don't understand," Nelson started. "I didn't do it. You've got to believe me."

"Nelson Hargreave," Hank began, "I arrest you for the murder of Maurice Hargreave on—"

"No, no," Nelson said, his voice now showing panic. "I won't take the blame for this." He tried to wrestle free of his police guard. "I won't take the fall for you," he screamed and tried to get loose to Tina's recoiling body. "You and your smart ideas. 'I can make it work,' 'I've got the perfect plan, it can't fail.' 'We'll get him away on vacation, he won't be suspecting a thing.' 'Your parents' anniversary is coming.' Always so damn clever. You. God, how I hate you!"

Tina was safe from his grasp, and she let him have it with all the power of her undisguised disdain. "To think I put my faith in you. I chose you because I thought you had some balls. I thought you

318

could be as good as Maury, but you will never be the man he was. I hate you, too!"

"You had to go and kill Harold," Nelson came back. "I had the nerve, I had the guts. I looked at Maurice and shot him. You had to lose your temper and pick up a damn flower pot! You're not so hot, Tina Willets. You are what you've always been, a little guttersnipe who got lucky and married a Hargreave."

Caroline shut her ears to the angry recriminations. They continued until both Nelson and Tina had been taken away by the police.

When they were gone, Hank turned to Emily Hargreave and asked, "Would you like to tell us now, Mrs. Hargreave, why you confessed to the murder of Maurice Hargreave?"

"Tell them, Emily," her husband said. "Tell them and let this end."

"It can't end here, Lionel," his wife answered.

"You saw him, didn't you?" Hank's voice was gentle.

Emily nodded and bit her lip. It went red from the force of the pressure from her teeth. She was not crying now, but rather her whole body was sagging with inner pain.

"Mrs. Hargreave," Caroline said, "I know what happened that day in the gazebo is painful for you, but you can't hide the truth forever. It happened." She looked at Brian. How much of the truth had he known? His eyes were fixed on his mother.

319

"Yes, my dear," Lionel said, "we both must face that." He turned to Hank. "My wife saw Nelson in the gazebo that day. She had come down from the taxi, just as you said it happened. My fault, completely. I mishandled my leaving the company just as I mismanaged my whole life. Maurice lied to me, and I didn't want to believe that."

Here Emily's hand reached for his, and they touched each other in a fumbling, adolescent manner. Kae was watching the gesture closely, her body rigid. Caroline tried to read her emotions. Had she been hurt by Nelson's complicity with Tina? Or was she thinking of the future embarrassment the trial would bring?

"As she approached the window," Lionel continued in a weary voice, "she saw Nelson. For a moment she was startled. His face, she told me, looked in a way she had never seen before. Not angry, but a cold hate. She stopped. It frightened her. It all happened so quickly. At first I couldn't even believe her." And now Caroline saw a tear glisten in Lionel's eyes. He tried to continue but gave up and silently began to fold himself in sorrow over his son's actions. Brian put his hand hesitantly on his father's shoulder.

"He killed Maurice." Emily said the three words in an empty voice that echoed her husband's torment.

Kae looked defiantly away as if she were blocking out the reality of the three words.

"Thank you for telling me, Mrs. Hargreave," Hank said. "I know it wasn't easy."

"I thought that by confessing I would accept the blame. But I would never condone killing another human being."

"Mother," Brian said, "I've told you that you can't blame yourself for Nelson's actions."

"When his mother was arrested," Lionel said, "I waited for Nelson to do something, say something. But even then, all he wanted to talk to me about was his future in the company. As if that could compensate for Emily's suffering. But I didn't know what to do." He put his head in his hands and began to weep.

"Your son was afraid," Hank said. "I've seen that kind of fear many times. He didn't want to lose his position, his place, perhaps even his wife. And, yes, the money was important, too. Tina appealed to his vanity." And with a nod to Caroline, he added, "And to his greed."

"He caused Harold's death. I've lost two sons," Emily whispered. With that she stood. Her husband composed himself and took her arm. Brian took her other hand.

"Good-by, Caroline," Brian said. The words came out quickly. "I'll send you a card from Italy."

Quietly Kae rose from her chair, and Mark put his arm around her. She let him, and he looked relieved.

Donna looked wavering, as if she wanted to speak to Hank.

"Come on, Donna," Mark said. "It's all over."

"I know," she said softly, and she rose and took hold of his other arm.

The Hargreaves' stay at the Inn at Kenwood Court had come to an end.

EPILOGUE

"But who did they think would be blamed for Maurice's death?" Louise asked.

She and Hank and Caroline were sitting around a corner table in the main dining room of the White Horse Tavern. It had been Hank's suggestion that they mark the end of the case with a dinner, his treat. "You young people go on," Louise had said. But Hank knew better than to let the mother of Caroline's first husband stand in the doorway to watch her adored daughter-in-law drive off with a new admirer. No, he had been very insistent that Louise join them. And, to her credit, it had taken little persuasion on his part. That was a good sign, he thought.

And now they were a congenial threesome, dining out in this cozy old Newport restaurant with its low ceilings and dark wood and candlelight. Caroline, he thought, looked sensational in the glow of the flickering white candles.

"To tell you the truth," Hank said, "I'm not sure. I don't think Nelson ever expected that his mother would be charged with the crime. My guess is that Tina hoped Mark would be implicated. He had easy access to the gun. She might have known about the affair between him and Kae and hoped for a chance that might lead to some guilty slip-ups. We found Kae and Mark's trysting place on the afternoon of the murder. It was one of the motels in Middletown."

"I began to suspect them," Caroline agreed. "I thought Kae might have been the intruder in Maurice's room that night." She paused and allowed herself a laugh at her own expense. "When I went sleuthing in the middle of the night."

"Tell me," Hank said. "You read Nancy Drew books when you were a girl. Am I right?"

"Yes," she said emphatically. "Yes, I did. But, Mr. Detective, was it Kae?"

"I rather think that was Tina looking for the Pemberton file. That's the piece of the puzzle she didn't have. She had gotten almost all her information from eavesdropping and snooping. Harold wasn't the only Hargreave afflicted with that disease. And she did find out that Maurice was going to sell the company to Townsend Crest, not merge it. That's why she could talk Nelson into helping her to kill Maurice. He wouldn't want Hargreave Industries to disappear, and with it his chance of running the whole show someday. She also had to know the contents of Maurice's will. Mark Fitzgerald said Maurice kept a copy in his desk files. Tina must have first hoped that after

Maury, Jr., died Maurice would change the will and make her his heir."

"Was she mistaken!" Louise said.

"Yes, she must have been quite surprised to read that it was Lionel who would get the company. Therefore she needed one of his sons to be her collaborator."

"And Nelson was the obvious choice," Caroline said.

"Definitely," Hank said. "Harold was most unreliable, and Brian had no interest in the business. Mark Fitzgerald was not a Hargreave. No, she had only one choice."

"I wonder if she did try to interest Brian in the scheme," Louise said.

"I'm pretty sure her charms were not for him," Caroline said. "I've a feeling he's a better person than you give him credit for."

Louise blushed, and Hank said, "I think Caroline's right, Mrs. Kent. Brian was interested in his academic research. I don't see him giving Tina the time of day. No, I think she had Nelson in mind from the beginning."

"I almost feel sorry for Nelson. Trapped in a spider's web," Louise said.

"He was a big boy," Hank said without a trace of empathy. "And, unfortunately, he also didn't know about Pemberton. Only Mark and Maurice knew the plans for the new consulting company. Tina suspected something was up, but she didn't know what. I think, by the way, Maurice knew she snooped and teased her with the prospect of the hidden information."

"He should have realized," Caroline said, "what he was risking by betraying his family. Look at Lionel Hargreave. He sold out, believing his brother's promise that he would provide his sons with a lifetime job."

There was wine on the table, and Hank took his glass and held it up to catch the candles' light. Caroline was watching as the flames danced sparkles on the crystal. The facets twinkled and glowed.

"A toast," Hank said, "to two marvelous women, who it is now my great pleasure to know." He sipped from the glass in tribute.

Louise smiled. She held up her glass in Hank's direction. "And now to you, Lt. Nightingale, our thanks for a job well done. You have given us our home back. Caroline and I will always be grateful to you."

Caroline raised her wine in toast, and she and Louise drank to Hank.

"What a mutual admiration society we've become," Caroline said as she put down her glass on the thick white linen table cloth.

Hank thought, "You don't know the half of it." Out loud, he said, "We'll have to keep meeting like this. Who knows? I may need to consult you on my next case."

"I don't know about using my new-found detective skills again," Caroline said modestly, looking contentedly about the room, "but we definitely have to keep this up." Hank's patience was rewarded when at last her eyes came to settle on him. Green. He loved the way the candlelight reflected in them.

Hank felt Louise watching him, too, and he hoped there was friendship in her thoughts, as well appreciation.

"You were right to come home to Newport, Caroline," her mother-in-law said. "This is where you should stay."

About the Author:

A journalist and marketing/communications consultant, Anne-Marie Sutton has lived in Newport, Rhode Island, and used her knowledge of the city and its Gilded Age mansions to craft her first mystery novel. She was born in Baltimore, Maryland, and graduated from the University of Maryland with a degree in English. Now residing in Connecticut with her family, she is at work on the second novel in the series, *Gilded Death*, also set in Newport and featuring the team of amateur sleuth Caroline Kent and Newport police detective Hank Nightingale.

Printed in the United States
37155LVS00004B/89